I0718386

Space Operatic

Books by Dale E. Lehman

Howard County Mysteries

The Fibonacci Murders
True Death
Ice on the Bay
A Day for Bones

Bernard and Melody Capers

Weasel Words
Rooftop Sonata

Science Fiction

Space Operatic
The Belt
Penitence

Short Story Collections

The Realm of Tiny Giants
Found by the Road
Manifest Secrets

SPACE OPERATIC

DALE E. LEHMAN

RED TALES

Space Operatic
Dale E. Lehman

Copyright © 2020 by Dale E. Lehman

All rights reserved. Except as permitted under U.S. Copyright Act of 1976, no part of this publication may be reproduced, distributed, or transmitted in any form or by any means, or stored in a database or retrieval system, without the prior written permission of the publisher.

NO AI TRAINING: Without in any way limiting the author's [and publisher's] exclusive rights under copyright, any use of this publication to "train" generative artificial intelligence (AI) technologies to generate text is expressly prohibited. The author reserves all rights to license uses of this work for generative AI training and development of machine learning language models.

This is a work of fiction. All the characters, organizations, and events portrayed in this book are either products of the author's imagination or are used fictitiously.

Cover and interior graphics by Proi
https://99designs.com/profiles/proi

Book design by Kathleen Lehman
Text set in 11 pt. FreightText Pro
Chapter headings set in 14 pt. Chantal

Published by Red Tales, 2020
Baltimore, Maryland
United States of America
https://www.DaleELehman.com

Trade paperback: 978-1-940135-94-6
Ebook: 978-1-940135-95-3

DEDICATION

For my daughter Elizabeth, the family musician, who plays violin. Not cello. Not marimba. Violin.

(She read the manuscript, so she gets it. The rest of you will get it soon enough.)

No AI tools were used in the crafting of this story. Seriously, where would be the fun in *that*?

CAST

SOPRANOS

Chelsea Liwanu
> *Oort Territory Thirty-Seven's gloomy Culture Minister*

Snow Hill
> *Roberto Maccarone's indescribable appointments secretary*

Taqtuk
> *Devious, monosyllabic props assistant*

Santamonica Amarillo
> *StarBright Energy CEO and Chairman of the Board*

Amelia Carbuncle
> *TDY-41093-RRP base director*

MEZZO-SOPRANOS

Lena Froebisher
> *StarBright Energy acting CIO*

Kaja Omdahl
> *Overbearing mining supervisor*

Miranda Miranda
> *Hyperefficient if sarcastic minder reporting to Artemus Worthington*

BonBon
> *Mercenary Gordo's mercenary wife*

CONTRALTOS

Mina Ramsden
> *Artemus Worthington's droopy Executive Secretary*

Darya Pasternak
> *Miner and lunatic rebel explosives expert*

Ophelia Tansaniya
> *Space Operatic principal conductor and board member*

Maisie Worthington
> *Artemus Worthington's perfectly perfect wife*

TENORS

Roberto Maccarone

Eternally optimistic owner of Space Operatic

Feng Shui Land, aka Mr. Fang

Space Operatic's malcontent Properties Manager

Ajit Tambe, aka the kid

Young rebel miner and budding explosives enthusiast

Manfred Mooseherder

Space Operatic lead tenor and board member

Perry Pauli

StarBright Energy advertising scriptwriter...among other things

Bob

Annoying android

BARITONES

Kazimir Kapitan

Space Operatic stage manager and board secretary

Arne Slocum

Miner and rebel technical expert

Chicxulub

Space Operatic lead baritone and board member

Soumanwolo Jue

Artemus Worthington's know-it-all financial expert

Jay James

Artemus Worthington's multitasking appointments secretary

Gordo

Mercenary leader and mercenary BonBon's mercenary husband

Vanderbilt Morgan Snodgrass

Decrepit StarBright CFO

Artemus Worthington

StarBright Energy Director of Marketing and perpetual plotter

Josh Murdock

Oversized miner and rebel leader

Harlan Peppermill

Smitten mining engineer

CHAPTER 1

A lush swell of music, a terrifying crash of orchestral thunder, and the makeshift stage scintillated with blue and gold lightning-sparks spraying down from on high. Draped in brilliant purple robes crossed by garish red and green sashes, dragging silver and gold trains behind, the baritone scurried stage left like a perfect-pelted seal pursued by cash-starved hunters, terror writ large upon his face. He slid to a stop before a bright orange door and yanked on it in vain. Turning to face the audience, he threw his forearm over his forehead to show just how vain the attempt had been.

"I am a prisoner!" he wailed in key.

He whipped about, robes swirling at his feet, and bolted stage right for another door, this one a warm, radiant yellow. He traversed the bare metal floor in a few giant strides, his magnetic boots keeping him on the floor in the feeble gravity, the fabric of his costume fanning as though caught by a divine wind. He nearly tripped over his hem not once but twice.

In the wings, stage manager Kazimir Kapitan, a short, rotund, balding fellow far less menacing than his name, bit his knuckles and averted his eyes. He knew what would happen. Any moment, the baritone would stomp on his own garment and face-dive on the stage. Nose gushing blood, writhing in pain, the singer would be rushed to the medical facility. Shaken by the disaster, his understudy would turn in a miserable performance. Refunds would be demanded. Reputations would be destroyed.

The curse! Kapitan silently agonized. *The curse!* The cursed curse had dogged the opera company ever since that stupid altercation on Titan. It could strike at any moment. Like, say, now. He closed his eyes and chewed his fingers a bit more, as though such chewing might forestall the worst.

Astonishingly, when he found the courage to look again, the worst hadn't happened. Not yet. Rather, the almost-falls added a curious verisimilitude to tormented King Nabucco's panic.

The baritone—a fellow inexplicably named Chicxulub, according to the program auto-downloaded to every patron's wrist computer—hauled on the yellow door. It, too, refused to budge. Anguished, he dropped to his knees, and the orchestra fell silent. A hush filled the theater. As though on cue, the entire audience held its collective breath. Then a single flute twittered.

"Mighty Jehovah, forgive me!" the king moaned, lifting his countenance not to God but to the balcony, or rather to what in a real opera house would have been the balcony. Here, four appendages resembling giant metal litter boxes had been bolted to the wall. Metal ladders ascending straight from the main floor provided access to the litter boxes.

Suffice it to say, no cats would ever visit them. No, in these boxes sat people, excessively important people who ordinarily wouldn't have consented to climb even one rung up a ladder, especially not to sit in a litter box. Dressed in brilliant reds, golds, blues, whites, pinks, oranges, and greens, they formed a virtual rainbow suspended above the dull gray theater.

Chicxulub—that is to say, Nabucco—shot an imploring look at the stage left box where sat Roberto Maccarone, owner of Space Operatic, alongside dignitaries from the Oort Territory Thirty-Seven government and the StarBright Energy Corporation. As he implored, the music softly rose. "God of Judah, your Temple and altar shall rise again! Save me from this torment and I will change my ways!"

And so forth and so on, all sung in Commonspeak for the benefit of those not familiar with Verdi's Italian, which was to say the entire audience.

Unlike Kapitan, Maccarone beamed. Act Four, and all was perfect! He loved how Chicxulub had pretended to trip several times. When had they last made it this far without catastrophe despoiling the production? He couldn't remember, nor would he dwell on it. This performance could finally put Maccarone on the artistic map, especially with these fine ladies and gentlemen in attendance. The Oort Territories infamously lacked for culture. Success here wouldn't just be a feather in his cap. It would be a coup of epic proportions. Appropriate, he thought, for the operatic form.

Nabucco finished pleading with God and rose, radiant with hope. Casting about, he spied an electric blue door at the back, stage center. He strode for it, head held high, as the music rose triumphant and his voice rang out: "Open, now, door of destiny!"

Whereupon the door tottered and collapsed, flexing in the middle just before it slapped the stage like a wet sponge.

Kapitan covered his face in his hands and moaned, "No, no, no, no . . ."

Chicxulub looked down at the shoddy door in surprise, but with his back to the audience he had time to regain his composure. Meanwhile, the collapse had revealed the dashing, black-clad, full-bearded singer essaying Abdallo, Nabucco's loyal servant. Abdallo hesitated but a moment before gathering himself up. He strode onstage followed by four soldiers in glittering gold and copper armor. "My Lord," he intoned, "where are you going?"

In Maccarone's box, the dignitaries turned inquisitive looks on their host. He didn't miss a beat. "Divine intervention. A miracle signifying that God has accepted Nabucco's prayer."

Artemus Worthington, StarBright's Director of Marketing, raised a skeptical eyebrow. "Really."

Once attention returned to the stage, Maccarone slumped for a moment, then quickly righted himself. He dared not let the sentiment creep into his conscious thoughts, but somewhere deep down he knew that it could have been much worse.

And the opera wasn't over.

"Mr. Fang?"

The voice was nervous and young, the voice of someone who knew he was too low on the totem pole to interrupt someone so high on the totem pole. Whatever a totem pole was. The voice's owner looked the part, too: five and a half feet tall, skinny, with a face that couldn't decide whether it was under or over twenty years old.

Mr. Fang sighed and looked up from the computer display embedded in his desktop. The lines on his vaguely Asian face suggested he had a problem. In truth he had several, the most irritating being his name. People called him Fang. Rather, people who didn't know enough to be afraid of him, people like Roberto Maccarone, called him Fang. Everyone else called him Mr. Fang because they'd heard Roberto Maccarone call him Fang.

That was *not* his name. His name was Mr. Feng Shui Land.

Actually that wasn't his name, either, but everyone in this lunatic business used pseudonyms. Feng Shui Land was catchy and clever—not that any of the cretins surrounding him understood its cleverness—and should have been easy to remember. Only due to a slip of Maccarone's tongue during the worst meeting of Land's life, he'd ended up having to answer to Fang, or at best to Mr. Fang.

"Yes?" He made it sound like air escaping a balloon.

The nervous young interloper shivered at the sound. "The curtain's down. You said you wanted to know."

"Damages?"

"Just the back door. It sort of, well, flopped." He made a vague flopping motion with his hand.

Land grunted. "No loss there. Cheap material, shoddy construction. I'm surprised it stood up at all." He returned his attention to the columns of numbers on his computer screen, not because he wanted to look at them but because he didn't want to look at other people, especially not insignificant other people.

The young man shifted his weight, apparently expecting something more: new orders, praise for a job well done, a cookie, anything. But nothing was forthcoming, so he finally made another vague motion, this one back the way he had come, and said, "I guess I'll, uh."

"Thought you already had," Land said without looking up.

When several minutes later he did look up, the messenger was gone. By then Land was pondering the second of his problems: he was the properties master for Space Operatic, a business perpetually plagued by cash flow problems. How he was supposed to keep them in props he didn't know, especially when Lady Luck regarded their productions with about as much favor as antelope regard lions.

The tale of woe told by the numbers on the screen was deeply tragic, but it paled in comparison to the third of his problems. He hated—no, he thought, hated wasn't strong enough. He *despised* life in the Oort Territories. He'd taken this position two decades before to become part of the culture scene. The culture scene in the Oort Territories ranked somewhat below that found in most petri dishes. Worse, the place was cold, dark, and especially dark. *When you're two thousand astronomical units from the sun*, he grumbled to himself, *you need a spotlight to see what you're having for lunch.*

All these problems would vanish like a nightmare upon waking if only Maccarone would take them back to Mars. On Mars they'd been building a reputation—specifically, a reputation not based upon disaster after disaster. On Mars it wasn't always dark, although it wasn't exactly balmy. On Mars, nobody had called him Fang.

Okay, they *had* called him Fang, but only at the very end, only after that meeting where Maccarone had said Feng but made it sound like Fang, and everyone laughed except for Land, and not five minutes later Maccarone told them he was moving the company to Titan where, it turned out, Lady Luck couldn't follow. In one meeting, his life had been ruined.

It dawned on him that it would stay ruined unless he forced Maccarone's hand.

"The music was passable. I guess." Artemus Worthington tested the imitation gravity by lifting his right foot a few centimeters off the metal floor and letting it thunk down of its own accord. The resulting clank of metal sole on metal floor disconcerted him, as did everything about facilities on dwarf planets and the smaller shards of ice populating the Oort Territories. As far as he was concerned, civilized people were meant to live on space stations, where everything including the gravity could be properly controlled. This wasn't even gravity. Magnetism. A cheap substitute. People only stayed on the ground if they kept their shoes on.

"Some bits were fairly dramatic."

Worthington didn't look at the fellow who'd offered that appraisal. Directors of Marketing didn't have to look at script writers, and this guy, this Perry Pauli, barely qualified as a script writer. He was merely some vague relation to StarBright Energy's Chair and CEO Santamonica Amarillo, which was the only reason he'd scored a ticket to this lame excuse for a party.

Besides Worthington and Pauli, four others stood before the gaping window overlooking the alleged spaceport. A barely adequate facility, it was the only spaceport on the oversized snowcone designated TDY-41093-RRP, a lump of soot-contaminated ices just large enough to be compressed by gravity into a sphere. StarBright mined places like this, extracting hydrogen and other goodies from the frozen organics. Here they'd built facilities to support mining operations, including dingy-cramped office space, dingy-cramped living quarters, and dingy-understocked commercial venues. The six visitors were as enamored of the place as they were of stomach flu.

"Dramatic," Worthington said, sotto voce. Instead of eyeing Pauli, he eyed the only other important member of their party, Chelsea Liwanu, Culture Minister for Oort Territory Thirty-Seven. A slight woman with an austere visage, Liwanu, unlike most people here in the cold dark of the next-to-last circle of hell, wore black all the time. Worthington suspected she liked to be invisible against the background of space, the better to ambush others.

"Some of it, I guess," she replied without interest.

Worthington glared at the tarmac which, in spite of the dark, clearly didn't harbor a spaceship. "Why isn't the transport here yet?"

"Useful for commercials," Pauli added, his voice filled with hope.

Liwanu eyeballed Pauli as a disappointed teacher might a daft student. "Space Operatic is here to raise morale, not make commercials."

"They're here to sell tickets," Worthington snapped. "Where's the facilities manager? What am I doing here, anyway?"

"You were invited." The Culture Minister offered him a grim smile, as though she thoroughly enjoyed watching him writhe under torture. Which, he knew, she did.

"No kidding."

"Didn't raise *his* morale," muttered Liwanu's appointments secretary, a plump fellow with a face bearing an odd resemblance to a manatee's. Liwanu smacked him on the arm, a rebuke he took with amazing aplomb. "Hey!"

Pauli drew himself up to his full height, which wasn't impressive but probably made him feel vaguely assertive. "We could use them. That Macaroni fellow—"

"Maccarone," Liwanu corrected.

"—would make a great spokesman."

"At least Nabucco had an escape door," Worthington grumped. He had no use for an opera company or the owner thereof, no matter how charismatic. What he really needed was one more body on the board of directors, a loyal sidekick who would unhesitatingly follow his lead, a yes-man too stupid or too desperate to question him. He wasn't going to find such a stooge standing around here.

Liwanu looked out the window and up into the darkness. She pointed. A pinprick light had appeared in the sky: the transport beginning a cautious descent in the feeble gravity. It brightened with almost imperceptible leisure. "Forget Maccarone," she told Pauli. "He's a purist. Even if he needs the money, he'd be too stupid to take it."

Watching the light grow, unsure that it actually was growing, Worthington pondered that, and thought, *Hmm.*

CHAPTER 2

Dawn broke clear and bright on TDY-41093-RRP.

Actually it didn't.

Rather, every light in every room in every facility anchored to the surface of that ball of ice snapped on at precisely oh-six-hundred hours. The automated event qualified as sunrise regardless of whether your particular room happened to be sun-facing or blackness-of-interstellar-space-facing. Location didn't matter. That blazing star in the sky on the sun-facing side was the only difference. True, it was bright enough to cast weak shadows, but who bothered to look at the sky here anyway, even if a window did happen to be available?

Somewhere in the labyrinthine guts of the administrative facility, the employees of an opera company groaned, rolled over, pulled sheets over their heads, cursed the light, and really cursed the lack of controls to shut it off. They'd had a long night creating a modest success and then celebrating it. Now wasn't anywhere near time to greet a new day, especially an imitation/artificial one.

Roberto Maccarone, however, was up with the "dawn" and loving it. Success! Glorious success! "All you need," he crowed at the walls, "is ignorance and confidence and the success is *sure!*"

Wait a minute. Who'd said *that*? He scrounged through his memory for a few moments before coming up with it: Mark Twain. Good writer. Nevertheless, probably not the most appropriate quote.

It didn't matter. He was happy! He quickly pulled on one of the dull green jumpsuits his company had been issued and felt a bit less happy. Standard work garb, he'd been told. Nobody wanted to soil their fancy clothes crawling through a mining facility. Maccarone hated the outfit, as would the rest of his people, but it didn't matter. He had to set a good example. Besides, he'd wrangled free lodging and meals in exchange for cut-rate ticket prices for the miners. His crew should be elated that they didn't have to sleep on board their cramped little ship, the *Ponchielli*, not to mention the facility's food had to be an improvement over ship's fare.

And speaking of food . . .

He ventured forth, drab jumpsuit and all, in search of sustenance, which proved to be no mean feat. Upon their arrival a few days earlier, they'd received the standard base orientation. Good thing, too, because Maccarone found the facility's layout as confusing as hypermodern opera. The tangle of identical corridors assaulted his eyes in cacophonous dissonance. Not to worry, they'd been told. They'd soon figure it out, and until then just tap a wall and name a destination. This would conjure navigation lines on the floor in fluorescent orange (administrative offices), yellow (work sites), or blue (amenities) to guide them to their destination. Maccarone wondered what chaos might ensue should the whole opera company simultaneously ask directions. The image of tangles of lines wending through the maze suggested an idea for an opera. Hypermodern, of course.

Whatever.

He tapped the wall and said, "Breakfast," and a soft blue glow lit the floor, snaking into the distance. He followed it down corridors, around corners, and up a flight of stairs, quickly losing all sense of direction. The endpoint proved to be a big silver panel in the wall.

Nobody had told him about this. Maccarone studied it for a moment.

There was nothing to study. It was just a big silver panel in the wall.

He tapped it and said, "Three eggs, sunny side up. Three slices of bacon, crisp. Orange juice. Coffee."

Nothing happened.

Tap. "Eggs."

Nothing.

Tap. "Bacon."

Nothing.

The next tap came on his shoulder. He jumped.

Whether the tapper was man or grizzly wasn't clear. Whichever it was, it was huge, towering over Maccarone by almost a foot, with a bushy mustache, a bushy beard, bushy eyebrows, and hair down to its shoulders. "Swipe your ID," the creature said.

"ID?"

The bear-man's eyes narrowed. "Got one, doncha? Shouldn't be here if not."

"Oh. Yes. Right here." Maccarone searched the jumpsuit's fifteen or so pockets and came up empty. "Maybe I left it in my room."

"You're with that music group, yeah?"

"Yeah, er, yes. Roberto Maccarone." He extended his hand, although he wasn't sure he relished the prospect of a handshake with the giant. "Owner of Space Operatic."

The other regarded him, possibly thinking, "I liked the performance," possibly thinking, "I'm going to eat you bones and all," then accepted the handshake. Maccarone's hand survived it, just barely.

The bear-man smiled, slightly. "Wasn't half bad. Here's how it works. Get your card, hold it up here, then the machine will give you the menu. Pick what you want, but you can't go over your limit."

"What's my limit?"

"It tells you. Gotta go. Wasn't half bad." And the bear-man trundled off.

Massaging his hand, Maccarone thought he might be well advised to start this day over again.

Rank apparently had its privileges out here in the Oort Territories. Maccarone's limit proved higher than that bestowed upon other members of his company. By the time he retrieved his ID and returned, others were lined up at the silver panel, so by nonchalant shoulder surfing he could see what the dictatorial device allowed them. Discretion being the better part of employee relations, he rationed himself as the machine rationed the least of them.

Reaching the head of the line, he placed his order. The device hummed as though happily knitting a pair of socks, then a portal silently opened and a tray slid out. The dining area, if it could be called that, was little more than a wider part of the corridor stuffed with abused metallic tables and roughed-up metallic chairs. Rotten ambiance, but then this was a mining colony. Stage hands and chorus members, anyway, looked happy, and it wasn't hard to guess why. They all talked in awed tones about how little had gone wrong the previous night. Maybe, just maybe—so the speculation ran—the curse had finally lifted.

Maccarone indulged in small talk for a time, then excused himself and made for the spaceport where *Ponchielli* was docked. On board, he wound his way to his cramped little office. As he entered, he waved to the lines of holophotos adorning the walls: past performances, great singers, great musicians, great composers. At the heart of the lineup, Giuseppe Verdi smiled serenely from the largest photo in the most ornate gold and silver frame. "Signore," Maccarone acknowledged. "You would have been proud."

Verdi seemed to nod approval.

But to work. He squeezed into the chair behind his desk and palmed the computer screen embedded in the desktop. The machine woke, illuminating his face with a friendly bluish light. With a few deft taps, he summoned his appointments secretary, Snow Hill. Then, while awaiting her arrival, he pondered his next steps.

He needed money.

Government money.

Lots of it.

Not that this was a problem. Nobody had mastered the art of courting public largess like Roberto Maccarone. Had he not charmed, wheedled, cajoled, and otherwise wangled sufficient funds to build an opera house in the middle of Mare Tyrrhenum—-the one on Mars, not on Earth—-where others had failed to wrest even a single obol from those tight-fisted bureaucrats who controlled the planetary coffers?

Yes, he had. Granted, the resulting facility lacked the palatial extravagance of his dreams: no grand stairways, no cavernous auditorium lit by massive chandeliers, no excess of space for cast and crew, no entrance flanked by massive Corinthian columns. The actual thing had been a blocky structure where the company fought over every cubic millimeter. A paltry two hundred could jam into its undersized seats, and only ten VIPs could squeeze into the two skyboxes. But it had been his very own opera house nonetheless, fully funded by the planetary government. That, to Maccarone's mind, was victory. Even Fang had pronounced it a coup, and very little ever impressed Fang.

Snow Hill's entrance interrupted these thoughts. Snow Hill's entrance always interrupted any thoughts that were being thought. Although probably somewhere in the vicinity of fifty years old, she looked no more than twenty, a shapely twenty adorned by the latest, most elegant, most form-fitting fashions, a cool smile always playing on her lips, a twinkle always in her brown eyes, her long dark hair always spilling down her back like a—well, not exactly like a waterfall, since waterfalls weren't that color, but yes, rather like a waterfall anyway.

"You called, sir?"

That was something—okay, another thing—Maccarone liked about her. She always called him "sir." Her efficiency, too. He loved that. Nobody in the universe could manage a schedule as she could.

"I need to meet with Culture Minister Chelsea Liwanu today, preferably over lunch. Reserve a table at the best restaurant available. My treat. Tell her I want to thank her for giving us the opportunity to perform."

Snow Hill tapped at a mysterious device hidden in her lapel. Maccarone had always wondered about it. What technological marvels lurked within its tiny innards? Whatever it was, whatever it did, it seemed to work magic. No matter how vague or confused his instructions, his secretary always understood, remembered, and executed without flaw.

"Anything else, sir?"

"That's it. Our future hangs on this meeting." He leaned back, then leaned forward, suddenly worried. "Don't tell the Culture Minister that."

She smiled her cool smile, and he wished he could take back that last part. She hardly needed to be told. But she didn't mind. She never minded. "I'll do what I can, but it's very short notice. Finding a table may be tricky."

"I know, but it's critical. Strike while the iron is hot, as the old saying goes." He narrowed his eyes in puzzlement. "Whatever that means."

"Shall I gather that intelligence?"

Maccarone laughed. "No, it's not important."

"Sir." She turned to go, but paused for a backward glance. The playful look in her eyes could have melted all the ice in the territory. "The trip to Territory HQ takes two hours. You'd better change right away. That jumpsuit wouldn't even seduce a lady miner."

Her choice of words hardly registered. Maccarone scrutinized himself as she slipped away. She was right. He cut a dashing figure if he did say so himself—and indeed he did from time to time: tall, lean, Mediterranean, thick black hair, Mephistophelean eyebrows, and a smile that could charm Ebenezer Scrooge himself into making a contribution to the rich orphan's fund. But this jumpsuit—horrid! Bulky, baggy, a monochromatic monstrosity. No woman could resist Roberto Maccarone when, properly dressed, he fired up the charm. In this getup he'd never ignite anything.

No, what he needed was his Sunday best—although it wasn't Sunday and he didn't know what the day of the week had to do with it anyway. Where did all these bizarre expressions come from?

Never mind.

What he needed, regardless of the calendar, was his best burgundy and blue suit. Cut in the latest style, pale gold frills scampering down the lapels, faux emerald and amethyst buttons flashing on the sleeves, it never failed to impress. Well before their luncheon was over, Liwanu would be throwing money, and possibly herself, at him.

Aglow in the warmth of such happy thoughts, Maccarone decided he could spare just a few minutes for more mundane matters: financial projections for the coming season. The computer screen responded to his touch, allowing him to wander through a sea of numbers, his mood inclining him to the good in them. They were friendly numbers, whispering that all was well with his world, just as he had known it would be. So in tune were they with his thoughts that he nearly missed the one black cloud on the horizon: a memo from Fang requesting three times the budgeted amount for properties.

What was this, now? A joke? But Fang wasn't half that jocular.

Maccarone sent a request for further information. The reply came so quickly it almost knocked him out of his chair:

> *"The failure of the door in last night's performance points out systemic issues in materials procurement and construction techniques. It's only a matter of time before a significant failure occurs during a performance, jeopardizing the reputation and perhaps the very existence of Space Operatic. If the budget cannot be reconfigured to provide an adequate level of support for properties, we must convene a meeting of the board to discuss repercussions and seek potential solutions."*

Oort Territory Thirty-seven Headquarters moseyed about the sun in a painfully long, painfully slow orbit not too far removed from that of TDY-41093-RRP. "Not too far removed" in the Oort Territories meant over 1.6 million kilometers, a journey of not quite three hours on a ship equipped with fusion-jet propulsion powered by hydrogen mined right here in the Territories by, of course, the StarBright Energy Corporation.

A sprawling complex of metals and plastics, HQ looked from the outside like a messy collision of giant bug-eyed monsters, limbs stretched every which way, transparent domes scattered about like creepy eyes pointing all the wrong directions. The whole assemblage rotated to provide artificial gravity, although the angles of the arms caused some areas to have fairly wonky gravity useful for research projects but not so much for walking.

HQ provided living and working space for Territory government officials as well as a home for the StarBright Energy Corporation. StarBright's executives and corporate staff lived, worked and played here, Artemus Worthington among them, although one couldn't say he ever played and some wondered whether he ever really lived. He did work, though, seemingly nonstop, and if ever he did stop, he quickly became miserable.

At the moment he wasn't miserable. He was plotting. Enthroned on the most advanced auto-ergonomic executive chair money could buy—a high-backed, navy blue contraption with positioning and movement controls hidden in each arm—he surveyed his vast office. Gold and silver chrome walls reflected the solar spectrum light emanating from LED panels in the ceiling. The carefully-crafted curves of the wall segments threw rainbows of color onto key points on the light green carpet and natural wood furnishings. Worthington fancied the effect to be reminiscent of a primeval forest on Earth, although he'd never seen one.

Today in his faux forest, two key staff members plotted alongside him.

"Froebisher won't play," Mina Ramsden told him. "She'll know you're up to something." Her face had a droopy cast, not because she was unhappy but because pretty much all of her pretty much always drooped. Even her golden hair drooped.

Worthington took her droopiness as a given. She'd served as his executive secretary for the past seven years and had proven her worth time and again. And of course she was right. Acting Chief Information Officer Lena Froebisher had more brains than the rest of the board combined, excepting only himself and Chairman Amarillo. Fingers steepled before his expressionless mouth, he mulled that over.

The other coconspirator, Soumanwolo Jue, sat straight and tall, distinguished, important, smirking with confidence. Even his bright red and gold suit smirked. Clearly if he didn't know it, it wasn't worth knowing. As Worthington's financial guru, he probably shouldn't have been here, but his fingers found their way into nearly every matter of importance to the boss. His assessment was simple: "We need her on our side."

Worthington pondered that, too.

"Impossible," Ramsden told him. "It's a meritless claim."

"So we find better merits."

"We can't make up facts."

Jue smiled. "Why not?"

"You're off your rocker if you think you can pull the wool over Froebisher's eyes."

Worthington unsteepled his fingers. "What was that?"

Ramsden drooped toward his desk. "What was what?"

"Rockers falling off woolen blindfolds. What does that gibberish mean?"

"It means he's crazy if he thinks he can fool her."

"Why does it mean that?"

Ramsden shook her head and drooped back in her chair. "How should I know? The point is, we can't convince Froebisher to back us with such a weak claim."

Jue cocked his head at Worthington but didn't press the argument.

"No," Worthington agreed. "But Lena is vulnerable. Without me she doesn't have sufficient backing to secure a permanent appointment, and I don't want her in charge of Information Command as long as she's against me. She'd have too much power."

"So offer her a deal," Jue suggested. "You back her if she backs you. She gets the position she wants, you get control of security. And thus you win. Guns always trump computers."

Ramsden pulled herself out of her permanent slump long enough to say, "Not good enough," and then fell back into it again. "She'll demand evidence. We don't have any."

"Some of these incidents are sabotage," Jue told her pointedly. "Management's pathetic denials notwithstanding."

"Which don't translate into rebellion. It could be one fool miner who doesn't like the color of his company-issue undershorts."

Jue waved off Ramsden's protest and addressed Worthington. "Spin it right and rebellion it is. Which leaves the board where? Earth refuses to spend money on security out here. The territory government only has under-trained cops with water pistols. Company security is a joke. They only worry about information systems. The mercenary network you've cultivated is the only force capable of putting down insurrection."

Worthington's gaze slid from Jue to Ramsden, who seemed to be pouting, although he knew she wasn't. She was deep in thought. He allowed her fifteen seconds before prompting, "Well?"

"We need a spy among the workers," she said.

"We have informants."

"We can't trust any of them with something this big. We need an outsider, someone the locals won't suspect but who owes you big time. With that you might—might, mind you—learn enough to convince Froebisher of the danger."

"And if there isn't any danger?" Worthington asked.

"There is," Jue insisted.

"But if there isn't?"

When Ramsden met Worthington's eyes, their intensity almost knocked him from his chair. "Then your spy will have to create it."

Hmm, Worthington thought to himself.

CHAPTER 3

To the bear-man, the facility's theater resembled a giant cargo container into which had been bolted seating, smaller containers dressed up to look like litterboxes—er, skyboxes—and a shelf big enough to serve as a stage. In fact he was right, but then nearly every room on TDY-41093-RRP looked like a cargo container of some size or another with odds and ends bolted into it, mainly because that's what nearly every room on TDY-41093-RRP was.

Moreover, he thought, the theater shouldn't be called a theater. Ninety five percent of the time, its function rotated from temporary equipment storage locker to recreation area to meeting room. Only rarely did a performance brighten its existence. Right now it hosted a meeting, albeit unofficially. Management knew neither that the bear-man was there nor that sixteen of his coworkers were with him. Had they known, the lot of them would have been packed off to the penal colony on Proteus, Neptune's second-largest moon.

"Let's get started, Murdock," someone grumbled.

The bear-man, Josh Murdock, nodded and motioned at the man who'd prompted him. "Go on, then."

"Okay, so slow work so far. It takes some thought to get around the security vids. This new generation is smarter than the last one."

"They finish installing them?" Murdock asked.

The other, Arne Slocum, was a man as physically different from Murdock as a salmon was from a grizzly. Shortish and wiry, Slocum had a good ten years on Murdock and was arguably the brains of the outfit. Murdock thought of him as a sort of father figure but never mentioned it to anyone because he knew Slocum would resent the suggestion of age. "About. A few old ones still cover the South Pole sector, but nothing much of interest is down there anyway."

A nervous hand went up a bit behind and to the left of Slocum. It belonged to Ajit Tambe, the youngest of the group, a dark-skinned fellow whose thin, nervous face matched his thin, nervous hand. Murdock called him "the kid." So did everyone else, which Tambe hated.

"Yeah, kid?"

"Well, the lifters, they aren't usually under surveillance. Why don't we hit them instead?"

Women were underrepresented in this group of conspirators, but at least one of the four present compensated for the imbalance through sheer presence. The men were all pretty much afraid of Darya Pasternak, and with good reason. In a room full of rather fair crazies, she was crazy personified. A woman accustomed to hard physical labor, she looked it and wasn't afraid to throw it around.

She also didn't understand personal space, or so the other miners theorized. In support of said theory, she moved next to the kid and placed an arm none too delicately around his shoulders. Brushing her thick, black hair against his cheek, she purred, "Five of the damn things break down every day. Nobody would notice. Now if we blew up a couple of them, maybe. But our pals here don't like making noise. Pity."

Tambe smiled a sickly smile and extricated himself from her embrace.

"Darya's got a fair point," Murdock mused.

Slocum's jaw about hit the floor. "Blow up lifters? You can't be serious!"

Murdock's gaze slid his direction and slumped into rebuke. "About them breaking down all the time."

"Oh."

Pasternak always wanted to blow things up, a longing Murdock tried his best to quell. People could get hurt, either in the actual explosion or when the air fled the building. But now that he considered it, blowing up a few remote lifters might not be so bad. "They're the weak link," he said. "Hit enough of them, leave a calling card. Could get some attention."

Slocum made a face. He'd spent months working out how to sabotage the extractors, the front end of the mining operation and the most expensive equipment used in hydrogen collection. StarBright couldn't ignore the loss of even one extractor. Lifters, though, they were mundane—old technology so ubiquitous that the loss of five or six would hardly be noticed.

"What kind of calling card?" Slocum asked.

Murdock grinned at Pasternak.

She punched her fists at the ceiling and whooped, "Yes!"

Feng Shui Land, aka Mr. Fang, bolted from his chair, grabbed the shoulders of the poor flunky who had just delivered the news, and shook him, hard. "To *lunch?*" he demanded and shook harder. "He went to *lunch?*"

The King's Ransom. That's what the restaurant called itself. A curious name, Maccarone thought.

Whatever she thought of it, Culture Minister Chelsea Liwanu, dressed in an elegant black dress with a black lace shawl draped elegantly around her pale, elegant shoulders, did not smile. She did thank Maccarone for the lunch invitation, which was something, but in doing so only mustered as much enthusiasm as if he'd handed her a new toothbrush instead of offering her a five-star meal.

It didn't matter. Maccarone knew how to turn on the charm. He smiled warmly and with a slight bow replied, "It's the least I could do."

A rotund waiter in a cream-colored suit with bright orange buttons down the middle and blue braid dripping from the shoulders appeared at Maccarone's elbow. "Your table is ready, sir," he said quietly and led the couple into the dining room. The atmosphere was sublime, with swirls of blue and green light playing about an alabaster ceiling, walls draped in swaths of cream and orange silk, and a brilliant red carpet beneath their feet. The tables looked for all the world like real oak, although they couldn't be. Not way out here in the Oort Territories.

The waiter held Liwanu's chair for her, then held Macarone's, then placed printed menus before them, menus that had no prices. This, Macarone thought, was the height of class. At most restaurants, the menus were accessed electronically through the tabletop. Here they were printed, and not just printed, but printed without prices! The arrangement fairly screamed out, "If you have to as much as wonder, you shouldn't be eating here." Maccarone didn't allow himself to wonder.

"May I bring you something to drink?" the waiter asked.

"Mineral water," Liwanu said while studying the menu.

Macarone met the waiter's eyes and smiled. "The same."

"Sir." He glided away.

Maccarone turned his smile on Liwanu. How could she fail to fall under his spell? "You've done Space Operatic an enormous favor. I consider it a personal favor as well. You can't know how much it means to me."

Liwanu's eyes remained fixed on the menu. "Nothing personal about it. It's my job to bring cultural programs to the Territories. You like calamari?"

Maccarone didn't think he'd ever had calamari. He wasn't even sure he knew what it was. "Love it," he said. "Nevertheless, the competition must be fierce, and you choose me."

That got her attention. She peered at him over the top of the menu. Oddly, she didn't appear to be under any spell, his or otherwise. She looked more like she'd gulped a mouthful of salt water. "I chose your company. I assume you know how many opera companies are touring the Oort Territories."

Maccarone kept his smile fixed but had the unnerving sense that he suddenly looked like an idiot. "Of course."

"Of course. Why would you be so happy to be the top pick out of a field of one?"

"What I meant was—"

"I know what you meant. Opera happens to look better in my reports than, say, an Ed Wood film festival."

"A what?"

Miraculously, Liwanu did smile now, although it was the sort of smile wolves smile at deer. "Exactly. Either you don't know what it is, or you know all too well. Those are the so-called attractions most often inflicted on us out here."

She set her menu down as the waiter approached. "Calamari," she told him, "and the seafood étuffée. And a glass of Martian chloros, vintage eighty seven."

The waiter bowed and turned to Maccarone, who so far hadn't even looked at the menu. Forcing cheer into his voice, he said, "The same as the lady." The waiter bowed and glided off again.

"So," Maccarone said, hoping to get back on track, "you're saying you choose to do me a favor knowing I could do you a favor. A happy arrangement for both of us." He winked at her, knowing that couldn't fail to hook her.

Except it did. "I had no thought of doing favors. I merely approved your travel permits and initial performance schedule."

Maccarone leaned forward, elbows on the table, hands folded, chin resting on his knuckles. He looked devilishly handsome that way. His ego had no doubt of that. "Tell me, Chelsea. May I call you Chelsea?"

"No."

Unfazed, Maccarone plowed on. "What can I do to make things good for you?"

She seemed to be pondering how the conversation, and possibly the rest of the cosmos, had morphed into surreality.

Maccarone waited. Would she petition him for more performances? Entertainment for the masses? For the elite? She must! What high praise she would win with Space Operatic on her side. Would she offer him the best venues available?

Nah.

"Make audiences forget where they are."

"What?"

"Mr. Maccarone—"

"Please, call me Roberto."

"No. Look. Everybody hates it here. It's cold. It's dark. The work is miserable. The conditions are miserable. Life in general is miserable. My job is to make them forget all that. My job is to make them happy for a few fleeting moments."

Maccarone blinked. The job of this black-shrouded ice cube was to make people happy? He pushed himself back. Without realizing it, he adopted the same posture as her. He felt some of the joy seep out of his life. He wished he were wearing black, too. And he understood why. "You hate your job, don't you?"

"Loathe it."

"Calamari," the waiter said, sliding a steaming plate between them.

Land messaged everyone on the board of directors, every board member's secretary, and every other everyone who might conceivably have data to supply to the board regarding the opera company's precarious financial condition. He demanded a meeting. Today. Something had to be done before the next performance!

The resulting chatter miraculously coalesced around a time: six o'clock that evening.

Only Maccarone failed to respond, which fact sent Land into a rage. He kicked the wall, hard, then spent the next couple of hours in the infirmary having a broken toe mended.

Having given the matter sufficient thought, Artemus Worthington decided it was time to act. He needed a flunky of particular qualifications: someone stupid enough to accept his largess in exchange for complete loyalty, someone who could mix with the masses without raising suspicion, someone who would eagerly and unhesitatingly report everything back to him.

He thought he knew who it was.

In the outer office, his appointments secretary Jay James was hard at work juggling the tangle of commitments pressing upon the great man. James' fingers flew over his desktop, responding to requests, rearranging appointments, sending regrets—many, many regrets. Mr. Worthington couldn't be expected to meet with all the jokers demanding a slice of his time.

"Find Maccarone," Worthington told him.

Jay didn't pause in his labors for even for an instant. "He's at lunch."

"Alone?"

"With the Culture Minister."

Not much surprised Worthington, but that did. "She's buying him lunch?"

"Other way around."

That made zero sense. Why would Maccarone buy Liwanu lunch? Everyone knew how unapproachable the woman was. One look at her should have told Maccarone it was hopeless. "Where are they dining?"

James pointed ceilingward. "The King's Ransom."

Worthington's eyes followed while his jaw went the other direction. If Maccarone could afford *that* place, maybe this scheme was about to fizzle. Still, one shouldn't jump to conclusions. Gather intelligence first. "Send him a dinner invitation."

"Yes, sir."

"And since he's got time to kill, arrange a tour for him. I don't want him wandering off."

"As we speak, sir." James' fingers danced on the desktop.

Upon leaving the King's Ransom and parting ways with Liwanu, Maccarone stayed in the restaurant atrium for a time, staring out the huge window at the blackness of interstellar space, a blackness made all the deeper by the shimmering web of stars stewn across it. To say things hadn't gone according to plan would be a gross understatement. The Culture Minister, proving impervious to his charisma, promised nothing beyond a paltry two more performances. After that, she said, she would review Space Operatic's status.

Status.

Broke, that was his status. Dinner for two in this place, it turned out, cost what a more rational establishment might charge for a party of twenty. He nudged back his sleeve to expose his wrist computer and gave the receipt a good, long, look of rebuke. It didn't care. Good thing he'd put it on his personal account and thus didn't have to explain *this* to Fang!

As if it had been reading his mind, the device emitted a faint beep and a message from Fang popped up on screen. Something about an emergency board meeting at six o'clock. Maccarone eyed that with as much enthusiasm as he had his lunch bill.

"Mr. Maccarone?"

The voice at his left shoulder was gentle, even timid, but being unexpected it startled him. He spun and sputtered, "What? Yes?"

The man addressing him was shortish and youngish and blondish. His face was so nondescript that he could have been everyone in a crowd of a thousand. But when he cocked his head, the motion seemed unnaturally stiff, and from that alone Maccarone knew the man was not a man but a robot.

The troubled history of humanoid robots had led to this: a device that looked almost human but not like any particular human, that acted almost human but gave itself away through little unhuman quirks. People didn't want robots to fool them. They didn't want them to be too mechanical, either. Basically, they wanted warm, fuzzy helpers they could interact with as friends but with a cold undertone that allowed one to kick them without feeling guilty about it. Maccarone couldn't help but think this said something negative about humans.

"Mr. Worthington extends his compliments and invites you to dine with him this evening," the robot said in its calm, understated voice.

"He does?"

"Indeed, sir. He wishes to thank you for the fine performance last evening."

"Oh!" Maccarone smiled in spite of himself. If Liwanu wouldn't be persuaded to bestow cash upon Space Operatic, perhaps Worthington might. "That's very kind of him. What time, and where?"

"Eighteen hundred, sir. Right here." The robot gestured toward The

King's Ransom's dining room.

With a hesitant glance in that direction, Maccarone said, "Here?"

"Yes, sir."

"Who's buying?" Had it not been a robot, Maccarone wouldn't have asked, which also suggested something negative about humans.

"You are to be Mr. Worthington's guest. And since there is no time to travel to TDY-41093-RRP and back prior to dinner, I am instructed to give you a guided tour of Territory Headquarters, where many fascinating facilities are at your disposal."

Maccarone relaxed. "In that case," he said, "I accept. But just one moment, please."

The robot nodded with a touch of a jerk and turned away to give him privacy for that one moment. Maccarone used his moment to send a reply to Fang:

Unable to attend. Important dinner appointment. Please reschedule.

In the infirmary, Feng Shui Land grabbed the sleeve of the doctor's scrubs and nearly yanked her into his lap. "*Dinner?*" he barked at the message on his wrist computer. "He's going to *dinner?!*"

The doctor slapped Land's fingers, hard, caring not a whit about professionalism.

CHAPTER 4

Pitted against a century of spacefaring, a billion years of evolution won without breaking a sweat. As much as they pretended otherwise by dispersing through the solar system, humans needed the gravity of Earth to keep muscle toned, bone solid, blood red, and face nicely shaped. Thus, scattered across the Martian landscape, the surfaces of dozens of moons including Terra's own, and the interiors of thousands of small rocks and ice shards where people had flung the detritus of civilization, one found gymnasia and sports facilities galore. Even those who hated exercise indulged. It was either that or die a slow, miserable death.

But not here. Rotating to produce, at least in its living areas, an artificial gravity closely matching that to which its builders were adapted, Oort Territory Thirty-Seven HQ needed no such amenities. It offered a few, to be sure, but only for the benefit of those who liked breaking a sweat. For everyone else, HQ offered libraries and restaurants and virtual reality parlors and canned holographic concerts. Touring it all with his robot guide, Maccarone found it weird. Fun, yes, but weird, as though a part of life as vital as food had gone missing.

The robot, whose name was Bob (what else?), had explained it, but Maccarone couldn't quite grasp it. Oh, he got the logic. That made sense. "But why," he asked for the third time, "don't you have them anyway? It's like, I don't know, like saying that since there's no logical reason for cellos, we should burn them all."

"There is a logical reason for cellos," the robot replied, polite and bland.

Maccarone blinked at the not-quite-human machine. "There is?"

"Certainly."

"I think you misunderstand. There's an aesthetic reason for cellos, but not a logical reason."

"With all due respect," Bob said with a not quite smooth and not quite humble bow of its head. "I cannot be wrong in matters of logic."

Now that was just irritating. "There is no logical reason for cellos," Maccarone snapped. "I own an opera company. I should know."

"Without cellos, there would be a noticeable gap in the acoustic spectrum of the orchestra."

The human longed to kick the machine but wrestled the urge to the ground. "There is no logical reason why that gap couldn't be filled by something else."

"Like what, sir?"

He thought for a moment. "Marimbas."

"But sir," Bob protested, aggrieved, "the timbre of the marimba is not at all the timbre of the cello."

"Of course it isn't, but the range is about the same." Maccarone rubbed his temples. Why was he having this conversation, and with a robot of all things?

"One would not use the marimba in the same context as one uses the cello. If you like, I can demonstrate with our library recording of Yo-Yo Ma's performance of Bach's Cello Suite number one in G major, substituting the marimba for the cello based on library recordings of Mika Yoshida Stoltzman's jazz performances."

"Now why would I want to hear *that*?"

"To clearly appreciate why the marimba cannot substitute for the cello." Somehow, Bob made the offer sound utterly sensible.

Placing a hand over his face, Maccarone shook his head. "I only said that the two instruments have about the same range."

"Indeed. Nevertheless, the marimba can't replace the cello, and therefore there is a logical necessity for cellos. Now here we have one of the finest theaters in the solar system."

While arguing, they sauntered along a gently curving walkway carpeted in gold inlaid with deep red swirls. A glowing green and white ceiling arched overhead. Beyond the silver railings on either side, space dropped away to a sprawling flower garden eight meters below through which people walked along stone paths, talking and laughing. The walkway and the robot had stopped before an ornate pair of double doors, presently closed—purple doors across which gold tracery swirled in abstract patterns.

"Indeed?" Maccarone asked, glad to be off the subject of marimbas. "What makes it so special?"

"It was built to exacting optical and acoustical standards. It provides comfortable seating and food service for one thousand people. It has one of the most advanced lighting systems in existence, and a stage large enough to contain both the most elaborate live productions and full-size LaserMax (trademark) holographic projections."

His interest more than piqued, Maccarone almost felt himself drooling. Now here would be a venue worth booking! He was about to ask who to see about it when the robot added, "Also, it is in mint condition. It has never been used."

"Never been used! That's criminal! Why not?"

For once, Bob floundered for a reply. It gazed blankly at the closed doors, then with an unnatural jerk of its head gazed blankly at Maccarone, then with another unnatural jerk of its head looked at the doors again. "I do not have that information. But it is a fine theater, is it not?"

"Could I go inside?"

"No. Follow me."

Maccarone watched the robot move back the way they had come. He looked at the doors. He touched the doors, gently, his fingers caressing one beautiful gold swirl. He tugged at the gold handle. Locked.

"Never been used," he muttered. "Absolute crime."

Hurrying to catch up with his electronic tour guide, he came alongside it just in time to hear it say, "It really is no replacement at all. A marimba for a cello? No, I don't think so. In addition to their very different timbres . . ."

"Oh God," Maccarone muttered.

Ajit Tambe's thin, dark face might have had a wan cast to it had the light not been so wan itself. He felt wan at any rate, and a tad sick, the sickness brought on by nerves, the nerves brought on by Darya Pasternak. Just inside TDY-41093-RRP's South Pole sector on the eastern hemisphere of the iceball, Tambe and Pasternak were jammed close together in a narrow service shaft that passed alongside a disused lifter. Every time he turned or shifted one way or the other, some part of his body connected with some part of hers, reminding him more or less constantly on the one hand that she was a woman and on the other that her musculature was more developed than his.

Upon their latest mutual graze, Pasternak laughed. "Why're you on edge, kid? Am I your first?"

Whatever words were trying to form in his throat nearly choked him.

She bumped his hip with hers. "Yeah?"

"Don't call me kid."

"Ajit," she said, her voice syrupy.

"Can we just get our work done?"

The work involved placing a series of small explosive charges on the wall separating them from the lifter, wiring the charges together, and attaching a radio-controlled igniter. They were nearly done. The remaining equipment lay concealed in the pockets of Tambe's tool belt, he basically serving as Pasternak's pack horse. She placed and connected the components, her expert fingers conjuring the completed device almost on their own with little need of her eyes for guidance. Good thing, Tambe thought. He could barely see what she was doing, although he'd felt plenty.

"We could get lots of things done, you and me, here in the dark," she teased.

"Why am I even here?" He tried to project anger but only sounded evasive. "You don't need me here."

"Don't say that. I might need you more than you know." She bumped him again. "Besides, this was your idea, babe. Gimme that last charge."

Tambe handed her the charge. Why was he so scared of her? Okay, she was basically a scary lady, although lady probably wasn't the right term. He'd seen her pick fights a few times. With men. And win. Murdock's agreement to this plan notwithstanding, more than anything they were here to blow something up because Pasternik thought it would be fun to blow something up. Worst of all, she seemed to enjoy teasing the hell out of him. Still, it was only teasing.

Wasn't it?

"Igniter, Ajit, igniter!"

"Sorry?"

"Don't fantasize when you should be working." She shoved her hand into a pocket on his belt and fished around for the igniter.

He was positive he was blushing and hoped she couldn't see. It sure is warm in this tunnel, he thought.

Pasternik connected the igniter. "Done. I need to send a test signal. Let's move up the tunnel a bit. Just in case."

"Umm," Tambe replied, his mind not quite on work anymore. *Is she just teasing? Or...*

"Up the tunnel," she said, slapping him on the rump.

He moved ahead with her right behind, her hand in fact still on his behind. Her touch raised the temperature another ten degrees, yet somehow he found the sensation curiously pleasant.

"Do you, uh, well, like me?"

Pasternik made a funny noise, almost a choking sound, and withdrew her hand. "Like you?"

Tambe wished he hadn't said that, but to his own surprise he let his mouth get away with making it worse: "You know. Like me." It sounded stupid once it was out, but there it was.

"Sure, I like you. I mean I like you, not I like you."

That, he thought, sounded even more stupid, and he was fairly sure Pasternik knew it. Which didn't stop him from perpetuating the stupidity. "Which kind of like is which?"

"Don't worry about it, kid. I just like you, that's all."

Impossibly, the tunnel narrowed as they moved along, and Tambe found he had to turn sideways to keep going. Pasternik was so close he could hear her breathing in his ear. "Don't call me kid."

"Ajit," she replied, not quite so syrupy this time. She placed a hand on his shoulder, her touch surprisingly gentle. "Stop here." She fiddled with some device he couldn't see but knew to be the controller for the igniter, and a pale green light blinked on and off three times. "We're good. Move on. The exit should be about fifteen meters ahead."

Pressing onward, Tambe decided he wasn't scared of her anymore, although he didn't know why. Something had happened inside his head, something inexplicable, something he thought just might change everything between them. He wondered if she felt the same.

"I like you, too," he said.

Half an hour later, a very safe distance away, he thought she must indeed feel the same, because she let him push the button to blow up the lifter.

For the second time in one day, Roberto Maccarone soaked up the ambiance of the King's Ransom, delighting in the cream and orange silk draperies stretching from the brilliant red carpet upward to the alabaster ceiling, a ceiling crisscrossed by blue and green swirls of light. He marveled again at the oaken tables, still wondering if they could possibly be oak, doubting that they were, hoping that they were. Following his host's lead, he ordered porterhouse steak, rare, with assorted vegetables on the side.

"How do you like our humble home among the stars?" Artemus Worthington asked, holding up his steak knife and minutely inspecting it for blemishes. He didn't find any, certainly, but he pretended to and took up the pale yellow linen napkin to wipe away the imaginary spot.

"I wouldn't call it humble," Maccarone said, eyes agog at the opulence. "I've never seen any place like this!"

"I suppose to an outsider it would look plush. Live here for a time, though, and you start to take it all for granted."

Maccarone figured he was lying. He had to be.

Apparently reading that assessment from his guest's face, Worthington nodded. "It's true. I eat here a dozen times a week. It's part of my routine." He put down the knife, lifted his salad fork, and gave it the same treatment. "I walk the rose gardens on my way to the office every day and notice neither blossoms nor fragrance. My office looks like an old-growth forest on Earth, and what do I do there? I work."

That can't be, Maccarone thought. "What, with trees and everything?"

"Not exactly. But the effect is similar."

"Similar to trees?"

"Similar to a forest."

"You can't have a forest without trees."

"I'm so rich I can have anything I want."

"But . . ." Realizing he was starting to sound like Bob the robot going on about marimbas, Maccarone cut himself off.

Worthington set aside the salad fork and took up the spotless teaspoon to administer a good cleaning. "You're a man of taste, Mr. Maccarone, like me. But unlike me, you don't have massive wealth. I envy you that."

"Why?" Maccarone gasped.

Worthington smiled knowingly at his spoon. "Because you can still see and enjoy what's around you. To me, it's just the drab backdrop of a boring life." Setting down the spoon and folding his napkin, he sighed pathetically. Over the top that was, Maccarone thought, but the thought sublimated when Worthington added, "Take our theater, for example."

"Ah." Maccarone nearly swooned. "Your theater."

"Finest in the solar system. But to me, just another room behind a set of closed doors."

"That's because nobody ever goes in. If you could set foot inside—"

"Oh, I can, anytime I want."

Leaning forward, Maccarone held his breath, hoping against hope that Worthington could paint a vision, however faint, of the glories that must lie hidden behind those doors. Those beautiful doors, those doors that deserved to be flung open to the universe!

"But I don't."

"You don't?"

"No."

"Never?"

"Never."

"Never ever?"

That knowing smile returned.

"But why not?"

"Mr. Maccarone. May I call you Roberto?"

"Of course. And may I call you Artemus?"

"Absolutely not. Such familiarity would disrupt the order of things. What you must understand, Roberto, is that we have never used that theater because way out here on the fringes of civilization there has never been anyone capable of mounting a production worthy of it. We wouldn't want to sully such a sublime surround with an Ed Wood Film Festival, would we?"

Maccarone felt his head spinning, whether because of Worthington's alliterative prowess or the pervasiveness of whoever this Ed Wood fellow was or the tragedy of such a stunningly beautiful theater sitting idle its entire life. No, he knew what it was: that theater!

"But an opera," he boldly suggested, "a Verdi opera, why, that would make for a truly grand opening."

"Yes." Worthington sighed again, even more pathetically, as though he shared Maccarone's vision.

Which Maccarone knew he did not, but that hardly mattered. Here was the golden opportunity Space Operatic needed, the payoff to his gamble. One performance in that theater and the future of the company was assured!

"Unfortunately," Worthington continued, "the Culture Minister controls the keys. Without her in our court, we can't get you in."

Talk about a letdown. Maccarone felt like his best friend had just punched him in the gut.

"I see from your expression that you've already tried to sweet talk her. It's hopeless, I'm afraid. She's as cold as space, that woman." Leaning forward, Worthington lowered his voice conspiratorially. "You know what she really wants to do with her life?"

Maccarone couldn't have cared less. He just wished she'd take her life anywhere but here.

Worthington told him. "She'd like to take her life anywhere but here."

"You say you're so rich you can have whatever you want. Maybe you should pay her way back to Earth in exchange for the theater." He'd meant it as the blackest of black humor, but once it was out, he realized Worthington was chewing on it.

"Maybe."

"She'd accept a deal like that?"

"Not exactly, Roberto, but she is occasionally bribable. Very occasionally. She's been persuaded to grant a favor or two in the past."

"Are we talking about the same chunk of solid nitrogen?"

Worthington laughed, his reaction for once genuine. "Hard to believe, I know. But it's true."

Maccarone was sorely tempted to ask Worthington to do it, but even the promise of the grandest venue in the solar system couldn't justify law-breaking. Yes, he could wheel and deal with the best of them, or so he imagined, but bribing a government official? That crossed a line he never thought he'd nudge as much as a toe over. Then again, all they were talking about was scheduling a performance. How illegal could that be?

The question proved moot. Worthington made the decision for him. "One thing, Roberto. If I do this, I'll expect a favor in return."

The word "anything" fortunately caught in Maccarone's throat before it spilled from his lips. There were enough rash promises in the repertoire that he should know better. He didn't need to end up like Wotan. "Such as?"

"I'm in need of two things which you can provide. On the one hand, I need someone loyal on the StarBright board of directors. As a skilled businessman, you would certainly qualify."

That didn't sound so bad; in fact, it sounded positively wonderful.

"On the other, I need eyes and ears among the workers on TDY-41093-RRP. There have been some unsettling incidents of late. I understand your performance there was well-received. You could mix with the locals and gather useful intelligence with respect to potential insurrection."

That sounded distinctly unwonderful. Bristling with indignation, he snapped, "You want me to spy on people?"

"Not at all. I only want you to let the board, and especially me, know if you hear anything unsettling."

"Now look Ar, er, Mr. Worthington. I admit I'd love nothing more than to play that theater, but I'm not sinking to that level."

Worthington shrugged. "Suit yourself. You can always ask Chelsea to dinner again. Maybe she'll even kiss you next time. On the elbow." He garnished that offering with a sarcastic smile.

The waiter arrived and slid their steaks before them, steaming slabs of perfection scenting the air about the table with their rich aroma. Maccarone had never inhaled an aroma quite like it. He imagined eating here a dozen times a week. He imagined Space Operatic performing to a full house in that amazing, brilliant, unparalleled theater.

He imagined Chelsea Liwanu telling him no.

"How much," he asked, "does a StarBright board member earn?"

Worthington shrugged, supremely bored. "So much the exact figure doesn't matter."

CHAPTER 5

Feng Shui Land was fed up to there. Or there. Or even there! Maccarone be damned! He would have his board meeting with or without their lunatic leader. Within seconds of receiving Maccarone's request to reschedule, he'd told everyone so. Okay, not seconds exactly, but as soon he'd recovered from the blows inflicted by that sadist nurse. The medical staff on this God-forsaken iceberg was the worst he'd ever encountered. He added them to the list of reasons to despise the Oort Territories.

Only stage manager and board secretary Kazimir Kapitan objected to meeting without Maccarone. The rest fell mutely in line, leaving Kapitan little choice but to acquiesce. While Maccarone dined in opulent luxury, his board assembled around a cold metallic table in a cold, cramped metallic room to talk business over cold pseudo-meat sandwiches. Most had ice in their veins before a word had been spoken, which suited Land's purpose exactly.

"You know the state we're in," he told them. "Disaster waits in the wings. The longer we dither, the greater the chance cataclysm will enter stage left and demolish our reputation." He leaned back, a smile playing through his mind though not on his lips. He thought he'd put that beautifully.

Kapitan shook his head. "We're living under a curse, and you're talking money. You can't buy off a curse." He picked up his sandwich. He'd taken only one small bite. He turned it over a few times before dropping it again. "Is this supposed to be turkey?"

Grumbles chased each other around the conference table, some about business and some about food, starting and ending with principal conductor Ophelia Tansaniya, a dark-skinned woman of grace and bearing who in her seventy eighth year of life possessed nearly all the energy she'd had in youth. "Curses only follow those who believe in them." She scrutinized Kapitan's sandwich. "What does it taste like?"

"Which is why we're under one." That, asserted by the company's lead tenor, Manfred Mooseherder. Feng Shui Land could never fathom why the guy had picked such a stupid stage name. Mooseherder's comment was met with more grumbles, mostly of assent.

"Enough grumbling," Land snapped. "This is a financial discussion, not a séance for doomed spiritualists. Our stage properties and fabrication facilities require serious upgrading. Now—"

Tansaniya returned his snap so deftly that had it been tennis, she would have scored the point. ""Don't be daft. We don't have the cash."

"Not like turkey, that's for sure," Kapitan said. He poked at the sandwich as though it might still be alive, although it probably never had been in the first place.

Ignoring the sidebar discussion, Land gave Tansaniya another serve: "The very question I was about to raise."

Chicxulub, the company's lead baritone, laughed. He laughed a lot and smiled even more, often at the most inappropriate times. "I'll see your raise and call your bluff," he said in an intense Mexican accent.

Land turned unamused eyes on him. Clearly, Chicxulub didn't know the difference between tennis and poker. For one thing, there was no bluffing in tennis. No wonder the baritone had named himself after the site of an extinction-level impact. Given the quality of his input at board meetings, the appellation suited him.

"You know exactly what you want," Chixulub said, grinning like an idiot. "Spill it."

Kapitan's eyes struggled to keep up, shifting madly from one speaker to the next. He would have made a poor tennis fan. "What's this now?"

Tansaniya shook her head. "Really, Kasimir. When has Fang not had his moves planned a year in advance?"

Land pounded the table with both fists and immediately regretted it. But the pain at least served to intensify his anger to a gratifying height. "Don't call me Fang, damn it! That's not my name!"

"It is these days," Chicxulub smirked. "So what about it?"

Kapitan gazed thoughtfully at the ceiling. "It could be equal parts day-old bread, lemon juice, and moldy cheddar."

Land closed his eyes in despair. No choice. This crew lacked the navigational skills to follow him to the door without a tracking system and a chauffeur. He'd have to take them in tow. "How many performances can we book out here? The locals probably equate Ed Wood film festivals with high culture. Right now we're talking props, but face it: soon we won't be able to pay staff, much less ourselves. Imagine unemployment here in Beelzebub's outhouse."

The silence was as silent as the Oort Territories were dark.

"Exactly," Land continued. "Staying here is a death sentence. Worse. It's consignment to an outer dark where even demons refuse to tread."

"What's an Ed Wood film festival?" Kapitan asked.

Chicxulub's eyes lit up. "You want to take the company sunward again."

Finally the light bulbs switched on. Whatever that meant. Not that Land cared. The point was—

Tansaniya leaned forward and fixed Land with a matronly glare. "Maccarone won't go for it."

"He will if we're united."

"Don't you remember how percentages work?"

Land glared a glare of his own right back at her. Glares locked, neither flinched nor spoke. The others held their tongues, afraid to blunder into the no-man's land between.

Finally, Tansaniya said in a voice suited to explaining something to a small child, "One hundred out of one hundred. That's how many pieces of the company he owns."

"Not," Land said. "If," Land continued. "He," Land added. "Goes," Land appended. "Bankrupt!" Land snapped, slapping the table once more. "Ouch!" He examined his palm. "I wish you'd stop making me do that."

Kapitan shook his head at the table. "Going sunward won't help. The curse will follow us. Bad karma, probably. It started on Titan. Ever since the chorus got into that brawl with that methane processing crew we haven't any luck at all. Since then, a cloud has hung over every performance." He shivered. "A methane cloud." Pushing his mystery sandwich aside, he added, "You can't outrun bad karma. You have to pay off the debt. But how? That's what I don't get. It was their fault. If they'd had proper signage, nobody would have ended up in the wrong shower facilities in the first place. Why did we get stuck with the curse instead of them? Also, I really do want to know what an Ed Wood film festival is."

Feng Shui Land set elbow to table, balled up his fist, and leaned his head against it. "My God. Chicxulub?"

"I think Roberto has a plan. I'll wait to see what it is."

"Manfred?"

Mooseherder shrugged. "I'd go back in a heartbeat, but I think we should give the boss a chance. Chicxulub's right. He's got a plan. He always has a plan."

"Unemployed in Beelzebub's outhouse," Land said as though threatening them with something vile, like a lawsuit. "You'll see."

"What about Ed Wood?" Kapitan asked.

Arne Slocum loved surveillance technology. He'd often thought that if he hadn't ended up a miner, he could have been a spy. The opportunity to do both thrilled him no end. He'd eagerly put his enthusiasm to work in the service of Josh Murdock and his band of malcontents. In short order, he'd blanketed the tunnels and corridors of TDY-41093-RRP with micro-imagers and ultrasensitive listening devices, all cleverly concealed where nobody would notice, and built a control center in an abandoned restroom off the rear of an abandoned storeroom from which he could eavesdrop on all operations on the iceball.

He sat there now, along with Murdock and Ajit Tambe and Darya Pasternak, playing in spite of his age like a child, showing them the views from his latest installations, demonstrating the superb acoustic pickup afforded by his newest audio gear, and generally having a grand time.

"Need to see the lifter," Murdock told him for the third time, growling vaguely like the bear he less than vaguely looked like. "That's why we came."

"That's boring," Slocum replied. "You blew it up. What's to see?"

"The wreckage," Pasternak snapped. "What's the point of blowing something up if you can't see the wreckage?"

With a weary sigh, Slocum fiddled with the controls and brought up a new scene: a dark tunnel with a darker hole ripped in its side. From the hole, bits and pieces of less dark stuff protruded without revealing their nature. Slocum thought the conglomeration looked like a mutant squid probing the tunnel with twisted, inky tentacles.

Pasternak whistled appreciatively. "Surgical, huh kid?"

Tambe opened his mouth as if to object one more time to his nickname, then closed it. He nodded. "Yeah. Surgical."

"What's the chatter?" Murdock asked Slocum.

"About what you'd expect. Some cursing about a breakdown followed by some cursing about an explosion followed by some cursing about worn out, outmoded equipment."

Pasternak looked like she'd choked on a fish. "They didn't get it?"

"Not at first."

"But now they do?"

Slocum fiddled with the controls again. "Listen."

A static-infected voice erupted from the speakers. "This ain't no breakdown, boss."

Another static-infected voice answered, "What do you mean? Of course it was."

"Whatever blew up wasn't in the lifter machinery. It was outside, along the service tunnel."

"Okay, so something else went bad on us."

"Like what?"

The boss snarled something unintelligible.

"Didn't catch that."

"You heard me."

"No, really."

"Just document what you think went bad and get back here. HQ is already breathing down our necks."

"But boss, nothing went bad. I think—"

"No, you don't. Don't say it, don't think it, don't broadcast it tele-pathically. Just don't. This is just some cranky old whatchamacallit gone bad. Understood?"

The worker snarled something unintelligible.

"Didn't catch that," the boss said.

"You heard me," the worker told him.

Slocum turned off the sound. "That's pretty much it."

Pasternak smacked her right fist into her left palm. "I'm gonna blow up the payroll office next. Just so they can't cover it up."

Murdock gave her a thoughtful look.

Already bored with the conversation, Slocum switched the view to something more interesting, a team of technicians calibrating a new extractor near the North Pole. *That puppy*, he thought, *would make one amazing target.*

Tambe tapped Pasternak on the shoulder and quietly asked, "Can I help?"

After dinner, which included a melt-in-your-mouth key lime cheese-cake that glowed green when the lighting was dimmed for evening ambiance,

Artemus Worthington invited Roberto Maccarone to tour the rose gardens. Maccarone wanted nothing more than to return to the *Ponchielli* to sleep off his culinary overdose, but Worthington wouldn't take no for an answer.

So they walked, or in Maccarone's case waddled, through air suffused with a hundred different rose scents, surrounded by a rainbow of blossoms. In spite of the scenery, Worthington appeared bored. Maccarone felt sure his own face broadcast gluttonous excess, but nobody they passed gave him a second look, so maybe not.

Worthington stopped at a bench and motioned his guest to join him in a break from their stroll. Grateful, Maccarone sank onto the seat and closed his eyes.

"I assume," Worthington began, but was interrupted by a series of frantic beeps emanating from within his lapel. He rolled his eyes. "Excuse me." Tapping at the unseen device, he said, "Go ahead." Although Maccarone heard nothing, Worthington listened with interest. "What measures are you taking?"

Maccarone studied the lapel, wondering about the communications mechanism hidden there, whether it was a relative of Snow Hill's lapel device, what Worthington was hearing. Maccarone had never used such paraphernalia, preferring old fashioned communications like wrist computers and face-to-face conversations.

"Send me full details." Worthington closed his eyes as though in pain. "Full details." He shook his head. "What don't you understand? Full, or details?" With a quick glance at Maccarone, he added, "I'll call back shortly." Tapping his lapel again, he leaned back and looked skyward, although no sky arched over them. The distant ceiling glowed pink and maroon.

"Trouble?" Maccarone ventured.

"On more than one score. But a golden opportunity for you, assuming you accept my offer."

Maccarone drew a long breath. Although his every instinct said no, his mouth said, "Yes."

"Excellent. Then I need you to return to TDY-41093-RRP and prepare for your next performance."

"That's it?"

"Yes."

There had to be more. Didn't there?

"Actually."

Of course, Maccarone thought.

"We have to execute a contract to make your position official."

"Doesn't the board have to vote on my appointment first?"

Worthington waved away the objection. "I own the seat you'll be occupying."

"Oh."

"Come. We'll return to my office and take care of it immediately."

Which they did. Once the electronic signatures had been recorded and the agreement properly validated and filed and distributed to all relevant company and government storage systems, and once a cosmological sum of money had been transferred into his bank account, Maccarone found out what Worthington *really* wanted from him.

Somewhere in the deep interior of Territory HQ, hidden away like an embarrassment such as a half-wit uncle or a three-year-old who still didn't know how to operate a wrist computer, the offices of various lesser government agencies clustered, a mass of boxy, grayish spaces with exposed pipes and conduits overhead. It looked nothing like the rest of HQ because it was nothing like the rest of HQ. This chunk of unattractive metal and plastic comprised the original HQ, the first bits and pieces bolted together twenty five years earlier when the need for some kind of government presence to bring order to the lawlessness of the inner Oort cloud became obvious. That, and there were tax revenues to be had. Lots of tax revenues.

As StarBright gobbled up smaller mining operations, growing fatter and fatter each year, it struck a series of deals with the Oort Territory Thirty-Seven government. Those deals allowed it to build and partially occupy successive additions to the space station: stunningly beautiful, stunningly expensive additions, with construction costs heavily subsidized by taxpayers (no kidding). Details of those deals never quite made sense to anyone, or at least anyone willing to talk about them, but StarBright certainly made out like the bandit it was.

Be that as it may, Culture Minister Chelsea Liwanu lived and worked in the oldest and most unattractive part of HQ. She pretty much hated both her living quarters and her office space, but most days that hatred stood grumbling in line behind a dozen other hatreds, scarcely registering as it lay frozen in the cosmic ice field of her mind. Particularly now, it was the least of her discontents. She knew because she had a list, conveniently displayed for perusal on her desktop computer screen.

One.

She spelled out the numbers. She always did that. She herself couldn't have said why. It was an old habit, likely begun in a fit of pique to irritate one of her early teachers.

One: I'm surrounded by idiots.

Two: The idiots are miserable.

Three: The miserable idiots are making me miserable.

Four: The only hope of making the miserable idiots happy for ten seconds lies with an even bigger idiot.

Five: The big idiot wants something. The scoundrel wants the big idiot to get it.

Liwanu knew that because the scoundrel had messaged her not ten minutes before. He told her the idiot needed something from her, but in his not so subtle way failed to mention what. Presumably he wanted her to ask, which she pointedly had not. She annotated item five.

Five: The big idiot wants something. The scoundrel wants the big idiot to get it. I hope they both get it.

Six: Whatever it is, the scoundrel will pay for it.

Seven: Lots and lots.

Technically, these last two points weren't hatreds. They fell under the rubric of "intriguing," but being necessary to her chain of thought, they had to stay.

Eight: I hate this place.

Nine: I hate this place.

Ten: I really, totally, completely hate this place.

The one thing Liwanu didn't hate was the list. She thought she'd summed up life remarkably well this time, better even than last month, and that had been a stellar list. What made this one better, made it more than a mere catalogue of complaints, was that it contained the seeds of a plan. Seeds were all she had, but maybe she could grow them into the cash she so desperately needed while sticking it to both the idiot and the scoundrel. Especially the scoundrel. The idiot, he was just a big idiot.

The scoundrel was the reason Chelsea Liwanu shrouded herself in black.

CHAPTER 6

On board Ponchielli they had a really big room.

Just one, mind you. For the most part, *Space Operatic*'s official transport, like most such ships, consisted of cramped quarters, and too few of them. In the sleeping quarters, bunks stacked like rungs on a ladder squeezed out almost all standing and walking space. In the dining hall, it required a Ph.D. in topology to pull a chair out far enough to sit down. As for facilities of a more private nature, one doesn't even want to discuss conditions.

But *Ponchielli* did have this one really big room, a circular multi-purpose room near the heart of the ship that could be configured for large meetings or rehearsals. Right there, right now, the day after he took a seat on the StarBright board of directors, Roberto Maccarone assembled every member of his company from board members to musicians and singers to the ship's command and support staff. An audience of one hundred fifty three in all. He stood before the assemblage, all present pumped up for his big announcement. He was, anyway. He found their level of pumpedness difficult to gauge.

"My friends," he began, wearing a huge smile that went brilliantly (he thought) with his snazzy red blazer, the one with the gold frills along the lapels, and his brilliant white trousers crisscrossed by green, orange, and purple squiggles. "You all know coming to the Oort Territories was a risk. A calculated risk, but a risk nonetheless."

He could see nobody believed he had calculated anywhere near that far, but that was fine. Soon everything would be fine. Life was so amazingly fine right now!

"I'm happy to tell you now, today, that thanks to your highly successful performance before an assemblage of prominent dignitaries, the gamble has paid off. Ladies and gentlemen, we have struck gold!"

He spread his arms wide and wiggled his fingers to suggest gold falling from the sky. On second thought (he thought) that wasn't such a good image.

Who wanted to be stuck on the head by falling chunks of metal? Never mind. By the time his presentation was over, they'd be hailing him as a genius.

Right now, very little hailing was in progress. The looks the company gave him suggested they didn't know what he was talking about. Only Fang, glowering in the front row, perhaps preparatory to lobbing a lump of that fallen metal back at the boss, seemed to understand. That guy was strange.

"Today I had the honor of dining first with the Culture Minister and later with Mr. Worthington, the Director of Marketing for StarBright Energy. In the course of our discussions, I learned that Territory Headquarters has one of the finest theaters in the solar system. This theater, believe it or not, has never been used. But I've concluded an agreement that will allow us . . ."

He spread his arms to indicate his people.

"Allow *you* to open that theater in the grandest possible fashion: a Verdi opera!"

Jaws hit the floor, all except Fang's. He looked like he was trying to bite off his own head. *What*, Maccarone wondered, *is wrong with that guy?* This should have been the kind of news he'd been waiting for.

Never mind.

"Details remain to be worked out. And as you know, we have a schedule to keep. We have an encore performance here on TDY-41093-RRP in two days' time, then we play another small venue on another ice cube next week." Maccarone smiled and winked. Nobody smiled with him. This crowd had grown tougher since that incident on Titan.

Never mind.

"But we must start planning now, and we begin by choosing the opera. As I see it, we have two choices: *Aida*, or *La Traviata*. Let's put it to a vote. All in favor of *Aida*, raise your hand."

Nobody raised their hand. Maccarone hadn't expected that but maintained his happy visage.

"*La Traviata*, then. Show of hands, please."

Still no hands went up, which puzzled Maccarone even more. Surely one of these great operas must be the favorite? What did they want, *The Bloody Nun*? Or maybe *Das Opfer*, with its victory dance of the penguins?

"Would someone like to suggest a different work?"

The silence was so deep, Maccarone could have believed everyone but him had been sucked out an airlock. Then one timid hand rose up, slowly, nervously, in the middle of the gathering. It was an elegant young hand attached to an elegant young chorus woman. Wendy, Maccarone thought, or Whitney, or something starting with "w."

He pointed to her. "Yes?"

"Why, well, that is, why hasn't the theater ever been used?"

Smiling indulgently, Maccarone said, "I guess they don't want to open it with an Ed Wood film festival." He added a chuckle for effect. It had no effect.

Well, just one effect. In the front row on the opposite side from Fang, Kazimir Kapitan's head snapped to attention. "What's with this Ed Wood guy? He's popping up all over the place."

Oh God, Maccarone thought, *please don't mimic that robot.* "It doesn't matter, Kazimir. What matters is we get to open a spectacular theater. Us. Space Operatic. Think of the prestige!"

"And where," Fang said dangerously, "do you think we're going to get the money for a production on that scale?"

Ah, that must have been it. Land's irritation surely had been born of a perceived lack of funds to mount a fame-inducing production. Poor, frustrated fellow. But Maccarone had the answer. "Excellent question. I've been offered a position on the StarBright board of directors. That means I can funnel gobs of money into Space Operatic. So have no fear, Fa . . . ah . . . Feng." (Everyone did laugh at that, although behind their hands.) "Your worries are over."

Fang snarled under his breath, not at all the reaction Maccarone had expected. *What in the world is wrong with him?* he wondered again.

Never mind.

"Okay, show of hands now. *Aida*?"

Still no votes.

"*La Traviata*?"

Nothing.

"Need time to think it over?"

Another hand went up. This time the inquirer was an older fellow who had something to do with keeping the *Ponchielli*'s engines running. Maccarone acknowledged him. He stood, cleared his throat, and in a gruff voice asked a seriously annoying question:

"How the hell much they paying you for being bored?"

Maccarone rubbed his forehead. *Aida*, he decided. And he hoped they'd all hate it.

As a general rule, Artemus Worthington did not make house calls. Anybody who desired the benefit of his wisdom could beg for an appointment and, if granted the honor, come to him. Anybody he wanted to confer with would, knowing what was good for them, also come to him. He allowed but two exceptions to these rules: StarBright board chairman and CEO Santamonica Amarillo and, although he hated to admit it, his wife Maisie. Chelsea Liwanu appeared nowhere on that list. She didn't even merit an honorable mention.

Thus, when he appeared in her office without an appointment, she knew he was up to something. Taking in the unfashionable surroundings with evident distaste, he gingerly sat in a gray plastic chair and regarded her with feigned disinterest. "I was just in the neighborhood," he lied—well, it had to be a lie, didn't it?— "and thought I'd stop by. Any noticeable improvement in the culture scene of late?"

Liwanu returned his look with her own frostier version. "No wonder you're still married. All your pick-up lines sound like that."

Worthington brushed some non-existent lint from his dark yellow and orange sleeve. "No improvement. How sad for you."

"I'm sending a new act your way." She pretended to study a file displayed on her computerized desk display. "There's a guy who walks a tightrope while juggling flaming kabobs and singing some ancient song about how beautiful America was."

Worthington winced.

Liwanu disfavored him with a sadistic smile.

"You could do better than that," he told her. "Much better."

She nearly asked how but then realized why he'd stopped by. She had never answered his message, never asked the question he'd goaded her to ask. Now he had no choice but to spill it himself. She decided to string him along. After all, he'd expect her to resist, and resistance came so naturally. "No."

"A million times better."

"Absolutely not."

"Now Chelsea . . ."

"Don't mimic my father. He had some self-respect, which is the one thing you can't convincingly fake."

Worthington's eyes widen in surprise. "But Chelsea—"

Surely he didn't expect her to fall for that innocent act? "Aside from at the performance, have you actually talked to Maccarone? He's a jerk!"

"As it happens, I have. Whatever your opinion of his personality, he has something you desperately need."

Okay, she actually did want to know. Who wouldn't? But Worthington would not have the pleasure of hearing her beg or even ask. Rather, she snorted a most unladylike snort and thought the question without speaking: *What could that idiot possibly have that I could care about?*

Either Worthington heard her think it, or he'd merely grown tired of the game. "An opera company."

That disappointed her. He'd massively underdone himself. "Is that all?"

"Is that *all*? Good God, Chelsea—"

"Oh, shut up. I'm touring him around. A little at a time, just to make him nervous, but around. When all is said and done, he'll make my reports look good."

Pushing his chair back and stretching out his legs, Worthington assumed a look of mock disappointment. "You're not thinking big enough. That's your problem, Chelsea: you never think big enough."

"No, my problem is that I'm stuck out here with you."

"When you don't have to be."

Ah, yes. He was, then, prepared to pay massively for whatever he wanted. Good. But she mustn't give in too readily. He could smell a victim's desires a million miles off. "Maccarone's pathetic little act can't get us out of here. Or did you actually swallow that line about the door? A miracle signifying God's acceptance of Nabucco's prayer? Come on."

Worthington opened his mouth to speak.

Liwanu didn't give him the chance. "That was a construction failure, pure and simple. They're a sham. The whole company. Sooner or later, they'll get their comeuppance." Satisfied with her prognostication, Liwanu assumed a superior pose and donned an expression that would have sent a chill down Nootaikok's spine. She briefly wondered whether Worthington knew about Nootaikok. Not likely. Then she wondered how *she* knew about Nootaikok. Oh, yes. That proposal for that bizarre play submitted by that bizarre playwright a couple of years back. Why he thought it would be a good idea to stage a production about the Inuit god of icebergs and glaciers out here in the frigid abyss of the Oort territories was completely beyond her.

Worthington brushed some nonexistent lint from his left sleeve. "Maccarone's problem is merely financial. With sufficient means, he could stage the most inspiring performances."

Liwanu laughed out loud before she could stop herself. Doubling over, she barely pushed herself back in time to avoid knocking her forehead on her desk. She laughed with such intensity her whole body hurt, but it felt somehow good, never mind it being at another's expense.

"Why is that amusing?" Worthington asked once her mirth had played itself out. A hint of evil smile broke through in spite of his effort to contain it.

"Seriously? Pairing the words 'Maccarone' and 'means'?"

"I've hired him."

All trace of laughter fled her soul, leaving her with a vague sense of choking on something old and foul. "Hired him?"

"I've given him a seat on the StarBright board. He's drowning in cash now."

"Why?"

"So he can do what he does best: produce operas. He only lacks one thing."

Her question stuck in her throat. She knew the answer. She knew the horrible, traitorous thing Worthington wanted. An angry tremor ran through her body. It wasn't fair. This was supposed to be the payoff, her escape from hell, and instead Worthington demanded her soul. How *dare* he ask her for that? "No," she said. "No. No!"

"You'll be a hero, Chelsea."

"No! A thousand times no!"

"You'll be able to do whatever you want. To go wherever you want. Even back to Earth."

Shaking with rage, Liwanu sprang to her feet, knocking over her chair, and stomped to the door. As it swished open, she turned a murderous glower on Worthington and pointed a trembling finger at the exit. Her mouth worked, but nothing came out. If she'd had a zap gun, she'd have fried him where he sat.

Worthington sighed as though he were the most misunderstood creature in the universe. He pushed himself heavily from the plastic chair and shuffled exitward. "I'm only trying to help."

Later—much later—once she'd regained some measure of composure, Liwanu decided Worthington's startled yelp must have been genuine. It was probably the first time in his life that anyone had dared kick him.

Although Josh Murdock bore a certain resemblance to a grizzly bear, his disposition tended towards Saint Bernard dog. Only rarely did he get angry, and when he did his temper would more likely manifest as sarcasm. Still, he had his moments, and Darya Pasternak had triggered one of them now.

He slammed his fist on the table so hard it jumped. "You will not!"

"We've been hiding under rocks too long, Josh," Pasternak snapped back. "We're not insects!"

"You're mad, you are. You'll get us killed. Or worse. You ever been in a penal colony? You wouldn't last two days."

Rising up on the balls of her feet, she tried to shove her face into his. Given their height differential, she came surprisingly close. "You wanna put money on that?"

"Ajit wouldn't last two days, then." Murdock poked a trembling index finger at Ajit Tambe, connected with the kid's clavicle, and nearly knocked him over. "Hell, he wouldn't last two hours!"

Tambe looked like he wanted to say something, possibly to protest that none of this had been his idea, so why should *he* go to jail for it? But no words formed.

Pasternak regarded Tambe as though considering Murdock's assessment. Whatever conclusions she reached regarding the kid's resilience didn't deter her. She poked her own index finger into Murdock's gut. "You're being a parakeet."

Murdock chewed up the insult preparatory to spitting it back in her face. Neither knew what parakeets had to do with anything, only that it was the worst thing one could call a miner.

"You're the one who organized us," Pasternak continued. "You're the one who said we needed to send them a message. So let's send one!"

"Not by killing!"

"Who said anything about killing?"

Murdock nearly pulled out some of his own hair. "You blow up management quarters, of course people get killed!"

"Not if we warn them first!"

Tambe risked whiplash trying to follow the back-and-forth. He rubbed his suddenly sore neck. "What good will that do?"

Pasternak's eyelids drooped. "It keeps people from getting killed."

"Not if they don't believe us," Murdock snapped. "You aren't doing this, Darya."

"Then tell me what I am doing, Josh! I'm not skulking in the shadows anymore! You got that?"

"I got it," Tambe said.

"Not you, him!" Pasternak jabbed Murdock again, and this time he grabbed her hand and pulled her off balance.

"Do that again, and I'll break your arm."

"You wouldn't."

Murdock shoved her away.

She stumbled but maintained her footing. "I thought we were on the same side, Josh."

"Me, too."

"And me," Tambe added, then squirmed under their intense glowers. "We need another idea, yeah?"

Pasternak slapped at the wall. "Like what?"

"So, er, how about we blow up the theater?"

Now Murdock and Pasternak looked like owls who'd sprained their eyes.

"The next performance is tomorrow night. Say we blow it up early tomorrow morning, while it's empty. Nobody would get hurt, and it would sure get attention." Tambe shrugged. "Couldn't we?"

Turning thoughtful, Murdock ran his fingers through his beard. "Have to find out when rehearsals are."

"Easy," Pasternak told him. "All we gotta do is talk to someone in the company, maybe ask for autographs. They'd tell us."

Murdock nodded, but looked sad. "Pity. Wasn't half bad."

"What?" Tambe and Pasternak asked in unison.

"The opera. Wasn't half bad. Oh, well."

Grinning, Paksternak punched Tambe in the arm and nearly sent him sprawling. "Come on, kid. Let's get some autographs!"

As he followed her out, Tambe objected, "Don't call me kid," but he was smiling inside and out.

CHAPTER 7

At the opposite end of the architectural and sociological spectrum from the offices of government officials like Chelsea Liwanu, those of top StarBright executives constituted the only fragment of heaven to be found in the Oort Territories. Such, at least, was the opinion of Lena Froebisher, the company's acting Chief Information Officer. In a realm of ice and emptiness, she had transformed her workspace into a tropical sea where swirling blue and green lights played over a pale blue ceiling and a sand-colored carpet, where furnishings of imitation coral took on all the colors of the rainbow just like real coral (or so she imagined), where one felt at peace with the universe and grounded firmly on Earth, or rather, on Earth's seabed.

Frustrations and irritations and all other negative –ations melted away once one set foot in her office, unless whatever –ation it was proved particularly –atious. As, in fact, it now had, although she couldn't decide on the right word for it. Displayed on her desktop, Artemus Worthington's latest missive allegedly documented insurrection on TDY-41093-RRP and pleaded for help in crushing it. Support him, he told her, and he would vote to make her position permanent.

He was up to something. Obviously. He was always up to something. But what?

She directed her intense blue eyes at the only other person present, the thinnish and shortish Perry Pauli, advertising department scriptwriter, some relation of CEO Santamonica Amarillo—although nobody seemed to know exactly what relation—and the best spy she owned. Sunk deep in a particularly plush coral chair with wide arms and a back angled far enough to put its occupant to sleep, Pauli looked like he implicitly understood the implicit question. Regardless, his answer was uninspiring: "Who knows?"

"You're supposed to." Froebisher's irritation with him didn't in the least color her voice. Her poker demeanor was legendary.

"How am I supposed to find out? Getting close to Worthington is, well, challenging." Pauli tried to look challenged. He failed. He just looked stupid.

"Locating your paycheck may soon prove equally challenging."

Pauli chortled. Froebisher didn't. He sighed and shook his head. "You know he doesn't like me. He barely tolerated me at the opera."

"He doesn't like anybody. People are just means to his self-serving ends." She stood and began to pace, arms behind her back, brows furrowed. "What does he gain by putting down a revolution that doesn't exist?"

Pauli twisted himself into an uncomfortable position to keep an eye on her as she passed behind him. She noticed—she noticed everything—but ignored his masochistic gymnastics. She knew people skulking around out of view made him nervous. As did many other things. Maybe his excellence in spycraft had something to do with how nervous and impotent he looked. Nobody would ever suspect such a wimp.

"Do we know . . . ouch!" He jumped to his feet, used his fist to unkink his back, and fell into line behind Froebisher, mimicking her posture and motions. "Do we know it doesn't exist?"

When she came to a sudden stop, he almost ran into her. "Don't be an idiot. Of course it doesn't exist. Even assuming a gang of disgruntled miners is prowling around that second-rate ice cube, how dangerous could they be?"

"They blew up a lifter."

"They probably did us a favor. No doubt it needed to be replaced." She paced again. Pauli followed until she whirled around and they nearly collided again. "Do you mind?" A hint of menace shaded her polite voice.

Pauli stepped aside. "Explosives, though. People could get hurt."

"Like who? Miners? Foremen?"

"Well."

"Exactly. Who cares?"

"Worthington cares."

Now she looked like a teacher disappointed in a dull-witted student. "Why would he? So long as he's not one of them."

"I mean he cares about whatever he cares about."

"Don't try to be clever. It doesn't become you."

Pauli shrugged sheepishly. Then he scratched his head, maybe hoping the act would jar loose some fresh thoughts.

But Froebisher suddenly had a loose thought of her own. "Oh my God."

Pauli looked up, hopeful. Maybe he'd inspired a worthwhile idea after all?

"Like who. Miners. Foremen." She looked Pauli in the eyes. "Opera singers."

Pauli opened his mouth.

Pauli closed his mouth.

"Chelsea Liwanu," Froebisher said, "would have a cow."

Pauli directed his puzzlement first at Froebisher and then at his shoes, and then asked the only logical question: "Why would she want one of those?"

Had it been Mars, *Nabbuco* would have played for eight weeks. On TDY-41093-RRP, the run maxed out at a single performance. By then, everyone who might attend already had. A second performance would either play to an empty house or end in riot when the audience realized they were being treated to a rerun.

Boredom could be dangerous in the Oort Territories. Really, really dangerous.

For that reason, *Don Carlo* was now in rehearsal in Roberto Maccarone's favorite version, the Quasi-Postmodern Milan Streamlined. He found that version better suited to lowbrow audiences than the Reinstrumented Moderna Augmented version, which included backstory never envisioned by Verdi and two ballets, neither of which bore any resemblance to the original ballet. Avant-gardists considered the Reinstrumented Moderna Augmented to be Verdi's greatest work. Purists dismissed it on the grounds that a fifth of it originated over two centuries after Verdi. The avant-gardists turned up their noses at such petty quibbling.

Oblivious to the disputes of such hyper-educated snobs, the performers were enacting act two of the Quasi-Postmodern Milan Streamlined—being act three of the original version, or act four of the Reinstrumented Moderna Augmented—on a stage decked out for a garden party, replete with greenery, classical Roman statuary, a bevy of well-dressed guests, and one ornate faux marble fountain gushing pink water. The young and fair maiden Eboli, wearing a veil she had borrowed from the queen, made a show of scribbling a note on a large piece of paper held in her left hand as she sang beautifully in Commonspeak:

"For one night I'm queen, sovereign over this garden, reigning until dawn! In these soft shadows I'll enchant sad Carlo with love!"

A few locals had chosen to spend their free time watching the rehearsal, which delighted Maccarone no end. Surely their interest presaged success for Space Operatic. If mere miners could appreciate such lofty art, the movers and shakers of the Territory could only be spellbound by it. He smiled warmly from his seat in the middle of the makeshift theater as Eboli signaled to a passing page and handed him the note destined for Don Carlo.

At that instant, the fountain began to gurgle fortissimo—not to mention badly out of tune. The racket overwhelmed the orchestra. On stage, all action stopped as the entire cast turned apprehensive eyes on the water, now spurting erratically. Their apprehension turned to dread when the spurts died away completely and an even louder noise sounded, this one rather like the rumble of an irritable dragon rudely awakened from a pleasant thousand-year sleep.

The orchestra slid messily into a deep silence. The musicians, too, now watched the fountain in horror.

With an explosive squeal, a jet of rusty brown water geysered heavenward, splattered the ceiling, and rained down upon the stage, soaking performers, the orchestra, and anyone unfortunate enough to be seated in the front five rows. The aqueous jet ran on and on, accompanied by screaming and cursing and wailing. Panicked shouts arose backstage. Maccarone, pale and shaking, watched helplessly as the horrid liquid rushed in streams over the stage and continued to pour down from the sky like the Noachian deluge.

Then as abruptly as it had started, it stopped. Screams and shouts and curses faded away, leaving a low background of sobbing.

Ebloi, dripping wet, her sodden hair plastered to her neck and shoulders, her makeup a runny mass of hideous color, turned stage left and sang—not said, but *sang*—"I'm going to kill you, Fang!"

Head held high, she spun on her heel and marched off stage right.

Paralyzed, Maccarone couldn't take his eyes from the disaster. He couldn't speak, couldn't stand, couldn't move. He hadn't a single thought in his entire brain.

"Wow," someone said behind him.

A thought tried to form in his brain but gave up. He never found out what it would have been.

"Is that supposed to happen?" the same someone asked.

"Uh." Maccarone twisted about in his seat. The someone was a woman in a tight black jump suit. She had a rock-solid look, like she could induce a concussion by tapping her little finger on one's head. Seated to her left, a skinny young fellow trained a pair of kilometer-wide eyes on the fountain.

"No," Maccarone told her. "I'm almost certain that wasn't supposed to happen." Then he wondered if he were mistaken. Maybe it actually was? No, that couldn't be right.

"Pity," the woman said. "I rather liked it. How about you, kid?"

The skinny young fellow said, "Uh."

Maccarone thought the guy might be a kindred spirit.

"How many rehearsals does it take to get it right?" the woman asked.

Maccarone turned back to the stage and slumped in his chair. "A lot."

"No schedule? You just do it until it's right?"

"Oh sure, a schedule. We don't always stick to it. It's probably safe to say we won't this time." Maccarone thought about what his mouth had just said. It sounded about right, so maybe his brain was coming back online. "Why do you ask?"

"I like watching rehearsals. I wouldn't want to show up when the stage is empty."

"I doubt you'll have to worry about that."

The woman laughed. "But you can't rehearse all the time!"

"We'll be done before oh three hundred, I'm sure. None of us can take it for that long."

She laughed again while stage hands with shop vacs began cleaning up the water. Kazimir Kapitan shuffled onto the stage, took a long look around, and called out, "All right, everyone, we'll take a break to get dried out and, and, and, whatnot. We'll resume in two hours." He considered the mess for about two more seconds "Or three." He shook his head and shuffled off stage.

Maccarone looked back, but the woman and her silent companion were gone. Slumping into his seat again, he wondered if it wouldn't be better if someone just blew up this poor excuse for a theater.

Safely ensconced in his backstage office with the door closed, Feng Shui Land smiled an unpleasant smile, a smile suggesting he'd just bitten the head off of something and found its death, if not its flavor, satisfying. He didn't need to be on stage to know what had happened. Sounds of disaster and its watery aftermath echoed clearly through the makeshift offices behind the stage.

Maccarone would cry for him momentarily, begging answers to the usual questions. What had gone wrong? Could it be fixed? How soon? At what cost? Can we guarantee this won't happen at the performance?

Land put on his best vexed-and-tortured face and rehearsed his answers. He'd have to investigate. No way to tell. God only knows. Just fork over the money, Mr. Board Member, you can afford it now.

But there would be more to Land's performance this time. This time he would ask questions of his own. What if we can't fix it? What if this happens every time, every rehearsal, every performance? What if Kazimir is right and we're living under a curse? What if money can't buy it off?

He'd make predictions, too, dire predictions. All the money in the solar system can't save us now. Disaster will follow inescapable disaster. We'll be a laughing stock. We'll have to leave, return sunward. Space Operatic may be doomed. We may have to change the company's name. Hell, we may have to change our own names. No more Roberto Maccarone. No more Manfred Mooseherder.

No more Mr. Fang.

As Land rubbed his hands with glee, someone knocked on the door. "Mr. Fang?"

Most of his glee boiled away. "What?" he snapped.

"Mr. Maccarone wants to see you immediately."

Composing himself, he rose and strode forth, prepared to give the performance of his life.

Within moments of starting, the conversation twisted, turned, and tilted at angles Land couldn't possibly have anticipated. His face arranged to suggest frustration with the balky fountain, he slipped into the seat next to Maccarone and shook his head at the damp stage.

"You see that?" Maccarone said without indicating anything.

"Unbelievable," Land said.

"That's the past."

There it went, already tilting. "Sorry?"

"That. The past."

Land's phony frustration transmuted into genuine puzzlement. "That's water."

"Water is only the agent. What it is is the curse."

"You said it was the past."

"Yes."

Facing his boss instead of the past or the curse or the water or whatever it was, Land snapped, "For God's sake, Roberto, make up your mind!"

"Oh, I have, and my mind is set on never, ever, ever having this sort of thing happen again."

That seemed to put them back on solid ground. "I suppose you're going to ask what happened."

"No need."

"I'll have to investigate."

"No, you won't."

"There's no way to tell yet whether it can be fixed."

"I don't care."

"And if it can be fixed, God only knows how long it will take."

Maccarone set a gentle hand on Land's shoulder. "Are you listening, Fa, ah, Feng? I don't care about any of that."

Land chewed on his lip. "You don't?"

"Not in the least. I'm a member of the StarBright board now. Do you know how much money I make in that capacity?"

"Er." Land searched the stage for some clue as to where they'd ended up so he could get them back to where they were supposed to be. But there weren't any clues there, only frustration and general sogginess.

"So much," Maccarone told him confidentially, "the exact amount doesn't even matter. Which means if something doesn't work, we don't worry why. We simply replace it with something that does work."

"Oh." That actually sounded like the part of the conversation that should have gone, "Fork over the money." Which meant it was time for him to interject his own questions, although he thought some of them might be irrelevant now. So he just skipped to the important one. "What if money can't buy off the curse?"

"We have a new curse now. Unfortunately, he's the source of the money."

Really, Land thought, absurdity had infiltrated too far. He started to say so, but Maccarone didn't let him.

"Have you heard anything about an insurrection among the miners?"

"Er."

"Artemus Worthington thinks one is growing. That's why he put me on the board. So I can report on it. I'm supposed to get cozy with the workers so I can watch and listen."

"He wants you to spy for him?"

Maccarone nodded, thoroughly miserable. "Not only that, he told me how to do it. I'm to hire them on."

"In what capacity? I don't suppose they ever took voice lessons."

"No. But this little . . ." He waved a hand at the stage. "It's given me an idea."

Land didn't like this new direction any better than the previous one. Both meandered into uncharted wilderness instead of along his carefully-plotted course. "Like what?"

"Hire miners to build us a new fountain. They must have the technical expertise on staff. They're getting interested in opera. They'd love to help, especially if they're paid for it. I don't imagine they make very good money."

"Bad idea!" Land practically shouted.

Maccarone almost jumped out of his seat at the outburst. "Why?"

"Because, because, well, because, um, well, because . . ." Land's hands flailed helplessly.

"You're usually more eloquent than that."

Try as he might, Land couldn't come up with a plausible reason. All he knew was that he couldn't give up control to a bunch of unwashed peasants. The reins must stay firmly in his own educated, skilled grip or he'd be ruined.

"I have to get close to them." Maccarone eyed the stage once more. "And this is the way."

"Insurrection!" Land blurted out, finally seeing an escape route.

"That's the theory."

"You can't let insurrectionists build your props! What if they sabotage the production?"

Maccarone pondered that, at least at first. But then his mouth curled into a strange smile and he laughed a strange, ironic laugh. Land had never heard Maccarone make that sound before.

"What's so funny?"

"Sabotage might be an improvement!"

Land stood and kicked the chair in front of him. That done, he limped away, cursing everything in the whole universe.

CHAPTER 8

Josh Murdock blamed his appearance. He knew people compared him to a grizzly bear, and he knew they sometimes attributed that creature's savagery to him merely because he looked the part. He didn't take it personally. Sometimes misapprehension could be useful.

But really, he thought, Kaja Omdahl took matters too far. She stood before him, drawn up to her full six foot five inch height, clad in orange body armor, flanked by a pair of guards in silver and black body armor and armed with zap guns capable of stunning or killing anything that moved. Her fierce blue eyes flashed fiercely. Her golden hair reflected almost enough of the artificial light to blind someone. She had singled out Murdock for a murderous gaze, although a dozen others stood around her.

Omdahl, who supervised a group of miners working prime shift, had called this hasty meeting of foremen and technical experts. The show of force, Murdock knew, was mostly for him. Nobody actually hated her enough to attack her, least of all Murdock. Yet somewhere in her fevered imagination he longed to maul and devour her, a fate she expected to befall her at any moment.

One of the guards met his eyes but quickly looked away, cowed. Murdock shook his head.

"Special assignment," Omdahl announced. "You're going to like it. Even if you don't. The opera company's fountain exploded this morning and they need a new one. We're going to build it for them."

The miners looked around at each other and muttered things they didn't want Omdahl to hear.

"Engineering is drawing up a plan. We'll execute on it. High quality. No shortcuts. And—" She looked square at Murdock. "—no funny business. Right?"

Nobody said anything.

"I need a volunteer."

Nobody said anything again.

"Well?"

"Volunteer for what?" someone in the back asked.

Omdahl's face screwed up in disgust. "What do you think? To be my whipping boy when things go wrong."

"Oh," the same voice said. "A foreman."

"Stupid thing to ask for in a room full of foremen, huh?" She spread her venomous scrutiny liberally over the gathering.

Murdock arched his eyebrows. The setup couldn't have been more perfect. Pasternak wanted to blow up the theater, and here they were, being asked to replace the theater's exploding fountain. He raised his right hand, slowly so as not to alarm anyone with guns, or anyone with bodyguards with guns.

Omdahl narrowed her eyes at him. "What?"

"I'm volunteering."

"Oh yeah?"

"Sure."

"Why?"

"Liked the opera. Wasn't half bad."

"I wouldn't figure you for a connoisseur of culture, Murdock." She laughed a vat-full-of-boiling-acid sort of laugh.

Murdock shrugged. "Never can tell about people," he said, and everyone around him nodded sagely. Some people, anyway, thought he was more sense than menace.

"I've had my eye on you for a long time." She stepped toward him, slowly. Her guards advanced in lockstep with her. "You don't fool me for a second." She stopped mere inches from him. Her eyes tried to bore into his, but they couldn't because his were just too impassive. It was like driving an axe into an ocean full of peanut butter. "Step a hair's breadth out of line and I'll personally throw you out an airlock."

Murdock wondered if she'd had an unhappy childhood. That might explain a few things. Or maybe she was one of those brats who always got everything she wanted, until through some inexplicable twist of fate she'd ended up out here where nobody ever got anything they wanted.

"So you want to build a fountain."

"Why not?"

"Fine. You got the job. Just remember, I'm hoping and praying it goes horribly wrong."

Murdock smiled easily. "Probably will. That opera company is living under a curse."

Kaja Omdahl might have been a snarling wolf. Some almost inaudible sound seemed to issue from her throat, anyway.

Murdock thought she was almost cute when she was angry.

Except for the gnashing teeth.

Those doors. Those beautiful purple doors. Royal purple with abstract designs traced in gold. Real gold.

Artemus Worthington gazed upon those doors, his countenance that of an artist appreciating their beauty.

Actually, he couldn't care less what they looked like. He'd said he could walk through them anytime he wanted, but he'd lied, just as his admiring eyes lied now. Chelsea Liwanu clutched the keys to these doors in her tight little balled-up fists, allowing nobody, most especially her nemesis Artemus Worthington, inside. The potent elixir of opera and money ought to have loosened her grip, and he still hoped it might, but what he really pondered as he gazed on those stubbornly locked doors was whether he had erred.

"What do you want?"

He turned. Liwanu stood three meters away, a black-shrouded ice sculpture with wary eyes and mouth set in a firm line.

"To talk." He had asked her to come. Pleaded, really, which for him was like performing an appendectomy on himself. He wanted her to think he was desperate.

"The answer will always be no."

Worthington turned back toward the doors and gave them a slow once-over. "I've never seen their like. And I've never seen what lies behind them."

Liwanu might not even have been there.

"Maccarone would give his life to play it just once." Worthington was desperate, Maccarone was desperate, everyone was desperate. Only Liwanu could save them. She could demand anything in exchange. Anything. He willed her to feel the desperation surrounding her and take pity on all the poor wretches groveling at her feet.

"You didn't call me here to state the obvious."

"Come here. Touch this door." He touched it himself for effect. "You don't have to wonder what's behind it. You're so very fortunate. Won't you have pity on the rest of us?" Anyone would fall into his trap. Anyone.

She neither touched nor, apparently, possessed a milligram of pity.

Pouting like a little boy, Worthington motioned to a nearby bench and sat. Liwanu refused to follow his lead. "Then have pity on yourself. Maccarone is your ticket home, Chelsea." Anyone. Even Chelsea Liwanu.

"I can't believe you'd sink so low." She thought about it, then decided, "Actually, I almost can believe it of you."

Damn. Anyone but Chelsea Liwanu, apparently. "It's only a theater."

Livid, she crossed the space between them so fast he swore he didn't see her coming. She fell upon him like a tornado and slapped him hard across the face, then stormed off.

Genuinely shocked for maybe the first time in his life, Worthington rubbed his sore cheek and gazed after her. It wasn't so much that she had had another outburst. He was used to that. It was that he honestly had no clue why.

As women went, Feng Shui Land thought, Taqtuk had more utility than most. Her pleasant round face drew no more than passing attention. No comment whatsoever could be drawn by that thin frame covered in those bland greens and blues. Timid and soft-spoken in social settings, she nevertheless had a devious mind. She also preferred to work alone, which gave her deviousness ample opportunity for expression.

Had anyone looked at her when the fountain turned psychotic—which of course they hadn't—they would have seen a quiet little smile playing on her quiet little mouth. Leaning easily against a pillar just off-stage, her little arms casually crossed over her girlish chest, she quietly chewed a stick of gum without once being noticed. Later she presented herself in Land's office, that same smile still in place, and asked, quietly of course, "Well?"

"Great," he told her although his face suggested the situation was anything but.

"So?"

"The boss hired some miners to build a new one."

"Cool. I got ideas."

"I'm sure. But since we're out of the loop, I don't see what good they'll do."

Taqtuk sniggered.

"What?" Land worried that the conversation had grown too mono-syllabic. *I'll be a gibbering idiot before this is over*, he decided, *unable to speak in anything more than grunts.*

"They build it, I hook it up." She had supreme confidence in her ability to cause mayhem.

He rose and paced, fists clenching and unclenching in angered irritation, or maybe irritated anger. "Impossible. We've been cut out completely."

"I can fix it," she insisted.

"Sabotage after the fact would be too obvious."

"I got a friend."

Land stopped short and skewered her with one of his trademark irritated faces. "Friend?"

She didn't seem to mind being skewered. She wasn't even looking at him anymore. She was picking at her fingernails and looking thoughtful. "Me an' him got a thing on."

"He and I."

"Huh?"

"Never mind. Who is he?"

"Techie. Fixes stuff."

"Can you trust him?"

"Far as I can throw him, but he's a rebel, so it's all good."

Land didn't like it. Too many things were moving too far from his grasp. Yet what choice did he have? Maccarone was determined to make the Oort Territories their permanent home, it seemed, curse or no curse. He nodded approval and returned to his desk.

"This'll be fun," Taqtuk said.

"As fun as double pneumonia."

"You're a grouch," she laughed.

"I wouldn't be if I could see the sun."

She pointed to her face and grinned. "It's right here."

Why, Land wondered, *am I surrounded by lunatics?*

Participants in the hastily-called meeting assembled on the stage, which had been stripped of soggy props save only the miscreant fountain.

They all stared at the fountain in solemn silence as though gathered for the funeral of a prominent scoundrel who deserved equal parts awe and disgust.

"So I guess," Kazimir Kapitan said. He didn't immediately follow it up with anything more informative. His dejection accentuated his shortness and baldness. He looked pathetic in spite of his happy green jumpsuit.

Josh Murdock, a towering hulk of bearded menace standing to Kapitan's right, offered another thought: "Smells like burned mice."

"No mice were harmed," a female stage hand assured him. Her long, golden hair shimmered electric against her own happy green jumpsuit.

"Okay," Murdock replied, relieved.

"But something in the works melted," the woman explained. "The water ran down there and shorted everything out." She pointed down and everyone looked, although there was nothing to see but the stage floor.

"So I guess," Kapitan tried again. "I guess what we want is exactly this."

Murdock raised an eyebrow. One of his mechanics stood beside him, a guy who could have been his little brother, equally bearded and bearish but a good half foot shorter, with darker skin and squintier eyes. The mechanic said, "Huh?"

"Okay, not exactly this, but something that looks exactly like this looked before the incident. Oh, and that works properly."

"You okay with that, Harlan?" Murdock asked the mechanic.

Harlan shrugged without enthusiasm.

"It should spray pinkish water," Kapitan added.

That seemed to disturb both miners. They looked at each other, then at Kapitan, then at the stage hand, then at Feng Shui Land, standing on the opposite side of the fountain not in a happy green jump suit but in somber purple and silver business getup. Land's expression suggested he wished he could tear out everyone's fingernails, and that went for the fountain, too. The miners even looked at Kaja Omdahl, positioned ninety degrees to their left, still in her body armor and still flanked by her guards, who still had their weapons and still looked like they might shoot Murdock just to be on the safe side.

"Doesn't sound healthy," Murdock said.

"For God's sake!" Omdahl snapped. "Nobody's going to drink it!"

He gave the boss an easy smile. "Took a bath in it last time, though."

"It's just food coloring," Kapitan explained. "I'll give you the recipe."

"What's wrong with normal water?" Harlan asked.

"It's an opera thing," Land said as though explaining to an obtuse child. "Just do it."

"But pink? I dunno, I'd think maybe purple. Pink is so . . ." Harlan waved his hands as though to demonstrate, but his idea wasn't demonstrable, apparently.

"Girly?" Taqtuk sidled up to Land and waggled her fingers at Harlan in greeting. "You like some girly things, babe."

Harlan nearly broke out in a grin, then coughed and turned aside.

"That's him?" Land whispered to her. "We're doomed."

She poked him in the ribs with her elbow. Playfully. It hurt anyway.

"We can't change it now," Kapitan insisted. "Pink water, working fountain, looks like that." He spread his hands at the fountain. "Installed and ready to test by eighteen hundred tonight. If all goes well, dress rehearsals will resume tomorrow morning."

Murdock glanced at Harlan, who nodded. "Can do."

"And no funny business," Omdahl added.

Kapitan looked up in alarm. Land looked simultaneously sick and intrigued. The lady stage hand's eyes grew wide.

"What's that mean?" Land asked.

"Private joke between me and the super," Murdock said. "I'm evil and she's got a finger on the smite button."

"Cool," Taqtuk said. "Where can I get one?"

Land ground his teeth and stalked off.

Alas for his beautiful cherry red and sunflower yellow blazer, Perry Pauli got doused when the volcanic fountain erupted. He'd taken a front-row seat for the rehearsal, hoping for a chance to meet and flatter Maccarone, but he never saw the opera magnate. All he saw, or all he could recall seeing by now, was a downpour of muddy brown water, sickly, disgusting, and very, very wet.

The coloring agents in the water had turned his blazer a sort of yucky reddish-pinkish-orange. He looked like a moldy carnation. He'd been forced to trade in his dressed-to-impress business attire for one of those happy green jumpsuits he loathed. A stagehand lent him one and let him change in one of the makeshift dressing rooms backstage, after which he inspected himself in the mirror. No longer a moldy carnation, he now had the appearance of a bratty little kid in a baggy school uniform. Just great. Worse, Maccarone might actually think he *was* a bratty little kid in a baggy school uniform and pat him on the head. What a nauseating thought.

Pauli hung around backstage, ignored by the crew cleaning up the mess, but Maccarone didn't appear. He watched the on-stage meeting of minds—if it could be called that—about the construction of the new fountain, and still Maccarone didn't appear. It looked as though Pauli would have to start with a lower rung on the ladder of devious accomplishment.

Hmm, he thought.

He pulled a palm-sized device from the left leg pocket of his jumpsuit and made a note: *Lower rung on the ladder of devious accomplishment.* Clever phrase. Could be useful someday.

Stuffing the device back into the pocket, he waited until the meeting started to break up. When it did, he picked the target who seemed most in charge: the angry-faced lady with the body armor and bodyguards. He didn't approach closer than ten paces before the guards trained weapons on him and ordered him to halt.

The angry-faced lady turned her angry face on him. "Who the hell are you?"

Fear gripped him and spilled out of his mouth. "Ah, I'm, uh, that is, err . . ."

"Yeah, that's what I thought. A moron."

Fear turned to irritation, and he tried to stiffen his back. He didn't cut an impressive figure anyway. "I'm a StarBright representative." His voice sounded equally unimpressive.

"Oh, good. I can blame you for being stuck in this frozen junkyard."

"I'm looking for Mr. Maccarone."

"You'll have to stand in line, little boy. I got dibs on him. Not that much will be left of him when I get done." She grinned a wicked sort of grin.

The bodyguards shifted their weapons and grinned along with her, like they hadn't shot anybody in a long time and were itching for target practice.

Pauli swallowed. "If you don't know where he is, you could just say so."

She approached and leaned down confidentially. "You could try looking here." She swatted him hard on the rump.

As she left laughing, her laughing guards in tow, Pauli reflected that she was certainly the most unladylike lady he'd ever met.

CHAPTER 9

T minus thirty minutes.

Feng Shui Land had retreated to his tiny office onboard the *Ponchielli*. A sterile place, it sported no decoration of any kind, merely cold gray metal walls, a plastic faux wood desk, and sufficient embedded computer displays to give him all the information he needed about the dire financial straits through which Space Operatic sailed. And comm links, too, so he could stay apprised of his plan's progress and monitor responses.

But no progress reports came through. His fingers drummed on the desk like Nibelungs forging at the anvil.

He should have heard something by now.

T minus twenty-nine minutes.

"You're sooooooo . . . " Taqtuk dragged the word out just like that, ". . . sooooooo good with your hands."

Harlan Peppermill grimaced as he snapped a clip into place somewhere inside a mechanism that looked rather like a knotted trio of boa constrictors holding together an incoherent pile of scrap metal. "You're distracting me, babe."

"You loooooove being distracted." She ran a finger across his cheek.

Assembly finished, he flipped open a small display panel on the underbelly of one of the boa constrictors and tapped on the screen a few times. A soft beep issued forth, then he closed the panel again. "Come to my quarters and say that." He grabbed her hand and pulled her along.

She hurried behind him and completely forgot to report in.

T minus twenty-four minutes.

"Okay, kid, the coast is clear."

"Don't . . . oh, forget it." Ajit Tambe followed Darya Pasternak to the fountain mechanism, carrying a black bag inside of which huddled a small explosive device she'd cobbled together earlier that day.

Pasternak studied the weird-looking contraption, located a space amid the coils of the boa constrictors just big enough for her "surprise," and got to work. She partially unzipped the front of her jumpsuit and reached into an interior pocket, where she had stashed a few small tools of the trade. "Control module," she said.

Hovering over her, Tambe took a small black plastic box from the bag and gave it to her. He alternately watched her install it, glanced around to make sure nobody saw them, and gazed with admiration down her unzipped clothing.

"Explosive."

He handed it to her. She worked with perfect efficiency, no movement wasted.

T minus sixteen minutes.

Perry Pauli never did find Roberto Maccarone that day, which got him to pondering his dilemma. Lena Froebisher wanted him to discover Worthington's evil plot. The only clear route to Worthington ran straight through Maccarone, who at this point Pauli was about ready to run through on general principles. Where had the man hidden himself?

There was Froebisher's suspected attack on the opera. Could he use that to his advantage? Maybe, but Space Operatic seemed accustomed to freakish disasters. He shuddered at the memory of all that horrid water showering down upon him.

In a flash of insight, he put two and five together and got somewhere in the vicinity of eighty-six: *That's it! All I have to do is sabotage the fountain, and Maccarone will* have *to come running!* Boiling over with excitement and without a thought for caution, he all but ran to the fountain mechanism below the stage and, finding it all alone in the world, undertook a task for which he had absolutely no aptitude.

T minus eight minutes.

On stage, Kazimir Kapitan had gathered the essential forces: a few stage hands with umbrellas and shop vacs at the ready; Josh Murdock; Harlan Peppermill; and . . .

"Where's your guy?" Kapitan asked Murdock. "Harlan, wasn't it?"

Murdock shrugged and looked around as though Peppermill might be skulking somewhere in the wings or snoozing in a back row seat. He actually knew what Peppermill was up to and with whom, having seen them fly at supersonic speed into the technician's quarters, but he didn't figure it was worth mentioning.

"What if something goes wrong?" Kapitan asked, wringing his hands. The look on his face assured everyone there was no "if" about it. Something always went wrong.

"Won't," Murdock said. "Harlan does good work." *Assuming*, he didn't add, *he's not distracted*. Which he surely was.

"Okay," Kapitan said. "Okay. Ready to switch it on?" He looked fearfully at one of the stage hands who, standing just off-stage, reached for the switch.

T minus five seconds . . . four . . . three . . . two . . .

Land pounded his desktop and shrieked, "Damn it, Taqtuk, where *are* you?"

Zero...

Pasternak and Tambe hurried in through the side door just before the switch was thrown. They slipped quietly into a couple of front-row aisle seats. Perry Pauli followed on their heels, but he stayed in the doorway as though anticipating a need to escape. The miners didn't notice.

The stage hand threw the switch.

Those near the fountain heard a whoosh, a swish, a faint gurgle, and then . . .

. . . a fine spray of pinkish water rose gracefully skyward, arced, and fell with a splash into the pool.

Kapitan held his breath. Murdock nodded in satisfaction. The fountain ran on, steady, serene, pink, perfect.

In their seats, Pasternak and Tambe watched, impassive. Tambe's hand moved slowly toward Pasternak's but didn't quite get there before it withdrew again, while nearby, unobserved by them, Pauli frowned and scratched his head.

Stunningly elegant, the fountain ran and ran and ran and did absolutely nothing that fountains weren't supposed to do.

"No burned mice smell," Murdock commented.

Kapitan gradually relaxed and, for a moment, even managed a happy face.

Pauli, not at all happy, slipped out.

"Not bad," Pasternak said quietly so only Tambe could hear. "But just wait 'til oh three hundred." She grinned at her sidekick, who tried to return the grin without looking stupid. He nearly succeeded, and she tweaked his nose. "Come on, kid, let's grab some grub."

When Maccarone received the news from Kapitan, he felt a swell of elation. In his office on board the *Ponchielli*, he stood and pirouetted, arms spread wide. Surely nothing would stand in their way now! A few more rehearsals, a final performance on TDY-41093-RRP, one more small performance on another frozen rock, and then off to that wonderful, beautiful, amazing, stupendous theater! He looked around his office at the holophotos adorning the walls, depictions of past performances, great singers, great musicians, and great composers. He addressed them as though they were an adoring audience: "We're taking the Oort Territories by storm!"

In his mind, they cheered and applauded.

Before long, though, a less happy reality settled upon him and nearly squashed the elation right out of him. Sinking into the chair behind his desk, he tapped the comm link and called for Snow Hill. She sashayed in, cool, elegant, ready to work miracles on her boss's behalf. "Yes, sir?"

Maccarone admired her and her shimmering gold and silver and violet dress for a moment. She waited patiently, giving him time to come to terms with her overpowering beauty. "I need to congratulate that Murdock fellow and his crew. Can we get them here and serve them dinner or something?"

"Or something. Ship's supplies are a bit low, but I think I can arrange matters. The TDY-41093-RRP facilities manager promised me a sweet deal on consumables."

"Oh yes?"

"He likes me," she said with no hint of sarcasm.

Who wouldn't? Maccarone thought. "Very good, let me know what time."

"Sir." She turned to go.

"You don't think they'd decline?" he asked, suddenly worried. He had no idea how miners would react to an invitation like his. He didn't suppose management ever gave them much thought. They might be suspicious, and in this case there was plenty of which to be suspicious.

Snow Hill looked over her shoulder. "Not if I ask nice," she said, all serious and businesslike.

And, well, who could argue with that?

Ponchielli's one really big room could sometimes be pressed into service as a dining facility, which it just had been. It didn't look the part, really. With chairs pushed to the sides and more or less stacked up in precarious piles, the place had all the ambiance of a low-budget meeting hall, complete with battered gray storage lockers along one boring gray bulkhead. But in the center of the room, a large round table had been set with four faux silver place settings, and something the galley had branded beef Wellington would soon be served up. Maccarone thought the aroma wafting in smelled okay, even though dinner was likely some kind of soy concoction. He just hoped his honored victims—or rather, guests—couldn't tell the difference.

When they arrived, a pair of Space Operatic ushers dressed to the nines—

Why nines? Maccarone wondered. *Why not eights or tens?*

Ahem. Ushers dressed to the nines in flashy gold, silver, purple, and sky blue monkey suits ushered them in. Maccarone welcomed the miners warmly and bade them sit. Salads, or the soy version thereof, were immediately served, and nobody said a word because nobody had any idea what to say.

"I was most impressed," Maccarone finally began when the salad plates had been removed and a soup course served. "Mr. Murdock," he added. "Most impressed."

"Just a fountain." Murdock squirmed a bit in his chair, which obviously hadn't been made for someone his size.

"Well, you should have seen what it did to us before your crew fixed it."

"Heard about that." Murdock shot a knowing glance at Peppermill, seated to his right. Peppermill snickered.

To Murdock's left, looking like she'd rather be about a dozen kilometers further out, Kaja Omdahl, no longer flanked by guards or sporting body armor and looking, Maccarone thought, almost attractive in her red and orange and white formal suit, slurped a spoonful of soup. "Not bad," she remarked. She glanced nervously at Murdock. "My guys do first-rate work. If they know what's good for them."

Murdock nodded and sampled the soup, too. "The boss keeps us in line." He seemed completely serious about that.

Maccarone sensed an opening and charged through. "You've had a bit of trouble, though, I hear."

Omdahl waved it away. "Things are always breaking down. But don't worry, your fountain is newer than most of the garbage we have to work with out here." After she'd said it, it struck her as funny and she laughed.

Spoons clanked on bowls for a few minutes as the diners polished off their soup. Their waiter, a stage hand pressed into service for the duration of the meal, served up the beef Wellington with a theatrical flourish.

"I suppose there must be a certain amount of tension," Maccarone said. "I just run a small business, and there's always tension. When things go wrong, everyone is just so, so, so . . ."

"Tense? Peppermill suggested.

"Yes, I guess you could say that."

"I did say it," Peppermill replied, perplexed. "Didn't I?"

"Did," Murdock agreed. "Heard it myself."

"The company treats us well," Omdahl told him. "About as well as they treat raw sewage." She laughed again, then scrunched up her mouth as though not quite sure the joke had worked the way it was supposed to.

"People get antsy," Murdock agreed.

Maccarone set down his fork and steepled his fingers under his chin. He looked quite the thoughtful fellow that way, he thought. "Antsy?"

"Sure. Sometimes a faulty machine goes over a cliff." Murdock shrugged. "Helps blow off some steam, and sooner or later we get a new one to replace it."

"What about more organized..." Maccarone had to search for an appropriate word. "Remonstration?"

Murdock cut a chunk of faux beef and stuffed it into his mouth, looking not the least interested in remonstrations.

Omdahl pointed her fork at Maccarone. "I'm the only organization these guys have or need."

He couldn't bear up under her frigid stare and focused instead on his plate. "I see."

She didn't relent, either in expression or words or jabs with her utensil. "The company put me here to get a job done, and I get it done. You got that?"

"Sure. I was just curious."

"We don't need off-worlders coming out here and starting trouble. I won't stand for it."

"I wasn't—"

"You're all alike, waltzing in here with your grand ideals, like you're delivering canned sunshine. Well listen up." Omdahl exchanged her fork for her knife and jabbed at Maccarone with that, maybe just for a change of pace. "We don't need your ideals. You wouldn't last three days here if you had to actually work, so don't tell us how to live our lives."

"I wasn't—" he tried again.

"Shut up. Just shut up." Omdahl stuffed a forkful into her mouth and chewed viciously.

Murdock looked up and grinned at Maccarone. "Glad you invited us?"

Maccarone didn't dare open his mouth.

"Shut up," Omdahl told Murdock.

"Strange thing," Murdock said. "*She's* afraid of *me*."

"Shut," Omdahl said, "up!"

"Sure thing, boss."

Maccarone sincerely hoped the galley hadn't thought to prepare dessert.

Had he stuck to scriptwriting, Pauli might have remained safe and secure. Poorish, but safe and secure. But nooooooo, he'd had to turn spy at the invitation of his step-great-uncle, the key financial advisor to Santamonica Amarillo as well as some extraordinarily convoluted relation to said head honcho. Now Pauli spent most of his time not writing but selling his stealth to various board members. He'd never known a more devious group of people, if people they could be called. Sure, the adrenaline rushes could be fantastic, but not quite sabotaging a fountain could get one sent to Proteus. The mere name made him tremble with fear.

In fact the fountain had worked, so no saboteur hunt was imminent. Yet he couldn't quell his jitters. He sat on the floor in the dark, cramped utility closet to which he'd retreated, his back against something unyielding that could have been either an implement of cleaning or torture, puzzling over what had gone wrong. Or right. Or both.

A thin sliver of light spilled into the closet under the door. Barely illuminating the objects within, it transformed them into menacing shadows. He had no idea what that cold, damp bulk at his left elbow was, nor did he care. His thought was bent toward understanding why rearranging those connections in the mechanism hadn't led to aqueous disaster. Surely a machine has to be wired properly to function properly? Surely it took no talent at all—precisely what he had for machinery—to wire a mechanism wrong?

He chewed on his failure there in the cramped dark until nothing remained of it. Then something horrible occurred to him. Maybe somebody had discovered his handiwork and fixed it at the last minute!

The dark grew even colder, and he shivered there for a long time, not daring to move.

Harlan Peppermill smacked his right fist into his left palm. His face screwed up in concentration, he paced back and forth, back and forth through his sleeping quarters, inducing collisions between hand and fist again and again and again.

Taqtuk, back in her jumpsuit, sat crosslegged on his bed. Her narrowed eyes suggested he'd ruined her entire life. "You knew what you were doing?"

He shot her a dangerous look then resumed pacing and punching himself.

"Easy, you said."

"I know what I said!"

"It didn't work."

"I know it didn't work!"

"You said it would. Piece of soy cake, you said."

"Damn it, girl, stop saying what I said!"

She sprang to her feet and pushed herself as much into his face as possible given that she was a good foot shorter than him. "So why didn't it work?"

"I don't know!" He turned away from her, hit himself a few more times, then said to nobody, "Maybe somebody fixed it at the last minute."

"Stupid! Who knew?"

"Well something went wrong!"

"I know!"

Peppermill grabbed his own head and shook it. "Okay. Look. Okay. Tell you what." He stopped there.

"What, already?"

"In the morning, I'll have another look. See what happened. If I made a mistake, I can fix it."

"Yeah," Taqtuk said, deadpan. "Do that." She crossed the room and palmed the plate to open the door.

"Hey, where are you going?"

"To sleep," she said without looking back. "In my own bed."

The door shut itself behind her. Peppermill stared at its flat gray surface. At most such times, he might have wondered if he'd ever see the girl again. In this case, he was merely relieved. She'd been good the first couple of times, before everything went wrong, but with her no longer in his face maligning his skills, he found it unnecessary to further bash his hands. And that was good, too.

Later, much later because working up the nerve took more effort than he would have thought, Maccarone cloistered himself in his office to place a very important call. Ten minutes passed while the disembodied voices at the other end of the transmission tracked down Worthington, woke him up, and convinced him that the call actually was that important.

"Do you have any idea what time it is?" the great man snapped by way of greeting.

"Not really," Maccarone admitted. "I talked with some of the miners."

"I'm so happy for you."

"As you suggested, I hired them, and they did such a good job that I invited them to dinner and tried to get them to open up about tensions between themselves and the company, and of course they didn't admit much but . . ."

"Point, please."

"Sometimes a piece of faulty equipment goes over a cliff."

"Meaning?"

"I guess they get mad and demolish something."

"You woke me up for that?"

"You said I should report as soon as I knew something."

"And so you woke me up as soon as you knew nothing."

"But . . ."

"You don't even know that you know nothing. Don't be a moron, Maccarone. Get me something I can use."

Roberto Maccarone, owner and CEO of Space Operatic, wasn't used to being talked to like that. Bristling, he fired off a snappy retort: "Like what?" Upon reflection, that really wasn't what he'd meant to say. For one thing, it wasn't half snappy enough.

"News of a rebellion."

"There isn't one."

As friendly as the vacuum of space, Worthington warned, "There'd better be."

The connection terminated.

Maccarone stared at the disconnect message flashing on his desktop. He imagined Worthington sitting on the bench in the rose garden, his smooth tongue uttering smooth words, offering a smooth, smooth deal. But now the Marketing Director's skin looked a bit red and scaly, and there were definitely horns protruding from the top of his head.

Still, there was that theater.

But was any theater worth this? Even that theater?

Maccarone really, really didn't want to answer that question. He knew what the answer would be, and he absolutely didn't want to hear it.

The clock struck oh-three-hundred, or would have had it been able to strike. Since no striking clocks existed on TDY-41093-RRP, such clocks as there were quietly slipped from oh-two-fifty-nine to oh-three-hundred without anyone much noticing. Those scheduled to sleep slept on. Those scheduled to work worked on. Those scheduled for recreation recreated on.

Beneath the makeshift stage in the makeshift theater, something buried deep in the fountain mechanism woke up. It, too, knew that it was oh-three-hundred. It was time to do what it had been created to do.

Electrons began to flow.

Had anyone been there to see it and measure time so precisely, a millisecond later they would have seen a brilliant flash of light and felt the searing heat that followed.

Fortunately, nobody was. But everyone within a half mile of the stage, whether working or sleeping or recreating, felt the concussion.

CHAPTER 10

Bombs and space colonies don't mix. If not for emergency systems, TDY-41093-RRP's theater/meeting room/storage area might have proven that with a vengeance. The force of the blast slashed open the roof, spitting a brilliant orange tongue of fire for a paltry few seconds as atmosphere spewed into the dark, airless landscape. The walls bulged and cracked, and air screamed through the holes as though a chorus of banshees had commandeered the stage. Seats and settings momentarily erupted in flame. Thick, acrid smoke poured into the void above while alarms screamed high-pitched screams, waking everyone that hadn't been shocked from sleep by the detonation.

In surrounding corridors, sensors registered the plummeting air pressure and fired off signals to relays that tripped, slamming shut massive airtight doors. Pressurization systems woke and quickly replenished the atmosphere. The booming of doors echoed as far as the explosion itself. As the remains of the theater settled into vacuum, the fire died a sudden death and smoke particles skittered willy-nilly across the bleak planetoid, never to return. Nothing remained but twisted metal and fragments of things that had once been the trappings of grand opera.

Emergency crews reached the scene within minutes and quickly verified that the facility was secure. The alarms stopped, but by then people were everywhere, chattering, passing information and wild speculation, reporting in to see if they were needed. A recon crew donned pressure suits and made their way out the airlock nearest the theater. They carefully traversed the jagged wastes and picked their way through a rupture in the theater wall. The blast pattern led them directly to the fountain, but so little remained they couldn't be sure what had happened. Reasonable fountains, the team leader opined, ought not to explode. So either this fountain had been extremely unreasonable, or it was an innocent bystander when something nearby went kaboom.

Their report, transmitted directly to top management, was received with considerable consternation. After two hours of bitter argument, the facility's bosses arrived at a decision and promulgated it throughout the colony, up the corporate ladder, and to all interested government officials and opera company owners.

The explosion, they decreed, had been an extraordinarily freakish accident.

"Liars!" Darya Pasternak, rage red and punching everything that held still for it, repeated the imprecation several times for emphasis. "Liars, liars, liars!"

Ajit Tambe nodded nervously and kept his distance from her, not wanting to be mistaken for something holding still for it.

"Calm down," Josh Murdock said. The three of them had gathered in Murdock's quarters to celebrate their victory only to have it snatched from them by unprincipled bureaucrats. Had the powers that be no conscience? What was the point of sabotage if management was only going to deny it? He gazed around the room, which although slightly larger was identical to most everyone else's. All he saw were featureless gray walls, a colorless bed, a desk, and chairs too small for someone his size. Each item displayed the same uninspired design: rectilinear boredom. One didn't do much living in one's quarters, so little was expended on making them pleasant. "Let's see what happens."

"What happens is censorship!" Pasternak griped. "What do we have to do, blow up the whole damn—"

An annoying electronic chime announced the presence of someone at the door. Murdock palmed the sensor plate to open it and found Kaja Omdahl, once more protected by flashy body armor and her two armored guards. "Mind if I come in? You do? Good." She stepped into the room, leaving the guards to figure out how to squeeze through and reflank her as quickly as possible. "Oh, look. The crazy chick and the infant. What kind of party is this, Murdock?"

Pasternak nearly blew a gasket, but Murdock shot her a warning glance which left her impotently clenching and unclenching her fists. "Now that you're here," he said, "it's perfect."

"That was your handiwork, wasn't it?"

"My crew's, anyway. Pity it got blown up."

"That's not what I mean."

"No?"

"No!"

"Then what?"

"The explosion!"

"Oh, that."

"Yes, that!"

Murdock scratched his bushy chin. "Heard it was an accident."

Omdahl looked around for a place to sit. There wasn't any, which she had to have known at the outset. She leaned against the wall instead. "The bigwigs say so, but nobody's going to believe it. And it was your guy who worked on the fountain. Funny he's not here."

"What'm I supposed to say, boss? We blew it up? You'll have me shipped off in irons. We didn't? You won't believe me."

Omdahl's piranha smile got jarred loose when the annoying door chime chimed again. She signaled one of her guards to see who it was.

The door opened to reveal Harlan Peppermill, confused to find it wasn't Murdock admitting him. He craned his neck to see what was going on and said, "Um."

"Better and better," Omdahl said. "May as well join us, Peppershaker."

"Mill," he corrected. He more or less slunk to the far side of the room and stood next to Pasternak, who didn't look pleased to see him.

"Nice job on that fountain." Omdahl complimented.

"Thanks," he said. "Pity it got blown up."

"How did that happen?"

Peppermill shook his head and looked at his shoes.

Pushing off the wall, Omdahl closed in on Pasternak. Her guards started to move with her, but she waved them off. The women were inches apart by the time she stopped. "How about you, Past, er, Past, ah, Pastrami? You've always been a malcontent."

Pasternak ground her teeth.

"Yeah, I could see you blowing up a thing or two."

Pasternak was that close to punching the boss in the face when Tambe stepped to her side. "I did it," he said in a small voice pretending to be big.

For a moment, nobody in the room breathed. All eyes turned on him, some blank, some astonished, some questioning his sanity. "You?" Omdahl squeaked.

He tried to puff himself up. It almost worked. He looked like a steely-eyed prairie dog. "Yeah, me."

The armored lady's eyes narrowed in confusion. Then they widened in understanding. She snickered. She chuckled. She belly-laughed. She doubled over with hysteria, clutching herself as though to keep her midsection from exploding as the fountain had. The guards frowned at her. Murdock took an astonished step back. Pasternak and Peppermill shook their heads.

Tambe stood his ground, his face almost fierce.

It took a couple of minutes, but Omdahl got a grip. Her guffaws faded back to chuckles and finally mere snickers.

"What?" Tambe asked, and that set her off again.

She finally stifled her mirth enough to speak. "I guess I asked for that." She wiped the tears from her eyes. "You got me good. I haven't laughed like that in years. Maybe in my entire life." Motioning to her guards, she strode to the door. "Okay, Murdock, you're off the hook for now. But . . ." She spun and pointed at him, her eyes still bright with humor. "If I ever find out you had anything to do with this, you're finished."

"Suits me," Murdock replied and waved her good riddance.

One of the guards slammed a fist into the wall as he passed through the door, possibly thinking it made a good parting shot. The door shut itself in his wake.

Murdock nodded at Tambe. "Nice move," he said with genuine admiration. "Gutsy."

Peppermill shook the kid's hand and, while he was still looking all confused, Pasternak closed in and gave him a quick peck on the cheek. "Thanks, kid," she said.

Tambe touched the spot where she'd connected. He frowned.

"What?" he asked.

They stared at a wall that hadn't been there before, a bright red wall with brilliant yellow diagonal stripes. Before, this had been an open corridor ending a dozen meters further at the theaterish room thingy's main entrance. Now this garish wall stood here, not truly a wall but an emergency door blocking access to the airless scrap heap that used to be the theaterish room thingy.

Maccarone didn't know what to make of it. He wanted the wall out of the way so he could assure himself this was all a sick joke. But the wall didn't move, and slowly realization crept through his addled brain: no joke.

Feng Shui Land nodded sagely. "So much for that," he said, not at all displeased.

"What are we to do?" Kazimir Kapitan asked nobody. "What can we do? We can't do anything. We'll have to cancel the performance."

"Of course we'll have to cancel the performance," Land said, even less displeased. "We'll have to cancel the whole tour now. We'd better start packing for the journey home."

"It's not fair," Maccarone said quietly. "Everything was going so beautifully."

Land nearly bounced on the balls of his feet. "No sense crying over spilled soymilk. The sooner we get away from this disaster, the better. I'll let the crew know." He was about to move on that when he caught the look Maccarone was giving him. "What?"

"You don't seem too upset."

"Er, well, just trying to stay professional in the face of adversity."

"I appreciate that. And you're right."

"I am?" Land actually grinned.

"Yes. You're absolutely right."

"I'm glad to hear you say that." Land's professionalism acquired an elated glow. "I'll get the ball rolling."

Kapitan's brow furrowed. "What ball?"

Land slid back into default irritability for just a moment. "Nothing. Forget it." Then he cheered up again. "Time to press onward."

"Exactly," Maccarone agreed. "This is just a minor setback."

Land and Kapitan frowned at Maccarone, then frowned at the emergency door, which didn't look entirely minor.

"Setback?" Kapitan asked.

"Setback?" Land asked, too.

"Exactly. We have work to do. Contact base facilities. Find out how soon they can set up another theater. I'll personally pay for the work. I'll pay double if they can build us a venue in three days."

"But . . ." Land sputtered. "But . . ."

Maccarone put a consoling hand on the property master's shoulder, which actually didn't seem to console him very much. "I'm rich, remember? Money is no longer an object."

He found it touching when Land began to cry what he assumed were tears of joy.

In the aftermath of the explosion, Kaja Omdahl found herself very much in demand. The investigation put the fountain at or near ground zero. She supervised the crew that had rebuilt the fountain. Ergo, a very precise question was repeatedly put to her in a variety of creative ways, all of which boiled down to this: how the hell does a fountain blow up?

She loved the attention. She hated not having an answer.

Upper management had asked it first and most succinctly. The message from base director Amelia Carbuncle had read thus: "How the hell does a fountain blow up?"

She replied that she'd investigate.

After that, her local operations manager, the area operations manager, and the hemisphere operations manager all checked in with rapid inquiries, to wit: "Get me an explanation, pronto," and "Please provide background data for assessing the likelihood of a fountain malfunction resulting in an immolation of this scale," and "Immediately expedite a response to the foregoing inquiries regarding fountain internals with respect to explosive decompression."

To each of these, and a flurry of others from technical staff, environmental staff, PR staff, and staff she never even knew the mining colony had, she replied that she was investigating. Which she was. She'd grilled Murdock and his team and come up empty except for an outrageous joke. (Every time she thought about that, she nearly succumbed to paroxysms of laughter. Ajit Tambe, master saboteur!) Then she'd returned here to her little office—utility closet might be a more apropos term—and called up as much information as she could find on fountain mechanisms. As near as she could tell, fountains couldn't explode. Indeed, electronics generally couldn't explode, unless a connection sparked in the presence of a combustible like natural gas or hydrogen. *Yeah, right*, she thought. That left sabotage, which apparently didn't rate very high on the corporate acceptability scale.

Growing desperate, she discovered that anxiety functioned like an aphrodisiac for creativity. That would have proven wonderfully liberating except that just as her creative juices started to flow, a new inquiry arrived in the form of a short, thin visitor. The man slinked through her door, glancing nervously over his shoulder, then peered about as though noting all potential hiding places in the room. Omdahl wondered if he'd been demon quarry for the past week. She didn't bother acknowledging his presence, not even when he came to a halt before her tiny plastic desk, hands clasped tightly before him.

"Um," he finally said.

"Um what?"

"Your people, that is, the fountain. Your people, you know . . ."

"Built it. Yeah. So what?"

"It blew up."

"So I've been told."

The little man hurried back to the door for a quick look up and down the corridor, then scurried back to her desk. He leaned on it as though it was the only thing keeping him from collapsing. "What happened?"

"How should I know? Who are you, anyway?" He looked familiar, but she couldn't place him.

"Perry," he replied.

"Oh sure, sorry, I'm such an idiot. Everybody knows Perry."

That seemed to alarm him. "They do?"

"No! I'm busy. Go away."

"Sorry. I'm . . . it's important. I have to know."

"Who's your boss, Perry?"

"Lena Froe—well. Nobody, really. Just nobody."

Startled, Omdahl sprang to her feet and rushed him. He yelped and backed against the wall, but she kept coming until he had nowhere to run and her nose was only an inch from his. "The board sent you?" she whispered.

"No! Not! No! Not at all! Really! They didn't! Not really!"

Dizziness engulfed her. If the board of directors had dispatched someone to investigate, some serious heads were about to do some serious rolling. She sure didn't want hers to be among them. Then she wondered why she didn't want hers to be among them, because actually she had no idea what the archaic phrase meant. But that hardly mattered. Rolling heads couldn't be good, so yeah, she was pretty sure she didn't want hers doing any such thing.

"Okay. Sorry." She backed off and put up her hands to signal a truce. Time to grovel. Not many people knew she had this talent. Perry would, unfortunately, be one of them now. She took another step back. "Sorry about that. Stress, right? But I'm investigating. I don't have all the answers yet. But I'm working on it. I'm working really, really hard. I promise."

Now the man looked even more scared. Maybe one of his demons had just tapped him on the shoulder with a fiery claw. Or maybe he preferred aggressive women?

"It's maybe something to do with a spark," she added, hoping to appease him or at least make him feel like he'd done his job. "And, um, hydrogen." She'd read something about that. Or at least she thought she had.

"In a fountain?" the man squeaked.

"Well . . ." A sudden, brilliant thought occurred to her. Those creative juices must have turned back on. "Water is, you know, hydrogen and oxygen?"

"Oh." He frowned. "Is that how it works?"

She didn't know, but she was pretty sure that's how it was going to work. "Maybe. I don't know yet. I'm still investigating."

"Okay." He shuffled back to the door, but something apparently occurred to him before he stepped over the threshold. His face scrunched in concentration. "It wouldn't be, like, maybe, a wire in the wrong place?"

Surprised, Omdahl shook her head. "I don't think so. The fountain was working before, before, before, you know." She made an explosive gesture with her hands.

"Right," he said, then added quietly to himself, "Right. Hydrogen. That's good. Yes. Right."

"Just out of curiosity, why do you ask?"

For a moment he looked like he'd choked on a fish bone. "Things happen. Things get put in the wrong place sometimes. You know?"

"Yes," she agreed, but no, she thought, she had no idea what this guy was talking about.

"Thanks." He'd spoken without enthusiasm, but then Perry summoned considerable enthusiasm and rushed away, still pursued by demons.

While she frowned at her magnetic boots and puzzled over the strange encounter, another strange encounter began.

"Hello, Kaja. Can I call you Kaja?"

She looked up to find Roberto Maccarone standing before her. This was *really* unfair. "I'm still investigating. Maybe sparks. And hydrogen. Or wires in the wrong place. Maybe even both. Or all three?"

"I don't follow you."

"I hope not." Composing herself, she marched back to her desk and plopped into her standard issue plastic chair. "What do you want?"

"I have to say, when a piece of equipment falls off a cliff around here, it does it in style." He smiled a winning smile, and for a moment she almost thought he must like her. But this was Roberto Maccarone, opera boss, and no boss could possibly like anyone. She knew. She was a boss and she didn't like anyone.

"I don't have time for games. I'm busy."

Maccarone nodded. "I understand. Let's speak plainly, then. The explosion wasn't an accident, was it?" He looked rather pleased with himself for that assessment.

"Fountains blow up all the time around here."

"No, Kaja, they don't. It took me a little time to work it out, but it's clear now. You're having personnel problems." He flashed her that smile again. She was beginning to resent it. "Aren't you?"

Pretending to enter something on her computerized desktop, she snorted. "Why do you care?"

"For one thing, they've messed up my performance schedule."

Oh, that was rich. "You're lucky they didn't blow up your cast and crew."

"So it was sabotage, then."

"Management decreed it an accident. I'm still investigating the cause."

He puzzled over that for a moment. "They're covering it up?" Before she could tell him to get lost, he added, "That's fine. I don't care. I'd like to know the truth for my own reasons. So please do me a favor, Kaja, and . . ."

She sprang on him, slapped her hands on his shoulders, and pushed him to the wall. "Stop calling me that!"

Eyes wide, he nodded.

"Now get out!"

Maccarone graciously complied with her most amicable request.

Returning to her chair, Omdahl dug up some information and

fabricated a report about bad electrical connections and sparks and hydrolysis. It sounded maybe one tenth convincing to her, but she knew how management worked. They'd sell it somehow, and the debris of the theater would be swept under a metaphorical rug.

The metaphorical kind would have to do. They didn't have any *real* rugs way out here.

CHAPTER 11

It was another black dress day for Chelsea Liwanu, much like every day except for those on which she donned a black jumpsuit or a black skirt with a black long sleeve blouse or maybe black pants and a black...well, you get the idea. But not just any black dress day. A special black dress day.

Today she had chosen her most elegant black dress, a dress reserved for a very particular occasion. Tight-fitting, low-cut, all fringes and frills around neckline, cuffs, and hem, dotted with a sprinkling of tiny sequins that shimmered glossy black just at the edge of vision, it transformed her from the minister of gloom into a vision of stark beauty. The universe itself couldn't rival her.

News of the mayhem on TDY-41093-RRP had reached her office before she did, forcing itself to the top of her official agenda. She ignored it. She had her own agenda today. Besides, if Maccarone couldn't even switch on a fountain without blowing his theater to bits, he was a bigger loser than she'd imagined. Triply so, since he was now rolling in money. Who had he hired to build the damn thing, a herd of squirrels?

So much for that. She had worn this dress for the true top item on her agenda. Once per business quarter, she was required to inspect Territory HQ's theater. She had no choice in the matter. Regulations demanded it. Okay, she herself had written that particular regulation, but that just meant she had no excuse to ignore it.

She quickly checked messages to ensure nothing more important than a fountain had blown up while she slept, then she stood and swept out of the office, saying to her secretary in passing, "You know where I'll be." A new hire and young male who had never seen Liwanu look anything but severe, he gaped after her. She didn't notice. She moved with single-minded purpose, seeing nothing, hearing neither the sighs of envy of the women she passed nor the sharp intakes of men's breath. She had a duty to perform. She was going to inspect the theater.

She marched up the gently curving walkway, the walkway carpeted in gold with deep red swirls, paying no heed to the glowing green and white ceiling arching overhead nor the silver railings nor the verdant flower garden spread out below. She moved through them and over them, a vision that put them all to shame, utterly oblivious to them, until she came to the massive double doors with the winding gold tracery. She paused. She gently set a hand upon them.

She was going to . . .

Tears formed in her eyes.

Going to . . .

She wiped the tears away.

Inspect.

The theater.

"You've got a problem," Maccarone told Worthington confidentially. Since the comlink was secure, the confidential tone was unnecessary, but somehow it added excitement to the proceedings. At least he thought it did.

"You, or something else?"

His excitement melted like a bowl of ice cream in a blast furnace. "You probably heard about the explosion in the theater last night."

"That's all I've heard about for the past six hours. I'm sick of hearing about it."

"Your managers are calling it an accident. It's not."

Worthington didn't say anything. His silence sounded alarmingly like he was strangling someone. At least Maccarone thought it did. *How could silence possibly sound like that*? he wondered.

It didn't matter.

"It was sabotage. Somebody blew up the theater on purpose. Your managers don't want to admit it. So really, you've got two problems: rebellious workers and duplicitous managers."

"And you know this how?"

"I talked to the supervisor of the crew that built the fountain. She was preparing a bogus report to fit the conclusion management wanted."

"Is she in on it?"

"On what?"

"The plot, Maccarone, the plot!"

"To blow up the fountain or to cover up the cause?"

"Argh!"

"Say again? There was noise on the line."

Again there was that strangling-someone silence. Maccarone wondered how many people Worthington could get away with strangling in a single day. Probably a lot. He was that rich.

"It's her job to cover it up," Worthington groused. "Is she in on the *plot?*"

Maccarone wasn't sure, but before he could say so the first part of Worthington's statement struck him. "Wait a minute. You *want* her to cover up sabotage?"

Now it sounded like Worthington had transmuted into a balloon leaking air. It was the longest, most long-suffering sigh Maccarone had ever heard. "Roberto. Listen. You're a business owner."

Maccarone waited.

"You are, aren't you?"

"Yes, of course."

"So you know employees have to do what their bosses want. True?"

"Well, yes, generally. But—"

"If the supervisor's manager tells her to fabricate an explanation for an explosion, it's her job to do it."

Maccarone wasn't too sure about that, but he didn't say so. Contradicting Worthington didn't seem helpful. Or safe. The jerk might reach through the phone and strangle him. Silently.

"Now that that's settled, let's move on to sabotage. Is the supervisor in on it?"

"I don't know."

"Then find out! And the answer had better be yes!"

The connection wasn't so much severed as obliterated.

I'm sure glad we had this little talk, Maccarone thought. But at least he had made progress. Specifically, he'd progressed from knowing what Worthington wanted to knowing what Worthington really wanted to knowing what Worthington actually, seriously, truthfully wanted.

He wanted a rebellion.

Whether one existed or not.

Using an electronic key, she unlocked the doors but didn't immediately pass through. She needed time to prepare. *Deep breaths. Think of nothing. Breathe. Breathe.*

Her mind clear, all thoughts of Worthington and Maccarone and exploding fountains and Ed Wood film festivals consigned to nonexistence, she pushed the doors open just far enough to slink through. Once inside, she gently closed them behind her and relocked them. Then she didn't move again. She stood unmoving just inside the doors with a vast, empty darkness before her, above her, and around her. She might have stepped out of a spaceship's airlock while cruising the intergalactic void and been engulfed by a universe invisible to her eyes.

Still Chelsea Liwanu didn't move, but her vision gradually adapted to the featureless dark. She closed her eyelids and put a hand to a plate on the wall to her right. She knew its location by feel. She knew every detail of this place. She could wander blind up and down every aisle and row, every step, every inch of stage with never a false step. But she needed to see, wanted to see, and so at her touch, a blaze of light flooded the theater.

As though crossing from life to death and coming into the brilliance of the next world, even with eyes firmly shut she was momentarily blinded. She waited for the sensation to pass, then slowly raised her eyelids. The blaze softened, and the theater at long last came into view. Her breath caught in her throat, as it always did, once per quarter, when she came to . . .

Came to . . .

Inspect.

The theater.

A thousand plush seats covered in deep red fabrics with gold and silver stitching, arrayed in perfect, gently curving rows spread out before her and lurked in the massive balconies above her head. Aisles carpeted in forest green with swirls of gold, silver, and deep blue parted the rows, pointing to the stage where a massive curtain hung, shimmering with all the colors of the rainbow as light played across it, changing its appearance from moment to moment. Liwanu thought waterfalls must look like this, although she'd never seen one.

At the base of the curtain, the hardwood stage—real honest-to-God hardwood polished to a soft glow—jutted forward from the curtain. An orchestra pit opened beneath it at the center. All around her colored light splashed on pale walls that hid massive speakers and many of the lighting fixtures that illuminated the stage.

The silence was so deep she could hear her own heartbeat. Its rapid rhythm thundered in her ears.

Liwanu stood by the doors looking down the central aisle toward the stage, taking it all in as she did once per quarter. Then slowly, heart still racing, she lowered her eyes to the floor, to a point about three quarters down the aisle, to a spot where the carpet flowed around a circle of soft white light. From that spot, a gentle beacon leapt heavenward and painted its image on the ceiling far above.

Drawing a deep breath, Liwanu moved slowly, timorously down the aisle to the beacon. When she reached it, she sank to her knees. She looked into the beacon as though it were the only light in the cosmos and she a moth drawn inexorably to it.

"Hi," she told it.

Tears tracked down her cheeks.

"I'm still here."

If Kaja Omdahl wouldn't talk, maybe that Murdock fellow would. He seemed, Maccarone thought, easy-going. Besides, he liked opera, so he couldn't be all bad even if he was involved in a plot to blow up everything in sight. But how to find him? It was pointless asking Omdahl; she and Murdock appeared to be rivals if not enemies. Did the facility have a directory? He looked around but saw nothing. Almost literally. He was in the middle of what served as a receiving area alongside the space docks: a four-meter square of unbroken white: white walls, white floors, white ceiling, white corridors leading off in three directions.

Maybe, he thought, finding people was as simple as finding the food dispensers. It was worth a try.

Maccarone sauntered to one of the walls, tapped it, and said, "Murdock." Nothing happened. What was Murdock's first name? Jim, wasn't it? He tapped again. "Jim Murdock." Still nothing happened. He tapped again. "Personnel directory."

"What are you doing?"

Startled by the husky female voice, Maccarone executed a shoddy half Lutz and landed almost facing the woman. He knew her. He could hardly forget her, under the circumstances. She'd been sitting behind him the night the fountain spewed muddy brown all over everything. Hands on hips, she stood smiling like she knew the punch line to a joke that was on him. "Sorry?" he asked.

"You can't find people that way, only facilities."

"Oh. Do you know where I can find Jim Murdock?"

"Josh." She spread her hands to indicate something really big.

"That would be him." Maccarone regained enough composure to beam his winning smile at her.

"Yeah, I know him. He's my boss."

"Excellent! I'm . . ."

"I know who you are."

"Of course. And what's your name, ma'am?"

"Darya." She leaned close and drew out the second syllable as though its luscious sound might seduce him. She turned her head slightly, and her thick, black hair stroked his face.

He knew he had a powerful effect on women, but this was nuts. All he'd done was ask her name. He shuffled back a step. "I'd like to talk with Mr. Murdock, if I could."

"I'll take you," she said, batting her eyes. She hooked her arm through his and tugged.

That's when he realized it was an act, because she wasn't really that good of an actress. But he decided to play along in the hope of eliciting useful information. "Thank you." He again bestowed his smile upon her.

She laughed. "Smooth. Were you an actor before you became a business tycoon?"

"I spent a few years on stage, yes."

She pulled him around a corner from one boring white corridor to another. "Opera?"

"Oh, yes. Principally Verdi. I love Verdi's operas." He leaned toward her confidentially. "Not that I was as good a singer as Manfred, but don't tell him that."

"Who?"

"Our lead tenor. Manfred Mooseherder. "

"Mooseherder?"

Maccarone shrugged. "A stage name. We all have stage names."

"But Mooseherder?"

Time to change the subject, he thought, before he found himself discussing marimbas again. "I couldn't help but notice a certain tension between Mr. Murdock and Ms. Omdahl." They turned another corner. He was lost already. All these corridors looked the same.

Darya led him to pair of double doors and tapped the wall. "Kaja hates everyone." A moment later, the doors opened on a lifter car. "It's a matter of pride with her. Come on." They entered the car, and as the doors slid shut she shook her head. "Level twenty six," she told the lifter. "Mooseherder. Wow."

The lifter suddenly dropped like spaceship with dead thrusters, leaving Maccarone's stomach behind. He grimaced. "Kaja's made up a story about the fountain. Bad wiring and hydrogen and whatnot."

"Yeah, I heard about that."

The suddenly dark undertone in her voice got his attention. She looked angry. "You don't approve, obviously."

"That's the trouble with this place. All the stories have too much angular momentum."

"What do you mean?"

Darya just shook her head.

"You value honesty," Maccarone ventured.

"I don't know about value, but a minimal amount might be nice." The lifter decelerated hard. Maccarone thought he was being squashed flat. "Here we are," Darya said unnecessarily as the doors slid open and a burning smell infiltrated the lifter car.

They stepped out not into a gleaming white corridor but a cold, dark tunnel barely illuminated by a string of chemlights along the left wall. The rough walls scintillated with embedded ice crystals catching the artificial light and throwing it around. In the distance, Maccarone thought he could hear a gang of Nibelungs hammering at their forges. Occasional shouts punctuated the noise of industry, while an incessant high-pitched whine echoed through the tunnel. The overall effect was unnerving, to say the least. He felt he'd literally entered the underworld and was now at the mercy of demons.

Darya led the way down the tunnel, not in the least bothered by the atmospherics. Maccarone caught up and walked beside her in silence until she shot him a sidelong glance. "You're sure that's not a joke? Mooseherder?"

"I'm sure." *Please let it go*, he silently pleaded.

As they moved down the tunnel, they passed others branching off on both sides, some of them emitting whines and bangs and foul smells, others as silent as tombs. Darya kept to the main tunnel for a good five minutes, then turned left down one of the branches, which itself split a number of times. She turned again.

"How do you know where you're going?" Maccarone wondered if he'd ever get out of here.

"How do rats find cheese in a maze?"

He had no idea and decided not to ask. The noises had grown louder and the stench thicker. Finally, he saw several huge shapes ahead, and detected movement all around them. Darya stopped and opened a cabinet mounted on the wall. From within, she took a pair of respirators. "Put this on," she said, handing one to Maccarone. "Breathing down here is like trying to inhale melted marshmallows."

He watched Darya don hers, then quickly followed suit. She waved him forward, and as they approached the shapes resolved into a jumble of huge equipment. Men and women swarmed around it, presumably setting up and operating and troubleshooting. A blast echoed through the tunnels and shook the very walls. After the noise and the shudders subsided, Darya called out, "Hey Josh! Over here!" Her voice carried astoundingly well, although it sounded quite nasal through the mask. A moment later, Murdock lumbered around from behind the machinery.

"Darya," he said easily as he drew near, his voice equally nasal behind his own mask. "New boyfriend?"

"Yeah, I'm collecting them. He wants to talk to you."

Murdock leaned against the wall, folded his arms over his chest, and studied Maccarone. "What's up?"

"I have to say," Maccarone replied, repeating the words he's spoken to Omdahl, "when a piece of equipment falls off a cliff around here, it does it in style."

Murdock scratched his bushy chin. "Don't think that was a cliff. More an explosion."

"Now Mr. Murdock, you know what I meant."

Murdock looked him over as though not sure he was worth the trouble. "You think it wasn't an accident."

"I know it wasn't. Your managers know, too. They're covering it up."

"Sounds like them."

"I'd like to know the truth." He smiled easily to signal he harbored no malice toward the saboteurs, whoever they might be, although he wasn't sure smiles could actually be seen in this getup.

"Why?"

Maccarone spread his hands innocently. "Really, Josh. May I call you Josh?"

"If I can call you Rob." Murdock smiled in a way that made him look not merely like a grizzly but a hungry grizzly trying to put a trout at ease.

It sure didn't put Maccarone at ease, but at least for once the answer wasn't no. "Sure, Josh." A screech from the equipment made him jump, but he kept his eyes on Murdock, who took his time considering his answer.

"Truth is, anything can and does happen around here." Maccarone didn't see how that was an answer, and his face apparently said so, because Murdock went on. "We got safety regs, right? Sometimes they're too cumbersome or expensive, so we ignore them. Then sometimes bad things happen and reports gotta be filed. Can't have a report saying we ignored regs. So, freak accident. Nothing to do with us."

Darya glared at the floor and nodded.

Murdock shrugged. "Lotta freak accidents around here. Your fountain was just one more."

Maccarone inched closer to Murdock and lowered his voice. "But there's a difference between negligence and sabotage." Another explosion rocked the tunnel. This time, Maccarone didn't react. It surprised him how quickly he was adapting.

"Why?" Murdock asked.

"One is a willful act."

"Which one?"

"Sabotage. It's a willful act of destruction."

"So's ignoring the regs. It just takes a longer before a fountain blows up because of it."

Maccarone had the feeling Murdock was trying to tell him something without telling him anything, or was trying to not tell him something while telling him everything, or . . . He shook his head to clear it. "So you're saying . . ."

Murdock waited, still impassive. Darya tapped her fingers on her thighs, impatient.

"The sabotage," Maccarone ventured, "is to force somebody to acknowledge there's a problem."

"That's one theory," Murdock agreed.

"Like who? Not management. They just cover up everything anyway.

Government regulators? You think they'll ride to your rescue if enough bad things happen?"

"Someone might think that, sure."

"So you blow up everything in sight and hope for the best."

"Bombs and space colonies don't mix," Murdock told him gravely. "Most wouldn't go that route." He glanced at Darya, who responded with a tight-lipped smile. "But a theory would be, enough things go wrong, someone in authority has to step in and fix it."

"Unless that someone is on StarBright's payroll," Maccarone told him. "They can buy off anyone, you know."

Murdock grinned. "Like you, maybe?"

"I'm only interested in opera." Maccarone hoped that would deflect the question. He sure didn't want Murdock knowing he was indeed on Star-Bright's payroll. He rather wished he didn't know himself just now.

Murdock looked back at the operation. Someone was shouting something, which caused someone else to shout something. The high-pitched whine intensified, then someone shouted again and another explosion, louder than before, set the walls ringing. The next shout reached them with full clarity: "Damn it, I told you to crank it down!"

"You ever do any mining?" Murdock asked.

Maccarone shook his head.

"Wanna give it a try?"

He didn't, but he said, "Sure, what do I have to do?"

Murdock sent one of his huge hands on Maccarone's shoulder. "Follow me. I'll show you the ropes."

On his other side, Darya hooked her arm through his. "This is going to be a blast," she said.

And sure enough, another blast sounded.

CHAPTER 12

That night, nothing blew up. True, Feng Shui Land melted down, but in pathetic fashion, rather like what might happen if nuclear fuel had the general properties of frozen yogurt. After handing off to Kazimir Kapitan the job of contracting construction of a new pseudo-theater, Land slunk to his quarters on the *Ponchielli* to ponder the demise of his hopes and dreams. Eventually, he pondered himself into something akin to sleep. Mental disturbances approaching nightmares then hounded him. He found himself adrift in interstellar space aboard a derelict shipping container disguised as a theater, lacking propulsion and food, his only companion the vessel's computer which kept interrupting his misery to inform him of the exact distance to the nearest star, an enormous number that never seemed to change.

When faux morning came, Land's mood was foul even for Land. He ordered breakfast sent to his office, then locked himself in with his soy eggs and soy bacon and soy coffee—it tasted like soy coffee, anyway—and sulked. He sulked for half an hour. For good measure, he sulked for another fifteen minutes. After that, he sulked for another five because he was in a groove and found it hard to stop. Sulking finally over, he activated the computer in his desktop, did some brainstorming, and compiled the results into a list:

1. Destroy the new theater.
2. Destroy the building supplies for the new theater before the new theater can be built.
3. Get the whole thing over with: destroy TDY-41093-RRP.
4. Kill Maccarone. (Note to self: brainstorming means recording everything that comes to mind, no matter how insane.)
5. Commit suicide. (Note to self: see above note to self.)
6. If we're stuck out here, at least go somewhere nicer than TDY-41093-RRP.
7. Quit and go home. The rest of them can freeze to death.

8. Embezzle as much as possible from Maccarone, then quit and go home. The rest of them can still freeze to death.
9. Embezzle as much as possible from Maccarone, use it to buy him out, and take the rest of them back home. Maccarone can freeze to death.
10. Get a job on StarBright's board, oust Maccarone, buy his company, and take it back home. Maccarone can still freeze to death.

After that, Land ran out of steam. Not that steam had anything to do with it, really, but none of these old expressions ever made any sense. He studied the list in silence, then mentally broke silence to ask a serious question: *Am I really that nasty?*

It was a tough question to answer.

Well, no, actually it wasn't.

But, he assured himself, *I've been horribly mistreated. It's not my fault.*

He deleted all of the really nasty items from the list, then considered the one that remained. Could there *be* any place in the Oort Territories that qualified as nicer? Not really. How could one slush pile slowly drifting through the dark be better than any other? Nor, he imagined, could the overwhelming majority of space stations drifting slowly through the dark be much of an improvement. Indeed, the only space stations that might rise above sewership were those serving as headquarters for major corporations such as StarBright. And of those, the one that played host to StarBright itself would undoubtedly prove best. So if he wanted to go someplace nicer without moving sunward, ultimately there was but a single destination.

As luck would have it, Maccarone already had his eye on that destination and the fabulous theater hidden within.

Suddenly seeing a light at the end of the tunnel—another puzzling expression, since he figured even tunnels should be properly illuminated—he carefully composed a message to Culture Minister Chelsea Liwanu requesting a preliminary inspection of the theater in preparation for their production. He smiled as he dispatched it. For once, he could actually look forward to somebody's reply.

Mining, Maccarone had discovered, wasn't much fun unless, like Pasternak, one happened to like blowing things up. And really, not even then. Each tightly regulated blast from the extractor vaporized a tiny hole into which a much larger surge of energy was directed a fraction of a second later, expanding the frozen material from within and causing a head-jarring explosion. Steam and fine debris would fill the air between the device and the collapsed wall. The operation was carefully calibrated to keep the miners safe so long as they stood behind the machinery, but even through his respirator the stench of methane and chemical soot filled Maccarone's nostrils. Without breathing protection, he figured, everyone down there would have asphyxiated in the first blast.

Then the machine lumbered forward and ingested the loose material, a long process during which it was impossible to hear anything aside from the crunch and rattle of ice and organics being reduced to fine dust and gas. Everyone wore hearing protection designed to prevent instant deafness, but nothing could stop the vibrations from penetrating the bones. Hydrogen—the chief goal of the operation—remained locked up in the dust, while the gas contained worthless elements like nitrogen, oxygen, and various impurities. Vented out the back of the extractor, this gas accounted for the burning smell he'd noted earlier. Ventilation systems would scrub and recirculate the gas throughout the facility as part of the breathable atmosphere.

Maccarone spent only an hour with the miners, enough for them to demolish and process just two small loads. After that, covered in soot and feeling like he'd been run through a food processor, he made up an excuse to leave and asked Pasternak to take him back up.

"What did you think?" she asked when she finally deposited him at the spaceport.

"I think you're made of stronger stuff than I am," he admitted.

"You'd survive it. Or not. Either way, it's about the same."

After she left to return to work, he boarded the *Ponchielli* and collapsed in his quarters, feeling like every brain cell had been rattled loose. He slept fitfully that night, dreaming of extractors chasing him about the stage, firing laser bolts at him. In the morning he shook the dreams off with the thought that an extractor-dragon might be interesting for a modern staging of *Sigmund*.

Over breakfast—equally as soy as Land's—he gave some thought to the mess brewing in the mines. Worthington wanted revolution. The miners wanted attention. They were on a collision course, with Maccarone stuck in the middle, a fine position from which to be squashed but otherwise not incredibly enviable. He just wanted access to a theater. How hard could that possibly be?

Chewing thoughtfully without tasting—something of a mercy, that—he pondered the likelihood that Chelsea Liwanu might grant him a performance at HQ. Rationally, she ought to. She wanted people to forget the misery of Oort life. The miners certainly could do with a bit of distraction from their routine. He doubted they were alone in that. In that theater he could transport everyone far, far from this horrid place. Worthington had cleverly planted a powerful negative expectation in his brain, but now that Maccarone thought about it, the Director of Marketing had a vested interest in making sure Liwanu didn't have a chance to say yes. The longer Worthington could keep Maccarone drooling for the theater, the longer he could use him for whatever other schemes his devious brain concocted. Once the theater opened to him, Maccarone had no reason to dance to Worthington's tune.

That wasn't entirely true, of course. The piles of cash paid to Maccarone as a StarBright board member kept him dancing, too.

Forget the money, he told himself. *Book the theater*. After that, he wouldn't need StarBright or Worthington or anyone. After that, he, Roberto Maccarone, would be running the show, and if Chelsea Liwanu wished to be Earth-bound, he'd get her there in style.

Pleased with himself for figuring it out, he carefully composed a message to the Culture Minister proposing a production of *Aida* in her theater. He smiled as he dispatched it, actually looking forward to her reply.

Among the cultural icons of what was once called western civilization, one finds the hefty woman in the Valkyrie hat—a sort of metallic funnel with pointy horns—singing a high-frequency note that almost but not quite qualifies as a dog whistle. The sound shatters an expensive piece of crystal glassware along with nearby eardrums. Everyone praises this fantastic achievement, except possibly the owner of the expensive piece of crystal glassware, and the singer smiles knowingly while whoever paid her to perform the stunt compares her sterling voice to whatever product they're trying to sell. Nobody watching the spectacle questions why they'd want to buy a product capable of destroying every window in the vicinity, but that's neither here nor there.

Here, rather, is the here and there: Chelsea Liwanu came very close to that glass-shattering pitch, and certainly matched the fabled singer's volume, upon reading not one but two messages from Space Operatic officials requesting access to her theater. Rushing into the room, her panicked secretary nearly tripped over himself, caught hold of a chair for support, and cried, "What's wrong?"

"Out!" she squealed. "Out!"

He outed.

The screaming stopped, but thumping and pounding ensued as Liwanu beat up on her innocent desk and the innocent walls and kicked an innocent chair across the room. Eventually she had to halt the tantrum because she now had a splitting headache. She dropped into her chair, folded her arms on the desktop, and buried her head in them.

That theater was *hers*. They couldn't have it! Besides, it was a theater no longer, except in name. It was a sacred place, a holy shrine that she would *not* permit hordes of filthy miners and rich buffoons and cheap performers to despoil. Nobody got in. Nobody!

Especially not Roberto [invective] Maccarone.

Most especially not Artemis [really long string of invectives] Worthington.

She straightened. She smoothed her black hair and her black dress. Projecting supreme calm now, she composed a single understated reply inviting Maccarone and Land to meet her at thirteen hundred hours.

She suggested they wear full body armor.

She deleted that last bit before sending the reply.

Leaning back and closing her eyes, Liwanu spoke to someone not present but always there: "We've got to get home," she told him. "Before I go completely mad. If only I knew how."

If her confidant made any suggestion, she couldn't hear it.

Invisibility was Perri Pauli's most notable talent. People usually didn't notice him, which meant he could move in nearly every circle. He didn't like to think too much about the implications concerning his personality, but he made good use of that talent on Lena Froebisher's behalf. For example, here he was, sitting alone, ensconced in a booth along the back wall of The King's Ransom, dressed in a subdued green and burgundy casual suit, dining on an elegant, fully expensible breakfast of real eggs, real bacon, real grits, real fruit, and real coffee while, seated in the booth right behind him, Worthington and Froebisher talked real shop. Froebisher knew Pauli was there, but Worthington didn't, nor would he bother to look, nor, if he looked, would he remember Pauli, nor if he remembered him would he think twice about it. Pauli was just some scriptwriter related somehow to CEO Santamonica Amarillo. Men like Worthington didn't pay attention to such small fish.

Now there, Pauli thought, *is a curious phrase. What do fish, big or small, have to do with people, aside from being their lunch? Oh, well.*

"My spy is investigating," Worthington rumbled in his deep voice.

Froebisher responded too quietly for Pauli to hear.

"You know better than to ask that. Just know this: trouble's brewing down there. Big trouble. These so-called accidents are no more accidents than I'm a peasant."

Froebisher said something along the lines of, "Yoombur slade end-ince." Pauli couldn't quite hash that out, but he thought she was asking about evidence.

"I'm working on that. But mark my words, facility management is lying to us. That theater explosion could have killed somebody. What's worse, my spy thinks at least one of the supervisors might be on the side of the miners. Maybe she even orchestrated the incident. Think about that."

"You're suggesting," Froebisher said, clearly for once, "it's escalating to open warfare."

"Exactly."

"Hmntroo propoe?"

Pauli wished she'd speak up. This would be a lot easier to follow if he had both sides of the conversation. Through the seat, he felt Worthington shift on his bench.

"On site security forces."

In reply, unintelligible sounds of astonishment.

"This is strictly confidential, just between you and me."

More sounds. Pauli grumbled to himself and carefully pushed his body up in an effort to raise the level of his ears. It wasn't easy, he being so short and the back of the bench being so high.

Worthington lowered his voice, but Pauli could still make out—just—what he was saying: "I've been afraid of something like this for a long time. I've quietly assembled a mercenary network to call upon in just such an emergency."

Froebisher's reply rang clear this time: "My God, Artemis, are you mad?"

"We both know company security is a joke, and Earth won't get involved. Shipping troops out here is too expensive."

"What do you want from me?" Froebisher was obviously worked up now, speaking loud and clear, at least from Pauli's vantage.

"Frankly, I don't think most of the dunderheads on the board will lift a finger to stop this. I can't propose this action until I have the votes. I'll only get one chance, so I can't risk being shot down. If I can count on you, I think it will happen. People listen to you."

More than they listen to you, Pauli thought. Worthington might be powerful, but he wasn't the most popular guy among his peers. Or the rest of humanity.

"I don't like it. It's dangerous."

"Lena, listen to me. This is far bigger than what happens on one small ice floe. Think domino theory. It could spread. If it does, it could take the company down." He slapped his hand on the table to demonstrate which way was down.

For a few minutes Froebisher was silent. Worthington let her ponder whatever she needed to ponder. Finally, she mumbled something unintelligible.

"Of course. And in exchange for your support, I'll do everything in my power to see you named permanent CIO."

"You'd do that?"

"Absolutely."

Again, Pauli couldn't make out Froebisher's reply.

"All right," Worthington said, "but please don't take too long. I'll give you more details when my spy reports in. After that, we must act swiftly."

Sensing Worthington rise to leave, Pauli bent over his breakfast and feigned obliviousness. Out of the corner of his eye, he saw a waiter glide up to Worthington as he extricated himself. "My treat," he told the waiter, who nodded and stepped demurely aside. Then Worthington was gone. Pauli continued to eat until he heard Froebisher snap, "Are you deaf?"

He turned to find her motioning him over. He switched booths and sat across from her. "I could only hear every fifth word you said," he complained.

"I didn't bring you here to listen to me. Did you hear him?"

"Yes."

"Well?"

"He wants your support in putting down a rebellion."

Froebisher's eyelids drooped. "No kidding."

Pauli didn't know why she asked him these things. She was a billion times smarter than he. He hadn't heard anything she hadn't heard. If she couldn't figure it out, what hope did he have? But she expected something, so he tried anyway. "Okay, let's back up. He wants your vote."

"So he said."

"Why does he want your vote?"

"That," she said dangerously, "is what I'm asking you."

See? She was fifty steps ahead of him, and they'd only started. Pauli tried to replay the conversation, but the only part he heard was the part about how the theater explosion might have killed someone. He'd never been much into guilt, but now it welled up inside him and nearly made him retch. "I gotta tell you something," he whimpered.

"No, you gotta answer my question."

"I did it. *I* blew up that theater."

She stared at him as if certain his brain had turned to mush before her eyes. Probably she'd never heard anything so insane. He wouldn't have believed it himself if he hadn't been there.

"I didn't mean it to blow up. I just wanted to break it so Maccarone would have to come out of hiding and talk to me. So I sabotaged the fountain."

"How do you accidentally blow up a fountain?"

Pauli shrugged. "I don't know. I just cut some wires. That's all."

"Don't be daft. You can't blow up a fountain by cutting wires."

"The supervisor said something about water and electricity and hydrogen and—"

"Shut up," Froebisher snapped. "It doesn't work that way. Whatever you did, it was coincidental. Somebody else blew it up. Now can we please get back to my question?"

Coincidental. That's what the lady said, and she should know. It wasn't his fault after all. Probably. So, okay, he felt better. A little. Maybe. "Okay." He thought about it for a moment. Actually, he didn't. He remained useless, having no idea whatsoever what Worthington was after.

No, that wasn't true. Clearly Worthingon sought victory for his security proposal, which gave Pauli something to start with. "How many votes does he have?"

"Two for certain: his and Maccarone's. Maybe one or two others, so let's say four to be generous. I'll have to check how many shares that constitutes. It changes all the time. I doubt he's anywhere near a majority."

"And if you back him?"

"That will garner him probably six more votes, with everyone who rides my coattails."

"What's a coattail?"

Froebisher ignored the question. "That would put him near a majority. Well over if I can persuade Santamonica."

"And then he brings in his troops."

"Yes."

"And," Pauli continued, trying desperately to work out where they were going, "they crush the rebellion."

"There is no rebellion. But he crushes something, that's for sure."

Something got crushed. So far, so good, if crushing some unspecified something could be good. It could be bad, too, depending on whether or not you were part of the something. But there, Pauli became hopelessly mired in the nothingness of his thoughts. "Then what?"

"Then he's a hero," Froebisher sighed.

"A hero with an army."

He was only stating the obvious, but somehow it was the right thing to state. Froebisher's eyes expanded about to the size of the plate before her. "Oh my God," she muttered, voice quavering. "A hero with an army."

Pauli frowned at her. "That sounds bad. He could get anything he wanted. He could take over the whole territory."

"Worse than that." He'd never heard her sound that worried before. "Far, far worse."

"What could be worse than that?"

Froebisher gave the remains of her breakfast a look that seemed to accuse it of treason. "A coup. He'd take over the company!"

Breakfast for the miners on TDY-41093-RRP lacked the elegance of that in The King's Ransom.

Well, duh.

A miner's breakfast consisted largely of variously shaped and colored artificially flavored versions of soy-something. Rather than eating at the tables near the food dispensers dotting the surface facilities, many workers availed themselves of the graciously appointed dining rooms below ground, stationed close to the work sites so nobody wasted time getting from food to job or vice versa. The ambiance featured soot-impregnated ice walls, furniture aged to perfection—you'd swear it was no less than a thousand years old and ready to crumble into your soy porridge—and the soothing music of extractors blasting new holes in the frozen matrix nearby. Had the miners not been so used to it, they might have thought with some excitement that one of those blasts would take out the dining room and them with it.

In this subdued atmosphere, Arne Slocum scratched his cheek and yelled pleasantly, "What's Maccarone's angle?" Everyone else was yelling, too. Aside from the occasional explosion, nobody could hear anything other than their own conversations, and sometimes not even that. Most of the yelling had nothing to do with anything important, but occasional juicy gossip might be picked up if one listened hard enough. Or, actually, not. One was lucky to hear what one said one's own self.

"Don't know," Murdock yelled back. "Could be working for the company."

"What does he know about mining? He's an opera manager."

"Don't know."

"Don't you know anything?"

The reverberation from an explosion underscored Murdock's gentle grizzly bear smile.

"Say he is working for the company," Slocum yelled. "Are we in trouble?"

"Nah," Murdock yelled with conviction. "I just told him what the company already knows."

"Which is?"

"Safety regs get ignored and we're not always thrilled about it."

Slocum pondered that for a moment, then yelled back an insightful comment: "Oh." He had too little information about Maccarone to have any clue what was really going on. He was inclined to tell Murdock to steer clear of the guy, but then his inner spy came out to play. "Why not use him? Feed him some line, see if the company reacts? Then we'd know."

Murdock nodded. "Good. What do we tell him?"

"Don't know," Slocum yelled. "Oh." A wicked grin spread across his face. "Tell him Kaja's stealing explosives and making her goons blow things up."

Returning the grin, Murdock said, "That'd be fun. But no." The grin slipped away. "She'd get hurt bad."

"She'd do the same for you, Josh."

"I know. But our real beef isn't with her."

"Real beef? What's that mean? There's no real beef here, only soy."

"Our complaint," Murdock yelled. "Not sure why it means that, but it does."

"Well that's dumb. So what do we tell him?"

"Something stupid. Like maybe—" Murdock's brow furrowed, which made him look a lot less friendly than a grizzly. "Like, the trouble would stop if we got real ice cream for dessert."

Slocum wondered if the noise had finally jarred some part of Murdock's brain loose. "That's stupid all right," he yelled. "Who would believe that?"

"Dunno," Murdock yelled back. "But if anyone would, it'd be Maccarone."

An explosion rattled shards of ice loose from the dining room walls. They chattered as they hit the icy floor, which might have added something to the ambiance had anyone been able to hear it over the yelling.

They just had time to catch the next shuttle bound for Territory HQ. More than a little astonished to learn that they'd each had the same idea, Maccarone and Land settled in—if it could be called that—for the flight. Even more utilitarian than most spacecraft, the shuttle jammed fifty skinny seats into its interior, packed in tight rows. A person could just about walk sideways down the narrow aisle along the side. An unpleasant shade of greenish gray coated the whole shebang. Clearly whoever built it didn't relish the thought of anyone actually riding in it and had done their best to make sure nobody wanted to.

Fortunately, Maccarone and Land were two of only seven passengers this morning, so they could sit in the front row where their knees scraped the forward bulkhead rather than someone else's back. Better still, they could sit two seats apart rather than in each other's laps. Best of all, they could speak in a subdued tone, as opposed to yelling at each other as certain miners had been forced to do, thus keeping their strange conversation private.

"I didn't realize you had matters in hand already," Maccarone said.

"What matters?"

"The theater, of course."

Land chewed his lower lip for a moment. "Yes, well, I wouldn't have come if I'd known you were already working the problem."

"What problem?"

"The theater! For God's sake, Roberto!"

Maccarone puzzled over that, not quite sure what Land meant. "The theater isn't a problem. The problem is Chelsea Liwanu."

"Why is she a problem?"

"Have you talked to her yet?"

"No. From what you said before, I thought . . . " Land waved his hands to indicate whatever it was he thought, but probably the thought didn't transmit well in that mode.

Or maybe it did. "When did I say that?"

"Is your mind on opera at all anymore?" Land snapped. "You told us you'd arranged to use the theater for a performance. You even asked us what opera we wanted."

"Yes." Maccarone did remember that meeting, all too well. "And you all asked the most irritating questions. But actually, I hadn't quite concluded negotiations."

"Obviously. What's the hang up?"

"I told you. Chelsea Liwanu."

Rubbing his temples as though in pain, Land shook his head. "Why," he asked in a remarkably dull voice for him, "is she a hang up?"

"If you'd met her, you'd know."

"Try. Explaining. It. To. Me."

With a heavy sigh, Maccarone leaned back in his seat. That proved about as comfortable as sitting on the sharp edge of a pointy rock, so he sat forward again. "To be honest, I have no idea. I'd say she enjoys making life impossible for others, except she doesn't actually seem to enjoy it. She just does it. Maybe it's a bad habit."

"How far did the negotiations get?"

"I didn't actually ask her about the theater. I only found out about it after our initial meeting, which went badly enough that I opted for a different approach."

"That being?"

"Artemis Worthington. He said he could, er, convince Liwanu."

Land closed his eyes and rubbed his temples again. Maccarone wondered if he was prone to migraines. Maybe he should take a medication. Several medications.

"What happened with that?" Land asked.

"I have a bad feeling about Worthington. That's why I'm going back to Liwanu." About whom he also had a bad feeling, but maybe not quite so bad a feeling as he had about Worthington. The situation could hardly be called felicitous.

"So what you're saying is," Land grumbled, "we're back to square one."

"Back to what?"

"Square one."

"Is that a location?"

Land studied the ceiling of the compartment and shook his head. "It's the beginning."

"Oh. Well yes, basically."

"Just when things can't get any worse," Land muttered, "they exceed my wildest nightmares."

"Come on, it's not that bad. We just have to ask nicely and offer her some incentives."

Land looked at Maccarone in surprise, perhaps realizing for the first time that, yes, the boss actually did have a plan. "What incentives?"

"I'm filthy rich now."

Gaping, Land clapped a hand on Maccarone's arm before realizing he didn't want to be that cozy and snatched it back. "Bribery?"

"I understand," Maccarone said without enthusiasm, "that she's occasionally bribable. Anyway, it's only a theater. It's not like I'm trying to buy votes or influence contracts. She can use the money to develop better programs. Or go back to Earth."

"Go back to Earth!" Land looked like Maccarone had slapped him in the face and then punched him in the gut for good measure.

"Sounds crazy, doesn't it? But that's what she wants to do."

For a good while, Land couldn't seem to find anything to say. Maccarone once again ruminated on his property manager's oddballness, but in the end decided he'd just have to accept it. Likely it was genetic.

"What's the opera?" Land asked with astounding lack of enthusiasm.

"*Aida.*"

"You're working overtime to make me miserable, aren't you?"

Oh good, Maccarone thought with equal lack of enthusiasm. *He hates it.*

CHAPTER 13

Oddly enough, Artemus Worthington had something in common with Feng Shui Land: people were working overtime to make the marketing director miserable, too. He enumerated those idiots as he got dressed that morning, surrounded by the pleasant reds, golds, and purples of his bedroom, a sprawling space done up to look like a terran sunrise or sunset, depending on the time of day. The colors migrated from one side of the room to the other with the clock. As bedrooms went, his tipped the scales in the heavyweight range, comparable in size to ten of those rooms in which the miners lived their existence. All he did here was sleep, occasionally eat, and occasionally work, but he needed elbow room. He couldn't possibly work with other people breathing down his neck.

His enumeration of idiots went thus: Maccarone, a miserable excuse for a spy if there ever was one; Liwanu, inexplicably guarding her theater as though it were the Oort Territories Central Bank vault; Froebisher, who although not an idiot would have better served his purposes if she was; and every other damn fool on the board of directors who either wouldn't listen to him or wouldn't trust him. How dare they?

Still another idiot barged in before he had his shirt on. "You're not the man I married," she commented, giving his excessive poundage a cursory glance.

"Indeed not," he said. "I'm a billion times richer. What do you want, Maisie? You know I don't like to be interrupted."

"Oh dear, did I forget to make an appointment again?"

There was no point. He pulled his shirt on and buttoned it up. Deep red with silver and gold tracery meandering all over it, this was his power shirt. He needed it today.

Maisie had aged better than her husband. She maintained her youthful appearance with careful diet, rigorous exercise, and the best cosmetologist money could buy, all that garnished with the finest fashions in the Territories. Today she outpowered her husband's power shirt with a tiny bright red skirt and a tight blazing gold top topped by a blazing green and silver blazer. One couldn't look at her without thinking the sun had descended into the room. She sat very properly on a ladder back chair near one of Worthington's four hardwood desks and smoothed her skirt. Her legs, he mused, were still gorgeous.

"You've been ignoring family responsibilities, Artemus."

"Family responsibilities are your watch, not mine. I have a company to manage."

"That's hardly an excuse for forgetting what today is."

Worthington gave her one of his fake long-suffering looks, then went to find a suitable suitcoat in the closet on the far side of the room. The distance being so great, they had to raise their voices at each other. He made her wait while he tapped the wall and the closet opened. "What's today?" he finally asked.

"Only your youngest granddaughter's first birthday."

"Tell her I said happy birthday."

"Really, Artemus."

"She's one, Maisie. She won't notice my absence."

"She certainly will, and even if she doesn't remember it twenty years from now, the rest of the family will."

"The rest of the family should find something more constructive to do than interfere with my schedule." *Light blue coat*, he wondered, *or bright red*? Either could be stunning with this shirt.

Maisie inspected the cuffs on her blazer, tugging at them slightly to position them just right. She needn't have worried; everything about her was always just right. "What could possibly be so important?"

"I have to meet with Chelsea Liwanu. Urgent business."

"What, you need her to trot out another Ed Wood film festival before Santamonica dies of boredom?"

Worthington pulled on the blue coat and inspected himself. Too subdued, he decided. "I need her theater."

Maisie laughed uproariously until her husband glared at her. "She'll die before she lets you in there!"

"So I'll murder her."

"Don't even joke about that. The board might punish you."

"Punish me how?"

"They might cut your compensation five percent."

Worthington glanced from the mirror to his wife. She was getting more sarcastic every day. He wondered why, but then decided not to be concerned. It made their conversations more interesting.

"It might be worth it," he told her, returning his attention to the mirror and how he looked in all that red.

"Here's an idea. Instead of killing her, why not bed her?"

"Last time I tried that, it ended badly." Actually, he'd never tried it. Whatever Maisie might say about him, she couldn't complain that he'd been unfaithful.

She inspected her perfectly manicured fingernails, painted in swirls of red and orange with silver sparkles. "I suppose you *are* getting old," she remarked. "But then, they have medications for that."

"I doubt they have one for her overwhelming darkness."

"Pheromones in a spray can," Maisie replied, sounding bored. "A bit pricey, but you can get them at the pharmacy."

"Do they work?"

"Now how should I know? I only have eyes for you, and we have no need of the stuff."

True, Worthington thought. Their romantic life had ended through mutual boredom about twenty years before. These verbal sparring matches kept the flame alive now. He finished preening and turned. "How do I look?"

"Like Artemus Worthington."

"Excellent. I must go."

"Go. Leave your tiny granddaughter in tears."

With a sigh, he relented. "I'll stop by once I've concluded my business." He strode to the door, passing by his wife without a glance. "For her sake, not for yours or anybody else's."

Maisie remained seated, now inspecting her toenails, painted in gold and purple. They were perfect. Of course. "You're a gem," she said, deadpan.

"As are you, my dear. As are you."

After Worthington was gone, Maisie got up, crossed the room to the mirror, and looked at herself, turning this way and that to inspect every angle. "He's crazy about me," she told the mirror. "The big jerk."

While forces converged on Chelsea Liwanu, a group of scheming miners convened a secret meeting not so deep in the bowels of TDY-41093-

RRP. Ordinarily a simple matter, today's arrangements proved vexing. Their usual venue had exploded the previous morning and was now wide open to the vacuum of space. *How many other clubs have that problem?*

Ultimately, Josh Murdock took possession of an equipment storage area five levels below the surface, squeezing his bearish frame into a corner so everyone else could crowd in among supplies and detritus: boxes of spare parts; cartons of lubricants; bundles of wires; cast off grinder gears; broken mirrors that once had been employed in focusing and guiding energy beams; fused computer chips; and, rather inexplicably, a very large box of imitation jalapeño and artificial gouda flavored soy chips.

"We got trouble," he said.

Arne Slocum, picking his teeth with something that looked unnervingly like a piece of bone but was probably plastic, said, "I'll say. These chips are terrible!" He dropped a half-full bag on the floor and stomped on it. It crunched satisfyingly underfoot.

"Worse than that," Murdock told him.

Darya Pasternak sat down on the carton of soy chip bags. It slowly compacted under her weight, emitting a steady crackling as it went, as though somebody had set off an interminable string of firecrackers. She talked over it. "Let me guess. Maccarone. Omdahl. Lack of proper meeting facilities."

"Sums it up," Murdock rumbled.

A mutter spread through the gathering, which included something like seven men and four women, although it was hard to count bodies in the cramped, darkish space. The shapes could have been people or supplies or refuse. All were liberally mixed together here. The only certain thing was that crackling noise, which hadn't let up.

Unable to take it any longer, someone snapped, "For God's sake, Darya, stand up!"

"Nothing's changed," Slocum told the group. "We have plenty of targets. Let's just keep hitting them until something gives."

Murdock didn't seem interested in the status quo. "Kaja's story worked out. Bad wiring, sparks, hydrolysis. Management ate it up. Maccarone thinks they won't ever listen."

"Morons," Pasternak grumbled. She hadn't stood, but the chips were finally reduced to a pulp and the noise abated.

"Sure, but Kaja's on the warpath. She knows it was our handiwork. Ajit's clever little diversion didn't fool her."

Ajit Tambe's perpetually confused face looked, well, more confused. "What?"

Pasternak patted him on the shoulder, then on the assumption that nobody could see in here patted his rump, hoping for another startled reaction. He didn't flinch this time. He might even have leaned into the pat. That, she thought, opened up some new possibilities for teasing him.

"You all know what happens if she finds proof," Murdock continued. "She doesn't need management to sign off. She'll ship the lot of us off to Proteus."

Slocum slapped the nearest unidentifiable object. "What proof? Any proof there might have been is in orbit by now, or splattered all over the ice fields out there. There's nothing to find."

Murdock eyed him. "Maccarone's digging around."

"Maccarone's a fool," Pasternak opined.

"But he knows. And he's on the company's payroll."

A collective "What??" sounded, so intensely collective it was impossible to say who had joined it.

"Think about it. First the guy hires us to build a new fountain. Now he wants a new theater. Where's he get the money? Wasn't filthy rich when he got here. You saw that door go flop." Murdock made a flopping motion with his hand, although odds were even nobody could see. Regardless, the general murmurs suggested they got Murdock's point.

"So," Tambe said, and everyone looked at him and waited while he tried to find enough courage to speak. "So."

"Spit it out, kid," Pasternak said.

"So the board is using Maccarone to learn our plans?"

"In a nutshell," Murdock acknowledged.

"In a what?"

"Nutshell."

"What's that?"

Murdock's considerable brow furrowed into considerable furrows. "Good question. Don't know."

"Forget the nutcases!" Pasternak barked

"Nutshells," Murdock corrected.

"Whatever! You're saying that between them, Kaja and Maccarone will figure it out and take us down? Ha!"

Murdock stroked his bushy beard as though pondering whether or not that was what he was saying. "Pretty much," he decided. "So we gotta deal with it."

Tambe might have looked greenish if the lighting had been better. "Short of killing them, what can we do?"

Pasternak nudged him. "Why stop short?"

"We can't do that!"

"I'm kidding, kid."

"Stop calling me kid! I'm not a kid!"

"Okay, kid." While Tambe threw up his hands in frustration, Pasternak continued, "How about we plant a spy? Find out what Maccarone's up to, feed him bogus intel?"

"Josh and I discussed that," Slocum said with some enthusiasm. "Beats the hell out of blowing up lifters."

"I like blowing up lifters," Tambe said, then looked like he wished he could grab those words and eat them.

Pasternak laughed and slapped him hard on the back. He might have flown across the room had he not grabbed onto the nearest object for support, which to his embarrassment turned out to be Pasternak herself. In the dimness, several miners chortled. He let go quickly, but behind the embarrassment he seemed surprisingly pleased.

"So who's gonna be the spy?" Murdock asked. Nobody replied. "Need a volunteer. Willing or otherwise."

The silence suggested it would have to be otherwise.

"How about the k . . . that is, Ajit?" one of the women who wasn't Pasternak suggested.

Tambe's eyes widened so far it's a wonder his head didn't split open. "*Me?*"

"Thanks for volunteering," Murdock said with a grin. "All in favor?" Everyone except Tambe said, "Aye!" or "I!" or "Me!" or "Yes!" or, in one instance, "Go, kid!"

Murdock pushed himself away from the wall, which forced everyone else to move toward the door. "Fair enough. Darya can get him started."

The room emptied with astonishing speed. Clearly nobody wanted to give either Tambe or Pasternak time to object. The pair found themselves alone together in the near-dark. Pasternak, who'd had about enough of restraining her urge to tease him unmercifully, slipped her arms around Tambe's neck while he stared after Murdock's vanished bulk. Pulling him really, really close, she put a hand to his cheek and turned his face towards hers. Her lips brushed his while she spoke. "So, kid, should I get you started?"

"Uh." He pulled back slightly—only slightly—and gave her face careful scrutiny. Then his hands went somewhere that said, "Please do!"

She easily pushed him away. "I got a great idea. We're gonna apply for jobs with the stage crew."

"Oh. I thought . . ."

As he followed her out into the marginally brighter tunnel, she glanced back. "You think I don't know what you thought?"

"I was wrong?" He looked crestfallen.

Pasternak winked at him. "I'll let you know later. Right now, we got work to do."

The ambiance fell rather short of Maccarone's expectations. He envisioned the office of a culture minister to be akin to a museum or an art gallery, filled with paintings, sculptures, framed original pages from famous scores and librettos. But Liwanu's office looked like, well, an old, forgotten government office. No wonder she wanted to go to Earth. He'd go nuts if he had to work here. Actually, his own office somewhat resembled this one, since offices onboard spaceships never afforded luxury, but he didn't have gardens and outrageously expensive restaurants and the greatest theater in the solar system a few minutes away. One adapted to cramped quarters on a spaceship because nothing else existed. Here, it must be sheer torture.

"Siddown," Liwanu told Maccarone and Land.

They obeyed.

"The answer is no."

Land frowned his trademark "why is the universe always against me?" frown. "We didn't ask anything yet," he said.

"Don't start that."

"Start what?"

"You can't have it, and that's final."

Land turned on Maccarone. "Why do all of my conversations start this way lately? It must be because you're in them."

"I haven't said a word," Maccarone objected.

"You just did." He turned back to Liwanu. "We can't have what?"

She slapped her desk in irritation. "The theater, you moron!"

Crossing his arms over his chest and leaning back, Land said out of the side of his mouth, "Your turn, boss. Make it sound good."

Liwanu shifted her frigid black gaze to Maccarone. "The. Answer. Is. No."

"Chelsea," Maccarone said, sliding forward on his seat and smiling his winning smile. "May I call you—"

"No! It was no before, and it's no now!"

Maccarone plowed ahead as though it had always been yes. "This is not a complex proposition. You have a magnificent theater. I have a magnificent opera company."

Liwanu snorted in fairly unladylike fashion, but Land found that unsurprising. She hadn't much ladylike demeanor to begin with.

"Whatever the obstacles are, I can remove them. I have almost unlimited funds available to make things possible."

Liwanu's anger transmuted into astonishment. "What."

Maccarone couldn't tell if that had been question or statement. It didn't matter. "I can and will pay handsomely to make this happen."

"That's not how it works."

"How does it work, Ch . . . ma'am?"

Her eyes said her brain hadn't caught up with events yet. "The standard use of facilities contract gives the ministry a percentage of the take. There are no up-front costs."

Maccarone's smile turned more knowing, more intimate, as he rested his elbows on her desk to get closer to her. "I'm not talking about the ministry." His voice flowed quiet and smooth, as smooth as silk must be.

Despite himself, Land watched the exchange with fascination. He had to admit, Maccarone could be amazingly persuasive when he put his mind to it.

Liwanu shook her head. "I don't—"

"We both know you hate this place. You want to get out of here. I want to help."

"That's . . . bribery," she whispered.

"Not at all. You let me put on the greatest performance that theater has ever seen—"

"It's never seen a performance."

"Its first will be its greatest. I guarantee it. *Aida,* as only Roberto Maccarone can stage it."

That, Land thought, *sounds terrifying.*

"After that, without any connection other than the timing, just because I like you, I'll get you back to Earth in style. Just as a personal favor, not in exchange for anything."

Liwanu licked her lips.

Land held his breath. *This just might work!*

"Why not get me back first?" she asked.

"Don't you want to see the performance?" Maccarone asked as though of course the answer would be yes.

"No."

"No?" He looked genuinely surprised. He might have been, Land thought. "Why not?"

"It's complicated."

"I can fix complications."

"Not this one."

"What is it, Chelsea?" He'd slipped her name in on the sly, asking her as though talking to a lover. *This guy*, Land thought, *shouldn't be producing opera. He should be writing it.*

Liwanu pushed herself back, suddenly angry again. "The answer is no. It was always no, it is still no, and it will always be no. Now get out of my office!"

"But—"

She sprang to her feet and pointed at the door. "Out!"

Maccarone refused to stand. He looked supremely injured, a victim of horrible injustice, and he asked the only question a pathetic, wronged child with no comprehension of the world's cruelty could ask: "But why?"

"Because!" Liwanu nearly screamed. "Because it's not yours! It's not—" Land nearly fell out of his chair at the lengthy recital of obscene adjectives that followed. "—Worthington's! It's not even a *theater*, Maccarone! It's a—" She clapped her hand over her mouth, but Land could tell it wasn't that her brain had caught up with the foulness her mouth had spewed. It was the word she hadn't uttered, the word she'd almost let slip, the word she didn't want anyone in the whole universe to know.

Maccarone could only gape, so Land, hoping he could suitably imitate the master, slid forward and said so gently it hurt, "Say it, Chelsea. Don't keep it bottled up inside of you."

Liwanu sank into her chair, and to both men's surprise began to sob.

Complete befuddlement overtaking him, Maccarone ran a hand through his hair. "I'm sorry, Chelsea. I don't know what this is about, but I'm really sorry. I had no idea it meant... "

Land had no idea, either. "Maybe we should go," he muttered, for once thinking nothing of himself.

Liwanu wept as they rose and shuffled toward the door. But then, just before they could exit, she muttered something.

Maccarone and Land paused.

They turned.

They waited.

"It's not a theater," she whispered, barely loud enough for them to hear. "It's a tomb."

Radiating power in his ultra-red outfit, Artemus Worthington barged into the Culture Minister's outer office. Ignoring the sputtering secretary babbling complete nonsense at him, he grabbed destiny with both hands and pushed by the blithering idiot into Chelsea Liwanu's office. "Good morning!" he said brightly.

The empty office didn't reply, but it did radiate its own feeling: hopeless despair. Worthington frowned at it, puzzled.

"The Culture Minister is not in!" the secretary cried, right at Worthington's elbow.

"So where the devil is she?"

Unable to find just the right gesture, the secretary went through his entire repertoire of inane hand motions before saying, "Gone!"

"Gone where, man!"

"I—I don't know!"

"It's your job to know!"

"I know! But I don't know!"

Why, Worthington griped to himself, *must I always be surrounded by idiots?* "I suppose she waltzed right by you without leaving word where she'd be?"

"No! I mean yes! I mean sort of!"

The great man in his greatly powerful suit uttered a great sigh and shook his head. "Do you have any idea how stupid you are?"

The secretary flushed with embarrassment. Then, engorged with anger, he drew himself up and fired off a scalding counter-salvo: "That's very unprofessional of you."

"Snappy retort. Could you guess where she is?"

"No."

"Why not?"

"She told me not, er, that is, she didn't tell me where she was going."

"Ah." Worthington smiled an unpleasant smile. "Thank you, hmm, what's your name?"

"Smythe," the secretary told him nervously, possibly not used to having important people ask his name. "Braxton Smythe."

"Thank you," Worthington repeated. "Whoever you are."

There was only one place Liwanu would go without telling anyone. For reasons he didn't understand, that theater held some special meaning for her. When he'd arranged financing for its construction plus a bit on the side to help her get home, he'd done it with one purpose: the Artemus Worthington Center for the Performing Arts would be his monument to himself for all posterity and, not coincidentally, a bargaining chip for use with other board members who'd be eager to secure the best seats and host the best events for all the best people. The plan had failed miserably, victim of a construction accident. Afterward, Liwanu had declared the facility unsafe. Nobody could get in. Nor, strangely, did she return home.

The whole business stank of some scheme. Repairs should have been made by now. Moreover, she was far too protective of the ruins. But for the life of him, Worthington couldn't fathom her purpose. Why would she maroon herself in the Oort Territories merely to deprive him of his monument? It was high time he got to the bottom of it.

As he strode powerfully towards the theater in his powerful red suit, he thought powerful thoughts about how he would ring, most powerfully, the truth from her.

No more Mr. Nice Guy.

A darkness as huge as the universe surrounded them. Maccarone felt as though the air was being sucked mercilessly from his lungs. For some minutes he didn't dare breath, and then, just when he was sure he would drown in the nothingness, the lights came up.

Illumination gradually waxed as Liwanu palmed the controls on the wall, revealing, spread out before them in all its glory, the finest theater in the solar system. If Maccarone's lungs had any air left in them, the sight stole the remaining few molecules away. The deep red of a thousand seats, spread out in graceful arcs before the polished glow of the hardwood stage; aisles of forest green inlaid with tracers of gold, silver, and deep blue; the curtain, shimmering with all the colors of the rainbow in the lights trained on it from above; the splash of subtle colors playing across the walls. This was the most beautiful place he'd ever seen, reducing the theater he'd always dreamed of to the status of mud hut.

Maccarone glanced at Land, who was gaping on his left.

Ahead of them, three quarters down the aisle, the carpet flowed around a circle of soft white light from which a beacon thrust upward to the ceiling. He'd never seen such a feature in any theater. Serene and beautiful, it nevertheless didn't belong there. He wanted to ask Liwanu what it was but couldn't find his voice.

No need. She motioned them forward and, as they reached the beacon, sank to her knees before it and gazed into its light. "This," she said quietly, "is where it happened."

Maccarone and Land gazed mesmerized into the light, awash in peace and serenity, far removed from the cares of business, the troubles of miners, the schemes of power-mad executives.

"This theater was designed by Irving Ignatius Irvine. You've heard of him, I'm sure."

Maccarone indeed had. No wonder the place was so beautiful. Irvine had designed award-winning public structures on Earth and later Mars before mysteriously vanishing during a trip to the outer solar system. This theater must have been among his last creations.

"It was nearly complete. He was standing right here, consulting with a supervisor on some of the final details, when the supports on a massive lighting fixture failed." Liwanu pointed a trembling finger toward the spot where the beacon illuminated the ceiling. "He was directly beneath it when it fell. After the accident, an investigation revealed cheap materials and faulty installation. Other cut corners turned up, too. Lots of them." She pointed down into the beacon. "The debris punched through two decks. Seven people were killed and almost fifty injured."

"My God," Maccarone breathed. "That's horrible."

She nodded absently. "It could have been worse. I'm told that some of the heavier debris fused with the structural supports a mere half meter from the station hull."

Maccarone and Land shook their heads in unison. It boggled the mind.

"It proved impossible to completely remove the tangle without cutting the station apart. The operation would have been insanely expensive."

"Worthington and most of the other board members could afford that," Maccarone said.

Liwanu shook her head. "This was supposed to be Worthington's theater. He talked me into the project and funded construction. It was his baby. He picked Irving. He picked the contractors. He told them to work cheap. Then when the accident happened, he refused to spend any more than necessary on cleanup and repairs. He somehow convinced the government to decommission the damaged part of the station instead. The mess is still down there, along with two bodies that couldn't be recovered. One was Irving's." Liwanu extended a hand into the light and studied it. "I built this as a memorial to him."

She suddenly slapped the floor, hard. "I used the money Worthington gave me—money intended to get us back to Earth—to finish the theater and build this memorial. He will *never* get it back!"

Confused, Maccarone asked, "Worthington gave you money?"

Liwanu squeezed her eyes shut. "Yes. A bribe. That's how he got my buy-in. Afterward, he suggested I take my money and leave. He made it pretty clear that that if I ever told a soul what I knew about the accident, word of that bribe might get out and I'd be implicated, too."

"And I thought *I* was nasty," Land muttered.

"Why didn't you leave, then?" Maccarone asked. "What kept you here?

"This theater is mine. Mine and Irving's. Nobody else can have it!"

Land opened his mouth, thought better, and closed it again.

Maccarone dared to set a hand gently on Liwanu's shoulder. "I'm sorry, Chelsea. You and Irving..." He nearly choked on the bitterness of the realization.

"Yes," she said as tears began to fall once more. "When we got back to Earth, we were to be married."

Outside, radiating more power than he'd ever radiated, Worthington pounded on the doors and demanded Liwanu admit him immediately. He knew she was in there. She couldn't be anyplace else. But the doors were too thick, and no ruckus he could raise could penetrate. In the end, he was forced to retreat, fuming at a universe that had so unreasonably conspired against him.

CHAPTER 14

Late that afternoon, according to clocks that insisted a bright sun hung in the sky when it didn't, two bizarre incidents occurred simultaneously. The coincidence might have suggested conspiracy had both happened to the same somebody. In fact, they happened to two different somebodies, so nobody made the connection, which was okay as there wasn't one. Sometimes a coincidence is just a coincidence.

First by only a couple of minutes, Kazimir Kapitan met an odd pair of miners seeking employment. Kapitan couldn't think why, given the plague of curses—or was it the curse of plagues?—spreading its dark, fierce wings over Space Operatic. A strange duo, he thought: a skinny young man with neatly combed sky blue hair, and a female bodybuilder with an unruly mop of screaming red hair. They didn't exactly go together. Nor could Kapitan fathom why the woman snickered at him behind her hand when he introduced himself, as though privy to some joke on him. *Maybe,* he thought, *they escaped from an asylum? No, this whole territory is an asylum. They probably just live here.*

Kapitan directed his first question to the young man, who'd said his name was George Porge. Kapitan had never heard such a stupid name before, except maybe Feng Shui Land. "What exactly do you do for StarBright?"

"Well, Mr. Kapitan," Porge said, and the woman snickered again, "We're miners. So we, you know, operate mining equipment."

"And what does that entail?"

"Mostly blowing things up."

Fountains spewed fire in the recesses of Kapitan's brain. "What?"

The woman—Felicity Nice, she'd said—elbowed Porge in the ribs none too gently. Her name, while not as stupid as Porge's, hardly seemed appropriate.

"That is," Porge said once he'd recaptured his breath, "the extractors do. That's how they extract stuff. Laser beams. Explosions. You know."

"Oh. You blow up ice and..." He struggled to find the right word, but only came up with, "...stuff."

"Yeah."

"Not much use for that on stage."

"We fix things, too. Machines are always breaking down. So we can do stuff like that."

"Yeah," Nice agreed nicely. "We fix things real good. Mr. Kapitan." She snickered again.

Kapitan narrowed his eyes and studied her. "You didn't work on that fountain, did you?"

She shrugged. "Nah, not us. Our foreman put someone else on that job."

"Because somebody sure messed up there."

Nice smiled at him. Nicely, of course. That woman was up to something.

"All right, we could use extra hands for the theater reconstruction. You're on probation for the first three weeks. If you don't work out, you'll be out."

Porge blinked at him. "We're out if we're not out?"

Nice nudged him again, less than nicely.

"Quit that!" he objected.

"Okay, kid."

"Stop calling me kid!"

"Okay, kid."

"Are you sure," Kapitan asked, "you can work together?"

"Oh yeah," Nice replied with a wide grin. "He loves it when I play rough."

Porge didn't look entirely sanguine about that, but neither did he contradict her. In fact, when he looked at her, Kapitan detected more than a little lust in his eyes. *This will be a disaster*, he thought. *Another manifestation of the curse. At least it fits our modus operandi.* "All right," he told them. "Let's get your data logged and get you started on something."

Nice smiled way too nicely at him, then smiled at Porge in a manner not nice per se but which most young men would appreciate. Porge did, until he remembered Kapitan was watching. Embarrassed, he folded his hands in his lap. "Thank you Mr. Kapitan," he said quietly.

Right on cue, Nice snickered.

The second odd occurrence that afternoon took place outside the StarBright board room. A summons to an emergency board meeting interrupted Worthington's temper tantrum outside the theater. Taken aback, he ceased fuming and hurried to join. He had just climbed the gently ascending ramp to the august chamber, a ramp carpeted in brilliant sun yellow with deep blue cross-hatching, when Lena Froebisher slipped to his side and whispered, "I need two minutes of your time."

He eyed the other directors who were seeping into the room, oblivious to her request. "Of course."

They slunk around a corner into a small alcove that served as shrine to StarBright Energy Corporation founder, Phoenix Bakersfield Amarillo. An oversized holoimage of the man—a harsh, seriously tanned giant clothed in unadulterated jet black—dominated the otherwise austere alcove. The father of current Chairman and CEO Santamonica Amarillo, he sneered down upon anyone who came to worship at his feet. A fair number did, mostly confused executives who'd lost their sense of direction or young wannabes seeking inspiration for the long scramble up the mountain of power over the fallen bodies of less capable souls.

"I've made a decision," Froebisher told Worthington quietly.

"Indeed." He steeled himself for bad news. She hadn't been convinced this morning, and he'd had no chance to work on her further.

"I'm backing your plan."

Worthington blinked in astonishment before realizing how not under control he was. He got himself under control. "Thank you. May I ask why?"

"I did some independent research. You're right. Revolution is brewing. We must nip it in the bud."

"Nip what bud?"

"The revolution."

"What does pinching off underdeveloped flowers have to do with revolutions?"

"It's an old expression. Never mind. I'm backing you."

She was right. Whatever the flower-yanking thing was, it could wait. "Is that what this meeting is about?"

"Exactly. Let me do most of the talking. I'll make the case. You explain your security proposal. I'll demonstrate its viability. I can make this a short meeting."

Looking up and meeting Phoenix Bakersfield Amarillo's steel eyes, Worthington felt a swell of confidence. At last things were turning around! "What about Amarillo Junior? Is she on board?"

"She will be. Leave that to me."

He had no choice. The rest of the board trusted him as far he trusted them. They didn't trust Froebisher, either, but at least her intelligence had earned their respect. If she said the situation was thus-and-so, most of them would fall mutely in line. Nodding ascent, Worthington motioned Froebisher to lead the way.

Half an hour later, he left with full authorization to employ his troops in putting down the rebellion. He was so happy, no question of Lena Froebisher's real motives ever crept into even the remotest corner of his devious mind.

No sooner had Liwanu locked up the theater than Maccarone got a pair of messages. The first called him to an emergency board meeting. The second commanded him to keep a healthy distance between himself and said meeting, while authorizing Worthington to vote his shares with regard to "a certain routine security measure." Maccarone didn't care about routine security measures. Liwanu's revelations consumed him. He acknowledged Worthington and shuffled toward the docking bays.

Icy silence gripped Maccarone and Land during the voyage back to TDY-41093-RRP and the *Ponchielli*. Once safe in the embrace of their own ship, they took refuge on the observation deck. A narrow strip of transparency running mid-spine along the ship, it afforded passengers a clear, radiation-shielded view of the universe.

The opera executives watched the stars in silence for longer than they knew.

Land spoke first, subdued. "Irving Ignatius Irvine. Who would have thought?"

Maccarone could only nod in reverence. *Now there*, he thought, *was an artist. If opera were architecture, Verdi would be Irvine.*

"We've got to get him out of there, Roberto."

Planning hadn't concerned Maccarone. He had merely soaked up starlight. Land's stridence jarred him back to some semblance of normal consciousness. "What?"

"We've got to get him out of that tangle of scrap so Chelsea can take him back to Earth."

True, Irvine's present burial arrangements were far from ideal. Still, Liwanu had built him a stunning tomb. Moreover, she'd said the debris had fused with the structural supports near the station hull. If Worthington's wealth and the station's engineers hadn't been able to clean up the mess and recover Irvine's remains, how could the two of them possibly do it?

"It's the only way," Land pressed, his voice suddenly severe.

"Only way to what?"

"Open the theater."

Shocked, Maccarone gaped at Land.

"What?" Land asked.

"A great artist killed, Chelsea's whole life destroyed, and all you can think about is getting your hands on her theater?"

"Damn it, Roberto, we can't bring back the dead! We have a business to run. Unless we play that theater, this company ends up as dead as Irvine. It's either that or we exit stage right and return to Earth." He arched his eyebrows hopefully.

Maccarone looked up at the cold, brilliant stars and in his gut knew Land was right. All his hopes for Space Operatic hinged on playing that theater. "But how? If it were possible, they'd have done it already."

"It's possible." Land sounded as confident as if he'd already worked out the engineering himself. "Just expensive, and Worthington is cheap. But you're insanely rich, too, remember?"

"This may be beyond my means. Beyond Worthington's means, even."

Land shook his head. "He could do it. He just won't."

"How do you know that?"

"Well think about it. What could he possibly gain for his money? Liwanu would gut that theater before tacking Worthington's name on it."

True enough. But if so, Liwanu could never leave, no matter where Irvine was laid to rest. Before her ship had fired its engines, Worthington would seize the theater, slap his name it, and bend it to his will. Maccarone told Land so and, while Land tried to gnaw off his own hand, added, "Let Chelsea have her theater. I could build my own, one just as good if not even better."

"By the time you did that, we'd all be dead from starvation!"

Actually, Maccarone could feed the whole company from now until doomsday, whatever and whenever that was supposed to be. Restoration of the TDY-41093-RRP theater—such as it was, or used to was—had already begun. Why not scale it up, create a venue even more grand than Liwanu's? He almost suggested it, but another idea crept into his brain and chased it off. A quicker way out of their jam. A far, far cheaper way, too. Land couldn't help but appreciate both points.

"The real problem," he said, "is keeping Worthington's name off of the theater. Right?"

Still grimacing like he was being eaten alive by a polar bear that had all the time in the world for dinner, Land said, "I guess."

"So let's put my name on it." He glanced sidelong at Land and, seeing no change in his expression, added, "Our names. The Maccarone-Land Center for the Performing Arts."

Land gaped at him.

"Land-Maccarone?"

"Worthington would murder us! Literally!"

With a shrug, Maccarone turned his eyes back to the stars. "But we'd have our theater."

"*What?* Damn it, Roberto, don't you know what 'literally' means?"

"Yes, but I didn't think you meant it literally."

"I meant it literally! *Literally* literally!"

Maccarone had to grant the point. Worthington had no scruples. Murder might not be beyond him. "That could be a problem."

Land shook his head irritably. "We should leave. Go home. Back to Mars. Back to Earth. Anyplace but here. This place is one giant mental hospital managed by the patients."

Maccarone set a comforting hand on Land's shoulder, a gesture that didn't seem to comfort Land all that much. "Don't despair, Fa, ah, Feng. Perseverance pays off. You'll see."

The look Land gave him suggested that Worthington wasn't the only one capable of murder.

You, Maccarone thought but didn't say, *are one weird character.*

George Porge and Felicity Nice proved, to Kapitan's surprise, a skilled, efficient, hardworking duo. The woman in particular had leadership skills. No sooner had she appeared on the scene than she'd marshalled the whole crew into pressure-suited work parties, marched them into the frigid vacuum along with all the necessary heavy and light equipment, and put them to work clearing debris and prepping the area for the installation of an inflatable pressure dome. The job completed in record time, the site of the old storage room/theater/insurgent's hideout had been repressurized and was ready for reconstruction.

Now, Kapitan thought, they just needed to complete the job without puncturing half a million holes in the balloon that confined the air. Not terribly sanguine about the odds, he ordered everyone to keep pressure suits on, just in case. That slowed work and elicited some less than nice words from Felicity Nice, but he didn't care. They had so much money and so many workers—both Space Operatic employees and miners eager to rake in some of the largess—that they could afford a bit of caution.

Two days later, one couldn't tell that anything had ever exploded. The place looked for all the world like the old storage room, except the balconies were more ornate than litter boxes, including access via actual staircases. Also, the seating wasn't temporary; at the touch of a button, it unfolded from the floor plush, purple, and inviting. At another it tucked itself away again, leaving a storage area or insurgent's hideout or whatever else one might need space for. Even the stage was *Don Carlo*-ready, featuring a beautiful new fountain that Kapitan couldn't behold without shaking in terror.

All that in two days.

Meanwhile, another sort of art was afoot . . .

A signal flashed through space at the speed of light, an encoded message directed to pockets of unrest where small-time thugs lived on protection money and under-the-table cash rendered in exchange for acts of violence. These thugs operated by a code, a law promulgated in the early days of Oort Territory colonization by their thug ancestors. The ancestors had called it "the wild west code," an obtuse appellation since by standard nomenclature west meant galactic west, in the direction of the constellation Vela, whereas the Oort Territories now included about thirty percent of the inner Oort Cloud in the direction of Hercules, Corona Borealis, and Boötes, nowhere near galactic west. Some speculated that the name was mere branding; it sounded snappier than "the wild northeast code."

Be that as it may, the thugs got the message and immediately made plans to descend like a famished swarm of locusts upon TDY-41093-RRP. The place—so they heard—was fomenting revolution. There—so they most especially heard—a mercenary could make enough for five generations of thug descendants to retire before they were even born.

Thus Artemus Worthington's army began to muster. Now he needed a general to keep them under control, and having personally scoured hundreds of personnel records, he had a pretty good idea who it was. Sheer genius, he thought, turning the alleged leader of the alleged rebellion into the very real leader of its very real demise. A defection of that caliber would fill his colleagues with admiration. They'd let him get away with anything after that.

Three hours before, he had dispatched a message calling the general-to-be to his office on urgent and highly confidential business. Now here she was, striding in, nervous as hell but hiding it almost well. Covered in orange body armor, she was accompanied by two guards in silver and black body armor whose zap guns nobody, not even base security, had been able to confiscate. Worthington authorized their admittance weapons in hand. The woman's blue eyes had the warmth of steel. Her golden hair shot sparks as she moved into the forest lighting of Worthington's office. Yes, she was definitely the one.

Leaning back casually in his chair, Worthington scrutinized her, then smiled broadly. "Ah, Ms. Omdahl," he effused. "How good of you to come."

"Like I had a choice," Kaja Omdahl said. "Is this about my report?"

"Your report was fine. Bad connections, sparks, hydrolysis. Very clever. Shows initiative." Worthington sat forward and leaned on his desk. "It is in fact your initiative that interests me. I have a proposition for you."

Omdahl looked shocked at first, then angry, then snarled while trying not to snarl, "I'm a professional, not your toy!"

The guards sniggered while trying not to snigger, but they couldn't summon Omdahl's control. She smacked them simultaneously on the tops of their heads. A no-nonsense woman. Perfect.

"A business proposition. I want you to lead a military force. In exchange, I'll pay you an obscene amount of money. Interested?"

Omdahl relaxed. "Obscene amounts of money always interest me. What's the deal?"

"As you know, the miners on TDY-41093-RRP are on the brink of armed rebellion. We—"

"That's a damned lie!"

Worthington donned his bland mask. "Kaja. Rumor has it you're the leader of the rebellion."

She gaped at him. "How dare you!"

Worthington inspected his fingernails. "I dare because I'm the Director of Marketing for StarBright Energy Corporation. I'm more powerful than anyone on the board of directors except the chairman herself." Not strictly true, but Omdahl couldn't know that. "That makes me more powerful than the combined Oort Territories government elite." Which absolutely was strictly true. "And that means?" He looked up significantly, figuring it would take her maybe five seconds to work it out.

It took only a second and a half. "I'm the leader of a rebellion," she admitted, no longer a ferocious lion. Her guards blinked, stunned by the transformation.

"You're a quick study," Worthington told her. "Now. Leaders of rebellions . . ." He motioned her to finish the sentence.

"Are executed."

"Whereas leaders of Artemus Worthington's armies . . ." Again he motioned to her.

"Make obscene amounts of money. I get it."

Leaning back, Worthington smiled a fatherly smile, to which she responded with a sickened look. "My forces are converging on that revolting little ice cube. You will organize them, seize control, implement martial law, and execute anyone who gets in the way. Miners, managers, commissary flunkies, vicious Chihuahuas. Anyone."

"What's a Chihuahua?"

"A little dog. Never mind. You get the point."

"Why?" Omdahl had recaptured some of her earlier defiance, which suited Worthington just fine. He didn't want her too compliant. She might turn soft and squishy, ruining her utility as a commander.

"Let's just say it's a demonstration. Do your job well and nobody will ever dare question me again."

"What if I don't do it well?

Worthington swapped his bland mask for his disappointed one. "Unimaginable wealth," he said, pointing to the right side of his desk. "Inescapable death," he added, pointing to the left. "Will you do it well?"

"I don't know," she said honestly, although not without trepidation. "I've never led an army. Just these two goons." She nodded at her guards, who needed some time to work out whether she was complimenting or insulting them. They never did appear decided on that score. "And a band of scruffy miners."

"Mercenaries are easy," Worthington lied. "They only care about two things: money, and bashing heads. You let them bash a few heads, I pay them well, and everything will be fine. Do we have a deal?"

"I can hardly refuse."

"Wonderful. We'll begin operations soon. Until then, you can stay here at Territory HQ as my guest."

Omdahl needed zero time to work that out. "Your prisoner."

"You're wasted down there in the mines," Worthington praised, and she actually liked it enough to almost smile before she caught herself. "Obviously I must keep an eye on you. But it won't be a bad prison. You'll have one of the best suites money can buy, with all meals prepared and delivered to you by The King's Ransom."

Omdahl's eyes widened. She'd obviously heard of the restaurant. "What about my guards?" she asked. They looked eager to join her, but her tone suggested she'd just as soon ditch them.

"Do you want them for your army?"

They looked at Omdahl, then each other, then at Omdahl, then nodded hopefully to each other and to her more or less simultaneously.

"Oh . . ."

They nodded again, this time desperately. Possibly they'd worked out their fate should she refuse.

"Yeah, why not."

"Then,' Worthington said, his face a veritable portrait of generosity, "they can stay."

The guards sighed in relief.

"Great," Omdahl replied. "Take us to our cells."

She hated risks. Risks were, well, risky, especially when they involved Artemus Worthington. But Lena Froebisher had little choice in the matter, given her adversary's craftiness. Worse, she must now trust Perri Pauli with something that didn't come naturally to him. She eyed him skeptically. He stood before her massive desk, every nerve in his little body twitching. "You understand what you have to do?" she asked gently so as not to send him through the roof.

"Um," he said. "Yeah."

"Do you need anything? Equipment? Backup? Tranquilizers?" She really shouldn't have added that last item, but she couldn't help herself.

"You got any?" he asked.

She could get anything. He knew that. But then, he'd already about expired from fright. "I'll have some sent to your quarters."

"Okay." He shuffled about for a few minutes, then made a pathetic attempt to stand his ground. "You know I could get killed, right?"

"Don't be absurd." Froebisher tried her best to sound reasonable. "Worthington wouldn't actually kill anybody."

Which was hardly a reasonable statement, and Pauli knew it. "He sure would!"

"This is just like every other job you've ever done for me." Which of course it wasn't. "Insinuate yourself into the situation, observe keenly, and collect the evidence."

Pauli looked paler than normal, no mean feat for him. "If I get caught recording—" He didn't go further. Apparently, the thought was too horrible to speak.

"You won't. You know what you're doing."

The scriptwriter turned spy gazed at his shoes as though wishing they'd take him somewhere far from this madness. "Okay," he finally decided.

"Okay," Froebisher acknowledged.

"Tranquilizers?" he checked.

"Okay," she confirmed.

But he stood there shaking until she'd tapped out the order on her desktop and showed him the electronic confirmation.

When he heard the theater would be ready in two days, Maccarone wasted no time scheduling a performance. Dress rehearsals sans stage settings commenced on board the *Ponchielli* in its one really big room. The lack of a fountain was keenly felt: for once Kasimir Kapitan was completely at ease, while the singers and actors seemed lost without it. But on the whole things developed smoothly, and Maccarone felt satisfied that they'd be in top form on opening night.

Two days passed. When the third dawned (or whatever), the theater stood completed. Maccarone inspected it and congratulated the workers, most especially their heroic leader Felicity Nice and her staunch lieutenant George Porge, although staunch might not be quite the word. He'd worked hard, to be sure, but he couldn't quite wipe the timid from his face. Maccarone puzzled over that face for a moment, as well as Nice's. They looked simultaneously alien and familiar. He didn't know anybody with Porge's sky blue hair, and surely he would have remembered that bright red mop on Nice's head. He couldn't have met them before. Yet something about them niggled at him.

Never mind. Their stunning success had given Maccarone an idea. He pulled the pair aside after the formalities were over and asked, "How would the two of you like to make an obscene amount of money?"

Nice smiled in a manner that wasn't nice at all. In fact, it was downright depraved. "Obscene activities are my forte."

Porge looked like he was about to pass out. She took his arm, not to steady him but to pull him into a tight embrace at her side. "And don't pretend you don't like it, kid." She grinned at him, sunk if possible even further into depravity. Now he looked like he might throw up on her.

"To business," Maccarone suggested.

"Sure, what's the proposition?" She arched her eyebrows suggestively.

"I need someone to fix up a slight mess underneath Territory HQ's theater."

Suddenly Nice wasn't so keen on depravity. Her grip on Porge loosened, and she took a step back. "You're joking."

"Not at all."

"That's impossible."

"You're familiar with the, er, situation?"

Nice grabbed Maccarone by the lapels and shook him. He was starting to wonder how she ever ended up with that name. "*Everyone* is familiar with that disaster!" she snarled. "That's why nobody talks about it! Do you know who—"

Porge, suddenly bold, jabbed her in the ribs to shut her up.

She shook Maccarone again. "Do you know why—"

Porge jabbed her again.

She just about slugged him. "If you weren't standing right next to me..."

Maccarone wondered why she suddenly couldn't finish a sentence. "I know the whole story. The culture minister and I had a long talk about it." He leaned close and whispered, just to impress her with the intimacy of his knowledge on the subject, "Inside the theater itself."

Porge gaped. "Inside? Like, inside the doors? Actually, you know, inside?"

"Yes," Maccarone whispered.

Felicity Nice responded with a collection of far from nice terms, then added, also in a whisper, "What do you want us to do?"

"Retrieve the remains of..." He looked around surreptitiously. If nobody else wanted to say the name, he probably shouldn't either. "You know."

"The engineers said it was impossible. Too much fused metal too close to the station hull."

"Obscene amounts of money," Maccarone reminded her.

She pondered that. Porge tugged on her sleeve. She slapped his hand away. "Money can't do the impossible."

Maccarone smiled his most charming smile. "You did the impossible with this theater."

Porge tugged her sleeve again and received an even stronger slap.

"But the HQ theater," Nice objected. "That's a completely different situation."

Porge, tired of being ignored, grabbed Nice by the head and forced her to look at him. Astonished, she looked into his eyes until a few sparks erupted from them. "Will you listen!" Porge insisted, then could say no more because Nice planted a powerful kiss on his lips.

Maccarone blinked, looked away, glanced back. Their faces still locked tight, Nice inexplicably melted into Porge's skinny arms. The guy probably wouldn't be able to hold her up, Maccarone feared, but as neither yielded any ground, he looked away again, embarrassed. "You have an idea?" he asked. Then, remembering what Nice had called Porge, he added, "Kid?"

That put a stop to the hanky-panky. Porge shoved Nice away and pointed a skinny finger at Maccarone. "Don't call me kid! Listen, both of you! We could construct a support framework outside the damaged area, seal it with an inflatable, just like we did here, and gradually cut apart the damaged sections."

Nice regarded him with something approaching professional respect. "The materials cost would be—"

Maccarone knew how that sentence should finish. "Obscene?"

"Yeah."

"I'll cover it."

Porge looked hopefully at Nice. "We could use little explosives maybe?" He looked *really* hopeful.

"Not inside an inflatable, kid."

"Oh. Yeah."

"I gotta ask you, Mr. Maccarone." Nice sounded uncharacteristically nice as she said this. "Where does all this money come from?"

"I've recently acquired a position on the StarBright board of directors," Maccarone said, not a little pleased with himself. "I can afford anything now."

She gave him a sly look. "Just between you and me, is the board doing something about all the unrest down here?"

He wasn't sure he should answer that, but since he had no idea anyway, it wasn't a problem. He just shrugged.

"'Cause, you know, all it would take are little things. Better food, more colorful sleeping quarters."

He shrugged again but made note of the suggestions, just in case Worthington cared. Which he almost certainly wouldn't.

"All right," Nice decided. "We'll do it, Mr. Maccarone. But Aj, ah, George and I want some of that obscenity up front."

"You got it," Maccarone agreed.

That's about when the explosions started. Not the ones the kid wanted. These explosions came courtesy of a swarm of savage mercenaries launching an assault.

CHAPTER 15

"You are *not* to attack until I say so!" Kaja Omdahl bellowed at the transmitter, which responded with a static-laden cackle.

"Too late," a growly voice answered with all the clarity of someone talking with their mouth full.

Seated at a chrome communications console in Territory HQ's chrome-filled communications center, assisted by a communications officer who, thankfully, wasn't wearing a chrome jumpsuit but a green and orange one, Omdahl punched the desk with her fist. "I'm in charge here! Disengage!"

"Can't," the voice growled back. "Got our rhythm going now. Have to finish."

It took her a moment to decipher his words. She wondered how technology could have become so powerful without improving in the slightest the sound quality of a transmission. "This isn't a concert!"

"Music to our ears, babe."

Omdahl glanced at the desktop computer display, alive with video and data readouts streaming in from TDY-41093-RRP's defense systems, most of which had already given up the ghost, unconcerned that Omdahl didn't believe in ghosts. The mercenaries had done as instructed, up to a point. They'd converged on the target, surrounded it, made preparations for an assault on the local StarBright headquarters, and issued an ultimatum. But they hadn't waited the requisite half hour for a reply. They gave it only five minutes before lobbing small explosives, knocking out primary defense systems and blowing up a few abandoned facilities. In spite of Worthington's command to let the mercenaries bash a few heads, she hoped to restrict the target heads to those on the shoulders of certain executives she didn't like. Tough talk aside, she really didn't want her fellow miners blown to smithereens. Not unless she was the one to do it, anyway.

"All we want," she told the mercenary in her coldest voice, "is control."

"All *you* want. We get our thrills our own way."

"Listen, idiot, you got two minutes to call off the attack. After that, I'll come out there and blow up your ship myself!"

"Yeah?"

"Yeah!"

"That could be fun."

"Two minutes!"

"Ten."

Omdahl blinked at the panel. "What?"

"Ten minutes. We been traveling for two days. The boys and girls here gotta blow off some steam, you know?"

She really wanted to punch this guy's face in, but by the time she got there, TDY-41093-RRP would be vaporized. "Five," she offered.

"Seven?"

"Fine, seven. But after that you wait for orders."

"You got it, babe."

How, she wondered, *did I land in the middle of this?*

"What say," the mercenary suggested, "you stop by for drinks when you get here. I got a real nice selection on board."

The communications officer lifted an eyebrow and smirked.

Omdahl slapped him, hard, and let his yelp be her reply.

The mercenary chuckled. "Some other time then," he suggested.

The walls reverberated with thunder. From somewhere a hint of charred plastic seeped into the air. Maccarone found himself running full tilt, pulled by his fingers which felt like they'd been crushed in a vise. The vise wasn't a vise per se, but Felicity Nice's powerful grip. Hauling on Maccarone's phalanges with her left hand and George Porges' with her right, she'd bolted down the corridor at the first concussion.

"What's happening?" Maccarone screamed.

Nice didn't respond. She kept going, threading around corners until Maccarone was thoroughly lost, which didn't take more than two turnings. Skidding to a sudden halt, she hung on as Maccarone overshot her position then yanked him back. He felt like his arm was being ripped off. The only thought left in his addled brain was that her parents couldn't possibly have been prescient or they'd never have given her that sugar-and-spice name.

Nice slapped the wall and a lifter door opened. She shoved both of her male companions through and followed. "Thirty!" she yelled at the device, and for the second time in two days Maccarone felt like the floor had dropped from under his feet. "We'll be safe below," she said, and Maccarone only then noticed that she was nearly as winded as he. Nearly.

"What was that?" Porge asked, eyes wide. As the thuds and booms quickly faded away, he studied the lifter car's ceiling as though it might hold the key to understanding.

"Sounded like a bombardment," Nice told him.

"What! How do you know?"

She gave the kid a sour look. "You don't think I know explosions?"

"Okay, okay. But why? There's nothing here worth attacking."

Suddenly feeling ill, Maccarone thought he knew, and when he realized that he'd probably voted for it, he nearly lost his lunch. Fortunately, at that moment the lifter decelerated as only it could, nearly slapping them all to the floor. The others didn't question his sickly face.

"Come on," Nice commanded as the doors rushed open. Explosions left far above, she led them on a whirlwind tour through tunnels of ice and soot lit by strings of bluish greenish chemlights and finally pushed open another door. Following her in, Maccarone discovered a modest room littered with scraps of unidentifiable stuff but otherwise empty. Like all rooms down here, it had been carved out of the dirty ice and rigged to look more or less like a room, but unlike the others he had seen this one appeared to have no function. Yet there was another door along the back wall, which Nice made for, never breaking stride.

On the other side of that door, incongruity reigned. Equipped with all the fixtures of a restroom, the place was jammed full of electronics equipment, most looking like someone had drop-kicked it off of the top of a tall building. On counter tops, in sink wells, and in the midst of piles of electronics stacked along the walls, a few gizmos glowed and crackled with energy.

As Nice pulled the door shut behind them, Maccarone found himself face-to-face with Josh Murdock, presenting more bearish and irritable than usual, as though he'd just been rudely awakened from a pleasant hibernation. Behind him, a wiry older man fiddled with controls and mumbled inaudibly.

"That was fast," Murdock commented.

"I always work fast," Nice told him.

"Brought our friend, I see."

"Yep, the big M himself."

Maccarone smiled distantly. "Friend?"

"You remember our little talk in the mines," Murdock prompted.

"Sure, I remember you, but . . ." He looked back at Nice and with a start realized why she seemed familiar. "Darya!"

She grinned at him. "Fooled ya!"

"And—" Maccarone scowled at Porge. He didn't think he knew his real name, only his nickname. "Kid?"

Porge turned as red as Pasternak's fake hair.

"Ajit Tambe," Murdock supplied. "Darya's—"

Now both of them looked scarlet, in color and temperament.

"Assistant," Murdock finished with an easy smile.

"And I," grumped the skinny old guy working his electronics from an ancient, wheeled office chair at one of the sinks, "am just about fed up with these power fluctuations!" He slammed his fist on the top of a console.

"That's Arne Slocum," Murdock supplied. "He keeps an eye on things for us."

"So what's up, Arne?" Pasternak slid toward him more gracefully than Maccarone would have thought possible.

"Mostly smoke." Slocum fiddled with some knobs and switches and squinted at a monitor that, to Maccarone's eyes, showed only blobs of gray. "They may have knocked out a generator or two. Defenses are impaired, not that they were ever good for much. And there's some strange transmissions flying around. I think someone at Territory HQ was talking to the attackers."

"Hear what they said?" Murdock asked.

"It was encrypted. The voices sounded less than friendly. I think there was a disagreement."

"Sounds like a conspiracy." Pasternak's voice was dark.

Everyone looked at Maccarone.

"What?" His voice cracked somewhere in the middle of the single syllable.

Pasternak might have been about to slug him. "You know all about this, don't you, Mr. Board Member?"

Of course not, he told himself. He repeated it several times to make sure he had the line down and could say it convincingly. When he was ready, he spoke it: "Um." *Good grief*, he thought, *that wasn't how I rehearsed it!*

Pasternak closed on him. He stumbled backwards against a pile of junked equipment, which tottered and creaked ominously. "Well?" she demanded, her nose suddenly half an inch from his. He hoped she didn't try to kiss him the way she'd kissed Tambe. He might not survive the ordeal.

"Um," he said again. Really now, how hard could it be to deliver one line?

Murdock's massive paw—er, hand—settled gently on Pasternak's shoulder. "Darya. You're scaring him."

"I know."

"Not nice to scare people."

She smirked back at Murdock. "That why you never do?"

"Not my fault," he said with a shrug of his shoulders. "People don't like my beard, I guess." He pulled her back and moved her aside. Maccarone thought she might be able to resist, but she didn't try. "Now, Rob." He smiled an easy, friendly smile. "What's the deal?"

Unfortunately, Maccarone had forgotten his line by that time and could only say, "Um."

Pointing a thick finger ceilingward Murdock suggested, "That's the work of company goons, yeah?"

"Um."

"They always wrote off our little nudges as accidents. Why come in guns blazing now?"

Maccarone just about said, "Um," again, but a new line popped into his head. A clever line that couldn't fail. "How should I know?"

On second thought, he thought, that wasn't half as clever as he'd thought, besides being almost certain to fail.

Given Murdock's skeptical smile, it had indeed. "C'mon, you can tell us. We're all friends of the opera."

Friends of the opera. That sounded good. "Yeah?"

"Yeah."

"Okay."

Murdock waited. Maccarone couldn't think of a single thing to say. After all, he actually didn't know anything. Well, not much, anyway. Only one thing, really. If that.

His friendly smile sliding towards carnivorous, Murdock made a "Well, come on," motion with both hands.

"Artemus Worthington," Maccarone told him, as though that explained all.

It didn't, of course. Murdock motioned again.

"Director of Marketing?"

"Yeah?"

"He put me on the board."

Somehow that didn't seem to surprise Murdock, but neither did it satisfy his curiosity.

"And, well, he wanted you folks to be insurrectionists. Bad guys. You know?" Surely that was good enough?

"Nobody else did," Murdock informed him very reasonably.

"No?"

"No."

"Um." Maccarone felt a bit of a letdown, returning to that point, but then he remembered something else. "Your boss. She's in on it."

Murdock raised an eyebrow. "Kaja? Nah."

Why should he doubt that? Omdahl had it in for Murdock, or at least that's how it had seemed. But of course Murdock was right; she wasn't in on it, not really. "Worthington wanted it to be her fault," he explained. "She's supposed to be the ringleader."

Tambe, who'd been forgotten in the midst of the threats and confessions, squeezed between Murdock and Pasternak, rather purposely scraping himself against Pasternak as he went. "What?"

Pasternak rolled her eyes. Murdock grinned at him. "Kaja's not rebel material?"

"She's company to the core."

"She's just in it for herself," Pasternak grumbled, then moved in on Maccarone again. "What's Worthington want?"

"How should I know? He just told me to vote for a security action. That's all he told me."

"You *voted* for this?" Pasternak had her hands around his neck before he saw her coming, but Murdock peeled them off.

"Easy, Darya. Rob's just an artist guy."

"A con artist!" she snarled.

"I just want the theater!" Maccarone squeaked. "Not carnage!"

"Theater?" Murdock asked.

"Territory HQ theater!"

Murdock stroked his bushy beard and look thoughtful while Pasternak balled her fists. "You managers are all alike," she spat.

"Guys," Arne Slocum said from his post at the sink, and for a moment the rest of them, having forgotten about him, weren't quite sure where the voice had come from.

Murdock figured it out soon enough. "What's up, Arne?"

"Rob's right," he said, unable to keep incredulity from his voice. "I picked up some traffic control transmissions at HQ. It *is* Kaja. She's been talking to the attackers. And now she's on her way to meet them!"

When he realized what bedlam had been unleashed, the shuttle captain just about turned tail and fled back to HQ, except that Perry Pauli pulled rank on him ("I'll tell Ms. Froebisher!"). Besides, four heavily-armed black ships had moved in to prevent the shuttle from fleeing much of anywhere. The captain therefore logically determined that it might be a good idea to follow Pauli's powerful lead.

Pauli didn't feel powerful. When the gang of five mercenaries boarded the ship—three huge men with scraggly beards and mayhem in their eyes, two women who looked like they could toss the men across the room without effort, all of them armed with very nasty weapons—the scriptwriter hid, trembling, in the back row. The tranquilizers Lena Froebisher had given him rested forlorn in a small bag in the front row seat he'd just vacated, along with his recording equipment.

"What's this?" one of the men said, picking up the bag and holding it out as though it were a dead rat.

"Bag," one of the women said, bored.

"You think?"

The woman pointed to the back. "It must belong to that little guy back there."

"What little guy?"

"He scurried for cover when we came in."

The man dropped the bag. "Go look," he ordered, then motioned his companions forward to the command compartment where, from such noises as Pauli could make out, they commenced intimidating and threatening the pilot.

The woman kneeled on the seat in front of Pauli's hiding place and peered down at him over its headrest. "Hi," she said.

He glanced up at her, then slid down even farther. He wasn't sure if he'd curled himself into a ball, but it sort of felt like it.

"My name's BonBon," she said pleasantly enough. "What's yours?"

The introduction didn't put Pauli at ease, but it certainly startled him. "Huh?"

She tapped herself on her substantial chest. "BonBon," she repeated. Then she pointed at him. "You?"

"BonBon? How—why—*huh?*"

She rolled her eyes in irritation. "Never mind that. You are?"

"Perry," he mumbled.

"Hi, Perry. You don't look like a miner. Administrator?"

He shook his head but couldn't answer. He couldn't even remember what he did or who he was, aside from being a really scared guy possibly curled into a ball on a space shuttle seat somewhere on the fringes of a gang of bloodthirsty mercenaries.

BonBon extended her hand. "Need help getting up?"

Oddly, she didn't sound half as bloodthirsty as he expected. Something wasn't right with the world here. He put one timid hand forward and let her take it. Without effort, she pulled him into a sitting position. Now that he was up where he could see, he found her surprisingly old, maybe old enough to be his mother, with tangled black hair and a stretched face that bespoke decades of hard living.

"There," she said reasonably. "Isn't that better?"

Pauli nodded, completely lost at sea. *Lost at sea?* The scriptwriter part of his mind logged that expression for further investigation and possible use. He was nowhere near a sea and so couldn't possibly be lost in one, but he knew the phrase must have some relevant meaning.

Or not.

BonBon cocked her head. "What are you doing out here?"

"Going there."

"Where?"

"There." He couldn't quite remember where there was, but probably she could figure it out. She looked like a woman who knew where she was and what was what.

And indeed she was. "We're attacking it. Why would you want to go there?"

"I'm a scriptwriter." Pauli frowned. Did that have anything to do with anything? He wasn't sure.

BonBon looked surprised. "You going to write a play about us or something?"

That seemed like a good idea. Action. Adventure. Bloodshed. Paralyzing fear. "Sure," he decided.

"You could get hurt down there, you know."

I could get hurt up here, too, he thought, *but at least I have tranquilizers, if only I could remember where I put them.* As he couldn't, he decided to think about something calming, something soothing, like maybe how nice BonBon was, especially given that she was a bloodthirsty mercenary, and maybe like how all bloodthirsty mercenaries were basically decent people who'd been badly misunderstood. He focused on her and uttered the first words that came into his brain: "Is your name really BonBon?"

She gave him a dark look that suggested maybe she wasn't so badly misunderstood after all.

"Okay," he said. "Forget it."

"Thank you." She eyed him suspiciously.

"I don't care. Really. It's not important."

"Fine. Are you really a scriptwriter?"

"Yes. Where's my bag? I have tranquilizers."

BonBon gave him a tight-lipped smile then went to retrieve the bag. She returned with it and set it carefully beside him. She watched him open it just far enough to thrust his hand in, watched him extract the medication and take it. *It's almost like she doesn't trust me,* he thought. He slowly closed the bag and set it aside, careful to make no sudden movements. Sudden movements alarmed people like her, didn't they? Caused them to start doing bloodthirsty things like shooting everything in sight?

Regardless of such thoughts, Pauli felt better already. "Can we go now? Me and the crew? We won't be any trouble. I promise."

"Not my call," she told him. "My husband Gordo is in charge. But I'll put in a good word for you." She rose and held out her hand. "Come on, I'll introduce you."

Pauli didn't think he wanted to meet anyone named Gordo, especially not any Gordos brandishing weaponry the likes of which these thugs carried, but he didn't see how he could refuse, and anyway he thought BonBon must like him and would probably protect him. So he gave her his hand and she pulled him up and together they walked forward to the command compartment, hand in hand, where they found the pilot and copilot cowering in their seats, surrounded by the other four mercenaries, while intrusion alarms beeped and flashed on the console. Not a very relaxing environment. *Good thing she let me take my tranquilizers*, Pauli thought.

The largest mercenary looked back as they entered. He gave Pauli a quick once-over and returned his steel gaze to the pilot. "Any trouble with him?"

"Nope," BonBon replied, releasing Pauli's hand. Pauli grabbed the now free hand with his other to keep it from shaking. "This is Perry. He's a scriptwriter. Says he wants to write a play about our little adventure."

The man snorted.

"He's no trouble, Gordo, just scared. He'll be okay. He took some tranquilizers."

The pilot craned his neck to see Pauli. "Could we have some?"

Before Pauli could assent, Gordo snapped, "Shut up," and the pilot sank back down. "A shuttle carrying only one passenger, a scriptwriter with tranquilizers. You searched his bag?"

"Not yet." BonBon said.

"Why not?"

"You in a hurry?"

Gordo cast an irritated look her way.

"He isn't carrying, Gordo. Look at him."

Gordo looked, and Pauli's legs nearly gave out. "Yeah, okay. Better take another dose, little girl." He laughed.

"Don't talk to him like that," BonBon snapped. "You're such a bully."

"I'm a mercenary! Of course I'm a bully!"

"Save it for someone your own size."

"Like who, you?"

BonBon's frosty glare met his, and for a moment deep, dead silence engulfed the command compartment. The other mercenaries seemed to hold their breaths while Gordo and BonBon played chicken (another phrase Pauli's brain filed for investigation) with their eyes. Then Gordo smiled a toothy smile and said, "I'll take you up on that later, babe. Right now it's time to meet the big boss."

On cue, a light flashed on the panel and static crackled on the speakers. "Request docking authorization."

The pilot looked at Gordo with wide eyes. The mercenary motioned him to respond, which he did, requesting electronic identification. Computers connected across the gulf of space and exchanged information, then the voice from the other ship announced, "Docking protocol received and verified. General Omdahl requests boarding at your earliest convenience."

General Omdahl. She liked the sound of that! Now if only these idiots would respect it.

She scrutinized the collection of spacecraft that had, more or less, blockaded TDY-41093-RRP, a mismatched conglomeration of junk piles that somehow managed to be spaceworthy. Mostly black with just enough reflectivity to be visible in the faint sunlight, each craft bristled with energy cannons and jagged transceiver stacks and other weird appendages jutting out at all angles. A solid kick would probably have dislodged half of their components, but they seldom got kicked or, for that matter, blasted. Security forces in the Oort Territories were limited to facility police. If you needed an armed spaceship, you called your favorite mercenary.

And here they were, waiting for her, although they'd captured a shuttle just for the fun of it. Omdahl was miffed that instead of boarding the leader's ship and taking charge, she had to board an insignificant shuttle. That just didn't seem half as impressive. But she would be taking charge, and that would do for now.

Docking accomplished, she led her ever-present guards to the airlock and waited for it to cycle open, then strode onto the shuttle where a gang of six mercenaries lounged in the seats without a care in the world. She eyeballed them. They should have snapped to attention.

Collectively, they were almost as she imagined: big and ugly and tough-looking. Two of them were women as sturdy as herself. One of the men, though, didn't seem at all to fit: scrawny and wide-eyed with fear. She almost ignored him until, with a shock, she realized she'd seen him before.

"Perry! What the hell?"

One of the big men raised an eyebrow. "You know this little girl, babe?"

The woman seated next to him smacked his arm. "I told you, don't call him that."

Omdahl bit her tongue. If the mercenaries didn't know Perry worked for the StarBright board, chances were the board didn't want them to know.

The last thing she needed was trouble with Worthington. Changing the subject, she snapped, "And who are you two?"

"What two?" the man asked, smiling easily. "There's five of us."

"You! I recognize your voice. You're the one I talked to earlier."

"Yeah, babe, that's me. Call me Gordo. I'm in charge of these gorillas. This here's my right-hand woman, BonBon."

"BonBon?" Omdahl nearly laughed, nearly said the first insulting thing that came to her mind, but BonBon's icy eyes suggested she might want to rethink that course. "Okay, Gordo, I'm the head gorilla now. Here's what we're going to do."

"Hold on," Gordo said, raising a hand to stop her. "We got protocols, you know."

"I'm your only protocol from here on."

"What say we cut a deal. You tell me what to do, then I'll tell the rest of the gang what to do."

She rolled her eyes. This guy obviously had no military background. "That's the idea. It's called a chain of command."

"Gotcha. So you tell me what to do, then I ignore it and tell my gang what I want them to do."

"No!"

Gordo grinned and BonBon shook her head. "So what's the plan?" he asked.

"We take control of the executive office and impose martial law."

"Sounds like fun."

"No random violence."

"No fun."

"Except when I say."

"Possibly fun," Gordo decided. "Assuming you do say. If not, well, I can't guarantee full cooperation."

Omdahl made a mental note to kick Worthington's lying teeth the next time she saw him. "Listen, idiot, this is an official security operation, not a field trip for juvenile delinquents."

"You always this dull?"

"Yes!" She drew a deep breath. Time to start giving orders. "Release this shuttle and return to your own ships. I'll transmit terms of surrender to the executive office and arrange for our takeover. You'll receive further instructions shortly."

Gordo gritted his teeth and gave Pauli a sour look. BonBon looked severe, but patted the scriptwriter's hands. "All right," Gordo decided. "But there'd better be some action down there."

Omdahl waited for the mercenaries to vacate the shuttle, then approached Pauli. "What are you doing here?" she asked, but not too stridently. This was, after all, Froebisher's man. Or whatever.

"I'm a scriptwriter," he told her.

"That's a stupid cover. What are you really doing here?"

"Um."

A thought occurred to her, a really nasty thought involving power struggles and people like her and Perry being squashed flat in the middle of them. Especially Perry, the thought of whose flattening wasn't half as nasty as the thought of her own, but still. "Are you a spy?"

He looked like he might throw up on her, so she backed up a step.

"Hell. Is Froebisher with Worthington or against him?" Omdahl was pretty sure she knew the answer. Who could possibly be on Worthington's side without a gun held to their head, as it had been to hers?

Pauli spluttered helplessly, then wiped his mouth with his sleeve, then looked in alarm at his sleeve.

"Look, just get out of here. Do what you have to do, but stay out of the way. If one of these goons steps on you, you're done for."

Pauli nodded vigorously and didn't stop nodding, at least not before she left the shuttle. For all she knew, he'd be nodding still when he arrived on the surface.

CHAPTER 16

The black fleet descended in a blaze of fire, settled carefully on the tarmac, and connected to airlock tunnels that extended like groping fingers from the spaceport. The ships disgorged their mercenary crews into the tunnels, then, work completed, settled in for a long sleep. The skeleton crews left on board maneuvered their craft out of reach of the tunnels, just in case anything went wrong. Nobody could get to them without pressure suits and definitely without being seen. The black ships were now safe, which was more than could be said for the mining colony.

Magnetic boots clanked on the metal floor as the invaders trooped into the facility with General Omdahl in the lead. She stomped to the executive offices and barged in without announcing herself, flanked by her personal guards and trailing two dozen savage brutes. In the small reception area bounded by bare metal walls and littered with uncomfortable chairs, a lone unarmed security guard faced her down for all of two seconds before swallowing and commanding forcefully, "Follow me, please."

Omdahl and her retinue followed down a long corridor studded with closed doors. They rounded a corner and came to a huge conference room that was little more than the reception room on steroids. Inside, TDY-41093-RRP's top management and their support staff were crammed, all looking as nervous as the guard.

Base director Amelia Carbuncle, an austere fiftyish woman dressed all in orange, stepped forward, feigning courage, and demanded, "What's going on?"

Omdahl pulled one of the chairs to herself and plopped into it. She raised her feet and plunked them on the table. "I'm in charge now," she said, realizing at the same moment that taking her feet off the floor had been a mistake. In the weak gravity, she and the chair bounced backward. She quickly set boots to floor again and felt the magnetic tug secure her position.

"This is illegal!" Carbuncle wailed.

"This is your board of directors fixing your mess."

Carbuncle paled.

"You're all under arrest. My thugs are locking you up in the detention center. This base is now under martial law."

Nobody dared protest. Looking like cowed sheep—or sheepish cows—the gathering filed out under the escort of ten mercenaries while Omdahl smiled a frosty smile. Her smile slipped when she noticed the little fellow slinking out near the back of the line.

She glanced at the remaining mercenaries. None of them had noticed. He might be a wimp, she mused, but Perry Pauli sure got around. And he had a knack for making himself invisible in a crowd. He must have known management would be the primary target. But what had he been doing here?

Arne Slocum's whole problem, which rapidly became Josh Murdock's whole problem and from there Darya Pasternak's whole problem, which guaranteed that it would become Ajit Tambe's whole problem—

Hold on. Start over.

Smoke was the whole problem. Slocum's monitoring equipment couldn't see through it, which meant Slocum himself couldn't see through it, which meant Murdock couldn't find out what was going on, which meant Pasternak had to—

Hold on.

"We need boots on the ground," Murdock said.

"Our boots *are* on the ground," Tambe astutely observed. He looked down to check. "On the floor, anyway."

Pasternak rolled her eyes. "He means we need to go up there." She pointed up there.

"Why?"

"So we can see something other than smoke."

Tambe considered that for a minute, then made another astute observation: "Seeing smoke is safer than breathing it." He considered further. "Or being disintegrated into it."

Murdock's enormous hand settled on Tambe's less than enormous shoulder. "Kid, this is our home. We gonna let somebody demolish it while we're still in it?"

The kid's sickly look suggested he might consider that option, but then he shook his head. "I guess not."

"Besides, you and Darya make a great team." Murdock grinned as though that might encourage Tambe.

Pasternak enclosed Tambe's shaking hand in her own rock-steady one. "C'mon, Ajit, you stood up to Kaja for me."

Her logic was impeccable, but that didn't stop the shaking. At the time, he hadn't been thinking about what Omdahl might do to him, only what she certainly wanted to do to Pasternak. This was different. Throwing himself in front of her with explosions exploding on all sides wouldn't significantly alter the outcome.

She tugged at his hand.

"Okay," he finally decided.

Watching from the sidelines, Maccarone said, "I'd better go with you."

That floored everyone, even Tambe. Why would a business tycoon stick his neck out? Shouldn't he be sitting safe and secure in an underground bunker while instructing everyone else to risk life and limb for an end that wasn't at all clear?

"You sure?" Pasternak asked skeptically.

"My ship is up there." Maccarone nodded upward. "I have to make sure it's safe." But as he said it, he seemed to pale, as though he just realized what he was saying.

"Okay," Pasternak told him before he could change his mind. "Let's go."

So they exited much as they had entered: the woman in the lead and the men following, wondering what they had gotten themselves into now.

Pauli slipped from the executive offices, buried among the management staff now being herded toward the detention area. Hidden on his person, he bore surreptitiously made recordings of said staff whining about the brutes who had descended upon them, whimpering about the ultimatum they'd received from General Omdahl—whoever she was; nobody had ever heard of a general by that name, although a few of them knew there was a supervisor called Omdahl, possibly a distant relative of the general—and biting their nails over her declaration of martial law. They'd all been so preoccupied with fright and misery and outrage that nobody had noticed Pauli in their midst.

Hiding was his style, invisibility his talent. Though headed for prison, he felt safe again, or maybe the tranquilizers had fully kicked in. Whatever the case, he slipped out with the base staff, body and recordings intact. And when, marching their charges around a corner, the mercenary guards slipped up and let a few stragglers vanish back the way they had come, Pauli slunk off with them. Though few in number, they remained oblivious to the stranger in their midst, which suited him fine.

But anonymity didn't last long. The group struck off in a new direction. Terrified that they would be missed, they rushed as quietly as possible around a series of turns until they came upon another lifter. As the car arrived and the door swooped open, who should barrel out but Roberto Maccarone with a pair of miners—a skinny kid and a sturdy woman who Pauli swore he'd seen hanging around the theater shortly before it blew up. At first the newcomers didn't recognize him. Terrified that they might, he couldn't take his eyes off them as they passed by, and that gave him away. The woman noticed his frightened gaze and looked back, puzzled.

"Do I know you?" she asked.

"No!" he answered in something approaching a falsetto.

Maccarone looked him over and shrugged. "Come on," he told the woman.

But she didn't budge, and the other guy stood there switching his gaze from her to Pauli and back again like he couldn't decide which of them was in charge.

"Who are you?" she demanded.

The executive minions frowned and scratched their heads. They didn't know, either, so they collectively mimicked Maccarone's shrug and loaded themselves onto the lifter, which closed and departed.

This wasn't where Pauli wanted to be. He wanted to be comfortably tucked away among a crowd, anonymous, invisible, unimportant.

"Well?" the woman demanded.

"Darya, let him go," Maccarone said. "We have to find out—"

The young guy elbowed Maccarone.

"Er," Maccarone added, "what's going on with—"

The young guy elbowed him again.

"Er, some stuff."

Before he could stop himself, Pauli blurted out, "You don't know?"

Which caused the woman's eyes to narrow into a mean sort of squint. She strode forward and grabbed him by the shoulders. "Know what? Who the hell *are* you?"

"I'm Perry!" he yelped, trying to back away but unable to free himself from her grip.

"Who's attacking us, *Perry?*"

"I don't know!"

"Wait a minute." The woman started patting him down. He turned beet red with embarrassment and fear. "You're wired! You recording someone?"

"I'm a scriptwriter!" he whined, hoping that would explain everything.

"You're a spy is what you are. Who's bankrolling you?"

Really, Pauli thought, this was over the top. The mercenaries had treated him more kindly. "Let go of me!" he snapped, or at least he hoped he snapped, and then for good measure added, "Please?"

The woman let him go. "Are you with the attackers?"

"No!"

"Against them?"

"Um!"

Maccarone came forward and placed a tentative hand on the woman's shoulder. "Darya—"

She shrugged him off. "It's not nuclear physics. Are you against them?"

"I don't know!"

"How can you not know?"

"I don't know!" Pauli backed himself against the wall. "I'm just Perry! I'm just a scriptwriter!"

"We could spend years lost in this conversation," Maccarone said. "And eventually we'd start talking about marimbas. Just let him go."

"No," Pasternak said. "Until I know who he is, he's staying with us." She turned on Pauli again. "Right?"

Pauli didn't want to go anywhere this woman was going. If she were going to the warmest beach with the bluest waters on the most secluded island on Earth, he wouldn't go with her. He'd rather descend into the mines and spend the rest of his life digging out ice with his teeth than go with her. On the other hand, the mines were probably where she was going. She had to be a miner. Maybe the beach idea wasn't so bad, after all? Maybe that nice mercenary lady BonBon would go with him? On the third hand, BonBon was the only nice member of her clan. The rest of them were thugs, and whatever miners were, they weren't thugs. Maybe this miner lady could be good protection against mercenary thugs, or any other nasty creatures inhabiting this horrible place?

Pauli drew himself up to his full unimpressive height and bravely said, "I guess. If you want."

"I want," the woman said. "Come on."

Pauli was given the privilege of going second, behind the woman and in front of the young guy, with Maccarone bringing up the rear. They hurried through the rat's maze of corridors, twisting and turning until he had no clue where they were anymore, and finally came to a lifter that carried them rapidly up several more levels and deposited them in a large circular room built entirely of windows.

"An observation deck?" Maccarone suggested.

"Yeah," the woman replied, "in case anyone wants to come up here and meditate on the beauty of this godforsaken hellhole."

They looked out over the dark, jagged, ugly face of TDY-41093-RRP. If it were a human face, Pauli thought, it could only be contemplating murder most foul. Scattered across the surface, buildings reared up from below, some connected by flimsy-looking passageways, others not. The landing pads sulked well off in the distance, jammed full of horrible black mercenary spaceships. To their right sprawled a huge debris field, as though a ship had slammed into the ice and disintegrated into billions of chunks of metal and plastic. Just beyond it, a section of new construction stood, not quite gleaming under the influence of the distant sun.

Maccarone pointed. "The new theater, with the old one splattered around it."

"Never trust a fountain that sprays pink water," the woman quipped.

Pauli felt a twinge of his former sickness rising. But Froebisher told him he couldn't have blown it up. It didn't work that way. "I didn't do it," he told himself, except somehow he hadn't only told himself. The words had slipped out through his traitorous lips. The others glanced at him, puzzled.

Fortunately their young cohort had something else on his mind. He nodded in the opposite direction, where dozens of small gashes had been opened up in a collection of disused outbuildings. "The attackers did that," he said with a nod.

"No loss there," the woman told him. "Maybe they just wanted to scare us before launching their pillaging party." Facing Pauli, she said,

"Introductions." Pointing to each of her party in turn, starting with herself she enumerated: "Darya Pasternak, Ajit Tambe, Roberto Maccarone." Then she pointed at him and waited.

"Perry." When her look darkened he added, "Pauli. Perry Pauli."

"Are you really a scriptwriter?" Maccarone asked so reasonably that Pauli felt compelled to answer fully and truthfully.

"Yeah. And, uh, stuff."

Pasternak just about lunged at him again, but Maccarone waved her off and miraculously she complied. "What sort of stuff?" He flashed a confidential smile that suggested he already knew anyway.

"Well—"

"Come on," Maccarone prompted. "I'm the owner of an opera company, and Darya and Ajit are miners. But I'm also a StarBright board member acting as a spy for Artemis Worthington, and these two are also rebels who go around causing havoc. So what are you, besides a scriptwriter?"

Coming from Maccarone, the whole thing sounded entirely reasonable. Of course, everyone from high and mighty opera company owners to lowly miners and scriptwriters had some dark side, some wicked secret, some reckless desire for subterfuge. "I'm Lena Froebisher's spy," he admitted.

"Ah." Maccarone smiled a satisfied smile. "And what does she want?"

"To stick it to Artemis Worthington."

"Excellent. So you see, we're all enemies here. Isn't that nice?"

Pasternak punched Maccarone's arm. He stumbled sideways. "Stop babbling like an idiot. Who's behind this attack?"

"Mercenaries," Pauli said at the same time Maccarone said, "Worthington," and then they both looked at each other in confusion.

"Great," Pasternak spat. "Just great. Any idea who's leading Worthington's mercenaries? Tell me it isn't a jerk named Gordo."

Of course she'd know the names of mercenaries, Pauli thought. She looked like she could be one of them. Maye she had been one of them in a past life. "Gordo," he said. She grumbled something. "And maybe BonBon."

Maccarone and Tambe stared at him as if he'd lost his mind.

"But now it's General Omdahl."

"*What?*" Pasternak and Tambe and Maccarone all screeched, and Pauli felt the world falling apart again and sank to his knees and covered his head, just in case anything heavy was about to hit him thereabouts.

Nothing did, but it took a few minutes for the others to recover their scattered wits. "Oh, get up!" Pasternak snapped. He complied, if sheepishly. "Why's Kaja leading a gang of mercenaries?"

"Oh," Maccarone said miserably. "I'll bet Worthington got to her. He wanted her to be the rebel leader. Now she's the security force leader."

"That makes no sense!"

"Turncoat. The other board members will think he's a genius."

Pasternak chewed on the thought for a moment, and Tambe decided for the both of them, "Yeah, it makes sense."

Pauli didn't get it, though, and he tried to say so but couldn't. Instead, he just looked pleadingly at Maccarone.

Maccarone took pity on him and explained. "We're all pawns in Worthington's game. He's after total control of StarBright, which will give him total control of everything out here. Including my theater."

That was completely off the wall. "Theater?" Pauli asked. *Off the wall?* he thought. *One more phrase to file away.*

"Never mind," Maccarone said. "This has gone too far. Somebody has to put a stop to it." He looked around as though maybe somebody in attendance could do so.

"You got anybody with brains in your company?" Pasternak asked him.

If Maccarone thought it a tactless question, he didn't show it. He just nodded thoughtfully. "Yes, I have one very smart guy."

"And that would be?"

Maccarone smiled, apparently realizing just how brilliant this was going to be. "Yes, one very smart guy indeed, and fearless to boot. He'd do whatever it takes to stick it to Worthington."

"So?" Pasternak said impatiently. "What's his name?

Maccarone's smile broadened until Pauli thought it would split his face in two. As though introducing a new act, he announced, "We call him: Mr. Fang!"

Mr. Fa, ah, Land had been brooding on board the *Ponchielli* when the first explosion sounded. Startled from his dark reverie, he sprang to his feet and made for the door, but the second explosion stopped him in his tracks. By the time the third came, he'd figured out that something was horribly wrong, that it wasn't onboard ship, and that if the ship got involved, it would quickly become tricky to breathe.

He bolted from his office and rushed down the narrow corridor to the airlock, already jammed with Space Operatic staff frantically escaping to the imagined safety of the terminal.

Only after pushing their way in did it dawn on any of them that whatever was blowing up was doing so inside the colony. Faced with two unsavory options—dying on their ship or dying in the building—they quite rationally stood around gaping at each other and the walls and the ceiling and the floor until, about seven noisy and terrifying minutes later, the thunder stopped.

"What do we do?" a woman wailed.

"Don't move!" another woman suggested.

"Get back on the ship!" a man countered.

"File a complaint!" another man, probably the guy who doubled as lighting expert and legal counsel, insisted.

"The theater!" a third woman cried. "They've finished rebuilding it, right? We'll be safe there!"

Everyone liked that idea, judging by the murmurs. They were so happy that Land hated to squash their hopes. Well, no, actually he didn't. "You mean that theater that vomited its guts all over the airless landscape a few days ago? Great."

Nobody listened. A stampede ensued, leaving Land all by his lonesome, pondering the cruelty of a universe in which everyone but him had lost their minds. At least he now had quiet and could think. First order of business, he decided, was to find out what had happened and whether it represented any danger to their ship. Assuming not, the second order of business would be to get everyone back on board and fly away before anything else could go wrong. He might have to conk Maccarone on the head and truss him up to do it, but he was okay with that.

First, though, information. "Executive office," Land told the facility, which obliged by lighting up a fluorescent orange line on the floor. He followed and within a few minutes strode boldly into a nest of huge, scruffy-looking men and women brandishing black steel weaponry while arguing heatedly about who got what percentage of whatever loot they found lying about the place.

This, Land thought, *can't be right.*

"Oh look, one of the opera flunkies."

The words, if not the voice, made him bristle, until he realized that the voice belonged to the supervisor who had led reconstruction of the exploding fountain. But instead of lording it over a bunch of miners, she had her body-armored body planted in a really big chair behind a really big desk that should have belonged to somebody really important. One foot on the desktop and the other on the floor, she chewed on a stick of foul-looking something and smirked at him.

"You!" he said.

"Wow. I'm so thrilled you remember me."

"What's going on? I demand to see the . . ." Noticing that the men had stopped arguing and were now eyeing him as though it might be fun to use him as a football, he changed his tone. "That is, I'd like to speak to whoever is in charge."

One of the mercenaries pointed. "General Omdahl." He sneered at Land as though daring him to challenge the assertion.

"Oh."

"You want to sell us tickets, I suppose?" Omdahl asked.

"No. I just, well, that is, I wanted to know if we could, you know . . ." He did have a purpose in coming here. He was sure of that. But he must have mislaid it somewhere. He looked around the room in confusion.

Omdahl nodded as though she did indeed know. "Nope."

"Nope?"

"Nope. Nobody leaves until this little matter is cleaned up."

Land didn't even know what this little matter was, although from the looks of things it couldn't be all that little, nor could he possibly want any of the cleaning implements to touch him.

Omdahl dragged her foot off of the desk and dropped it with a clank to the floor. Standing, she clumped over to Land and looked down at him. She was a good foot taller than he, which he found disconcerting. "Besides, you got a performance coming up, right? It said so on the computer."

"Are you an opera lover?" Now why had he asked her *that*? And why did all of his conversations seem to go this way of late?

"Oh yeah, I'm a big fan. I loved it when the fountain blew up. So, what are you really doing here?"

He found his purpose again. At least, he thought he had, so he tried it on for size. "I heard some explosions." It sounded right but needed a bit of clarification. "Not fountains. Just explosions."

"And?"

So much for that. "Nothing," he decided. "Can I go now?"

Omdahl drew closer to him, real close, like she was considering stepping on his head. *She could do it, too*, Land thought. She looked nearly as tall as Godzilla at short range.

"General," another woman said, and Land was surprised to see her standing there, right beside him. Where had she come from? "You're scaring him."

Omdahl glared at the woman, and one of the men rolled his eyes and said, "Not again, BonBon."

There's that conversation issue again, Land thought. "BonBon?"

The dark look she gave him suggested he should quit while he was ahead, so he did, although he wasn't sure he was.

"I just don't see the point in pushing around guys who are obviously no threat."

Land wasn't sure how he felt about being called "no threat" but decided that in these circumstances it would be prudent to play along, so he nodded as sagely as he could.

Omdahl considered that. "Yeah, okay. I guess I'm just used to dealing with guys like this." She nudged the man who had spoken to BonBon. He raised a hand as though to strike the general but lowered it again. "Good boy," Omdahl told him. "You remember who's in charge."

"You won't be forever," the man warned.

"So," Land said, taking a few steps backward toward the door, "I'll just be on my way then."

Omdahl watched him go but didn't try to stop him, and once in the corridor he found to his amazement that he could run pretty darn fast with the proper motivation. He ran and ran, blind to his surroundings, clueless as to his location, devoid of all sense of time. Eventually he stopped, doubled over, and gasped for breath. When that was over and he could walk without greatly hurting or panting excessively, he blundered along a few more corridors, wondering how to escape this madhouse. Finally he set his hand to the wall to steady himself then fell over sideways when the wall proved to be a lifter car door just swishing open.

The car wasn't empty. Trying to right himself, he stumbled into the arms of a woman who could have been Omdahl's twin, except she wasn't wearing body armor.

"Aaaieeee!" he apologized.

"Who're you?" the woman snapped.

"That," Roberto Maccarone said, although Land couldn't fathom why the hell *he* should be here, "is Mr. Fang."

CHAPTER 17

Since the bombardment had stopped, management had been locked up, and the mercenaries had spread out to thunk into all available heads the message that martial law had been imposed, Maccarone decided the safest place was within the secure and serene hull of the *Ponchielli*. Quickly, quietly, and surreptitiously, he led Pasternak, Tambe, Pauli, and Land this way and that, changing course only when Pasternak snapped, "*That* way!" and eventually they stole on board without being thunked even once.

He then led them to his office—he knew how to get *there* without help, at least—where they crammed themselves in, decided the place was too small for the five of them, and left again. They took up residence in the deserted dining hall instead. The facility wasn't so much a hall as a longish closet filled with tables bolted to the floor and chairs that slid in and out on tracks. Clustered at the end of a table at the end of the room, they gazed hopefully at Land.

After a moment, he snapped, "You look like a bunch of zombies."

"What do we do with this mess?" Pasternak demanded.

Land could suggest several possible things for them to do with it, but he withheld comment. "Who are you?"

"Let me introduce you," Maccarone said as though they had assembled for a networking luncheon. "Darya Pasternak and Ajit Tambe are miners and insurrectionists. That's Perry Pauli, scriptwriter and spy for Lena Froebisher. I'm Roberto Maccarone—"

"I *know* who you are!" Land snapped. "Unfortunately," he added under his breath.

Maccarone continued as if Land hadn't interrupted. "Owner of Space Operatic, Starbright board member, and spy for Artemis Worthington." He paused to wave a hand at Land, "And this is Feng Shui Land, Space Operatic properties manager and so far not much else."

Land squeezed his eyes shut in a show of emotional pain. "Thanks a lot."

"Feng Shui Land?" Pauli barely suppressed a snicker. Land shot him a warning scowl, which didn't seem to warn him. "I thought you said his name was Fang."

"Inside joke," Maccarone said smoothly to the accompaniment of his famously smooth smile. "It's not important now."

While Land fumed, Pasternak cut to the chase. "Short version. Worthington's taken over our little slush pile. His mercenaries are running amok."

"Thunking heads," Pauli said, aghast, and put a protective hand over his head.

Pasternak ignored him. "You need to stop them."

"*Me?*" Land calmly screeched.

"Yeah. Give us a plan. Your boss says you're smart."

What a rotten time for him to think well of me, Land grumbled to himself. "I don't know anything about fighting mercenaries. What about your security people?"

"They already surrendered," Pasternak told him.

"The miners?"

"Down in the mines so they won't get blown up."

"Territory security forces?"

"What security forces?"

Land shot Maccarone a menacing glance. The boss's talent for taking them from catastrophe to disaster had swollen to legendary proportions.

Maccarone apparently misread the look. "That's the spirit!"

On the other hand, this could force matters. "Let's go home," Land told Maccarone. "Take off. Set course for Earth."

"Kaja will blow you to smithereens before you're ten meters up," Pasternak said. "She's been itching to blow something up for a long time."

"Just like us," Tambe commented with a private little smile.

"Why would explosions cure itches?" Pauli asked, confused.

"Why am I even here?" Land muttered.

Pointing pointedly at Land, Pasternak snapped at Maccarone, "Who told you this guy had brains?"

"If only we could pipe some soothing music through the facility," Maccarone mused. "That would calm the mercenaries so we could have a rational talk with them." Then, with everyone directing confused and murderous glares at him—it's not hard to figure out who wore which—he added, "What?"

Without warning, Pasternak slammed her fist on the table. The men jumped a foot into the air. "Brilliant!"

Land didn't blame her for cracking up. Everyone else already had. It was probably contagious. "Music doesn't really tame savage beasts," he told her as though instructing a hopelessly stupid student.

"Not music," she said. "Commands."

"Commands?" everyone asked at once.

Already halfway to the door, she said, "Yeah, commands. Come on, kid, we got to get below."

"Why?" Tambe asked, rising and following her.

"'Cause that's where Arne is. He's gonna love this!"

Pauli longed for the protective cover of his herd. The office staff he'd escaped with hadn't minded his presence, hadn't even noticed him. Confused and scared, they were the perfect cover for a confused and scared spy. But Maccarone and Land could hardly be called a herd, nor were they confused and scared. Maccarone seemed hopelessly optimistic, as though revolts and explosions and head thunkings were everyday occurrences in the world of opera, while Land spat venom at the universe and its contents. And here he sat, an innocent young scriptwriter spy—well, okay, spies couldn't be entirely innocent, he supposed—alone, exposed, helpless before whatever terrors might be perpetrated by these purveyors of culture.

"You've ruined my entire life," Land told Maccarone. "You know that, don't you?"

"Be of good cheer Fa, ah, Feng," Maccarone reassured him. "We haven't lost that theater yet. I'll get us in there somehow."

The assessment seemed to spur the production of Land's venom glands.

"What theater?" Pauli asked, failing to see what any theater could possibly have to do with a military coup.

"The Territory HQ theater," Maccarone explained. "We want to perform there."

"Nobody performs there."

"I know. And I know why, and I know how to fix it. All we have to do is disgrace Worthington."

It was a good thing Pauli wasn't eating or drinking or he would have choked to death. "You're out of your mind!"

Maccarone shrugged. "Could be, but it must be done."

It occurred to Pauli that Froebisher wanted exactly that, too, which tossed him into the same boat as Maccarone, although it was more of a spaceship than a boat, and really neither type of vessel had anything to do with anything just now. When he looked up, he found Maccarone eyeing him thoughtfully. "What?" he asked.

"You, ah, wouldn't have any ideas on that score, would you?"

"No. I'm just making recordings."

"Right," Maccarone muttered thoughtfully.

Land squinted his eyes at the boss. "Oh God, Roberto, please don't start thinking now. Please don't drag us further into this insanity."

"No," Maccarone said, but Land didn't relax. "No." The repetition didn't appease his underling, either. "No. But—"

Land sprang to his feet and paced furiously—well, pushed and stumbled his way down the narrow space between the chairs and the bulkhead, then returned much the same way. Pacing wasn't quite the word. But Pauli could imagine him pacing furiously, had he had the space to do so. "I refuse!" Land declared.

"I haven't said anything yet," Maccarone told him quite reasonably, since he actually hadn't.

"I don't care. Whatever you're thinking of saying, whatever you're going to say, whatever you want to say but won't until you think I've calmed down, the answer is no!"

"The theater," Maccarone suggested gently.

"No!"

"The Maccarone-Land Center for—"

"No!"

"The Land-Maccarone Center for—"

"No, no, no, no!"

Pauli, however, had grown curious and couldn't help himself. "What's this about?"

"No!" Land proclaimed for good measure.

"I'll help you get your recordings," Maccarone told him.

That didn't sound so bad, Pauli thought.

"Don't listen to him!" Land warned. "It will be the ruin of your whole life and probably your whole afterlife, too!"

"He's just upset," Maccarone said confidentially. "Playing that theater means a lot to him."

Pauli had never witnessed anyone tear out their own hair, so Land's attempt at such astonished him. At least it proved a short-lived attempt, possibly because it hurt so much. "How will you do that?" he asked.

Maccarone leaned forward and smiled that smile of his. "Easy," he said so convincingly that Pauli was aching to get started before hearing step one.

"For the sake of your immortal soul!" Land insisted while gingerly touching his head. He checked his fingers for blood. There wasn't any.

Maccarone waved off Land's hysteria. "I'll take you straight to the horse's mouth."

"What do we want with a horse's mouth?" Pauli asked, astonished. "That sounds gross."

Maccarone's own mouth, which was nothing like a horse's, twisted into a puzzled frown. "It's an expression."

"Why would anyone use *that* expression?

"I don't know. Never mind. It just means we're going to—"

"Run away as fast as you can!"

"—pay a little visit to –"

"You'll be sorry for the rest of your life!"

"—Kaja."

"Argh!"

Pauli looked from Maccarone to Land and back during this exchange and a beat or two beyond. He watched Maccarone smile encouragingly and Land grimace horribly. Finally, he said the only thing he really could under the circumstances.

"Okay."

He wasn't sure whether Land had actually passed out was just faking it.

The meaning of life seldom ranked high on Arne Slocum's list of concerns. He'd grown up in the Oort Territories, born of the union of a notorious claim jumper—his mother—and an equally notorious con artist—his father, obviously. Josh Murdock was still learning to say "mama" when Slocum built his first zap gun. More technically, he'd disassembled three of his father's weapons and creatively reassembled them into a newer, more powerful unit, leaving myriad spare parts strewn about the workshop on the family spaceship. The contraption worked; he blew a hole in the workshop floor and disintegrated the control unit to the trash processor, which happened to be in the utility section just below. Mom and Dad weren't too pleased by his creativity, but he was elated.

A year later he saw his first commercial mining operation and, amazed that a person could get paid for blowing things up, set out to learn all he could about the subject, especially the equipment. Although his mother had done her fair share of mining, always on somebody else's property, she'd never let her precious child help or even watch. But Arne persisted in pestering her, and the day came when he convinced her. She agreed that at the ripe old age of thirteen he was mature enough to learn her half of the family business.

One fateful day, she left him in charge of the equipment inside a small bore on the back side of a modest irregular—somebody else's, of course. He couldn't help himself. He took apart mom's well-worn extractor to study its innards, reassembled it slightly wrong, and blew a good cubic kilometer of ice and hydrocarbons out into space. It was a miracle he wasn't killed. His mother fumed at having lost so much saleable material. His father had simply had enough. The kid would never learn to make an honest living as a scoundrel.

Dad griped about him to his fellow scoundrels. In short order, word of his son's little exploit reached a nearby mining colony. The owners, envisioning young Arne's talent and audacity propelling their third-rate company to second-rate status, gleefully took him on, almost as gleefully as his father handed him over as an apprentice. Henceforth, he mastered increasingly complex equipment of all kinds until today here he was, working not for a third or second-rate company but StarBright Energy, the biggest, baddest company in existence where, in the midst of a coup, he had just been asked to—

"You want me to *what?*"

"Broadcast commands to disable the mercenary ships," Pasternak told him as if it were the easiest and most reasonable thing in the universe.

That's about the time the meaning of life became a question of some importance to Slocum. "I'm not ready to die," he told her. "I have too many things left to do."

If she'd been wearing glasses, she would have looked at him over their rims. "Name one."

That was hardly fair. He deflected. "Are *you* ready to die?"

"Of course not. Somebody's gotta take care of Ajit." Pasternak nudged Tambe in her usual rough way.

"Oof," Tambe said, although possibly not in agreement.

"Anyway, you can do it all from the safety of this room. Just do your electronics magic."

That, Slocum thought, was the problem with people who had never taken apart a machine, put it back together wrong, and blown a hole in something with it. They always thought it was easy to get machines to behave as you wished.

"A virus," Pasternak added, as if that would help.

"Darya, it doesn't work that way. Spacecraft communications and control security is nearly unbreakable."

"A bomb would break it," Tambe suggested hopefully.

Ignoring him, Pasternak put a supportive hand on Slocum's shoulder. "But you can do it. Right, Josh?" She glanced over her shoulder.

Murdock stood in the background, looking like he hadn't heard a word, but Slocum knew he was taking it all in. "Arne would know," he opined.

"Okay, maybe not a virus. But there's gotta be some way to knock them out."

"Like a bomb," Tambe suggested again, still hopeful.

Pasternak gave him a long-suffering look. "Some quiet way."

"A quiet bomb?"

Obviously, Slocum thought, *nobody has thought this through, not even as far as step one.* "And what do you think those goons will do if we blow up, disable, or otherwise mess with their ships, which by the way happen to be their homes?"

Tambe thought about it, then came up with a brilliant alternative. "A quiet bomb that looks like an accident?"

Pasternak pulled over a chair and sat next to Slocum. "Look Arne, just say you were going to do this."

"I'm not," he assured her.

"But say you were. Say revenge of the gorillas wasn't an issue. How would you do it?"

He nearly hated her for that. She'd pushed one of those buttons that, once pushed, couldn't be unpushed, irrevocably committing his brain to solving the problem. Silence engulfed them while his gray matter chugged along, and within a few minutes the light bulb went on and the chime sounded and the result came out: "EMP."

"What's that?" Pasternak asked.

"Electromagnetic pulse. An energetic enough EMP can damage electronics. They can have natural causes, too, so it might look like an accident."

Tambe looked up, eyes bright. "A quiet bomb that looks like an accident!"

"Yeah," Slocum drawled. "But we couldn't create one with wide enough coverage short of setting off a nuclear device, which isn't at all quiet or accidentish."

"Counterproductive, that," Murdock observed.

Slocum pondered further. "Maybe a small device on or near each ship." Unfortunately, revenge of the gorillas was indeed a real possibility. He couldn't ignore it. "No, forget it. Too risky."

"Ajit and I can do that part," Pasternak said soothingly, and patted Slocum on the shoulder.

Tambe paled. "Huh?"

"Too risky," Slocum repeated.

"Nah, we're good at sneaking in and out."

Raising a finger to get everyone's attention, Tambe added, "Huh?"

Slocum looked helplessly to Murdock, hoping he could inject some sense into the proceedings. Taking the cue, Murdock lumbered forward, stroking his beard thoughtfully. "How close to the ship?"

That didn't inject any sense at all. "Josh, these would be little devices. Toys."

"Yeah?"

"Yeah."

"So how close?"

"Ten meters at the most. Maybe five."

"On the hull?"

Exasperated, Slocum glared at Murdock. "You trying to get people killed?"

"Nope. I'll handle it. Put electromagnets and small explosives in them. After the EMP, switch off the magnets so the devices fall, then after a couple of seconds detonate them."

Slocum's eyes widened, but Pasternak laughed with glee. "Destroy the evidence," she said. "Perfect!"

"You still have to attach them to—"

"Said I'll handle it," Murdock interrupted easily, and smiled.

Slocum shook his head. "Fine. But don't say I didn't warn you."

Murdock winked at Pasternak, then lumbered bearishly on his way, presumably to handle it.

She'd finally perfected it. Left leg sprawled casually on the desk, right foot on the ground where the magnetic boot could anchor her, chair leaned back just kissing the wall behind her. Absolute equilibrium, and it made her look powerful and seductive and in charge and she didn't know what other cool kinds of things. Flanking her, her body armored body guards stood ready to kill anything that even thought about messing with her image, and only occasionally—like every five to ten seconds—snuck glances at the junction of her thighs.

That's when Maccarone waltzed in with Pauli at his side, and she just about choked on her own smug satisfaction.

"Hello, Kaja," Maccarone said cheerfully.

"You!" Whipping her leg down, she fell forward and caught herself just before her chin smacked the edge of the desk. "And you!" She stared wide-eyed at Pauli.

"You know each other?" Maccarone asked, surprised.

Pauli slid behind him to hide. "Sort of."

Maccarone rearranged his face into a cheerful smile. "I hear you're a general now. Congratulations!" He reached behind him and tugged on Pauli, who stood as unmovable as a mule.

The guards exchanged a glance as though trying to figure out if Omdahl's image had just been messed with. They shifted their zap guns, just in case.

"You shouldn't be here," she said. She squinted as though that would help her see Pauli through Maccarone's body. "Nor should you. Don't you have something you—damn it Perry, come out where I can see you!"

Maccarone tugged Pauli again, and he reluctantly complied.

"Don't you have something you should be doing?"

"Um," Pauli replied.

Maccarone put his hand on Pauli's back and, pushing the scriptwriter, moved forward to stand before the desk, still smiling that smile. "So Kaja—"

"Stop that! It's General Omdahl!"

The guards gripped their weapons more tightly.

The smile froze for a moment, but only that. "General." The guards relaxed again. "I was wondering if..." Pauli tried to slither behind him again. Maccarone grabbed his arm to stop him. "I was wondering if you could enlighten me."

Time to reassert the image, she thought. She carefully leaned back, settled her left leg on the desk again, and put on the smuggest of her smug looks. "I doubt anyone can."

His smile froze again. It almost made Omdahl want to check the temperature in the room.

"So what's your problem?" she prompted.

"It seems the facility is under new management." Maccarone motioned around. "And I have an opera to prepare."

"How is that my problem?"

"You're the new management."

"I'm just the ambassador."

"Oh? So who is in charge?"

Omdahl's cold smile broadened. She loved being in charge without really being in charge. It felt so liberating. "The StarBright board arranged this stunt."

"I'm on the board."

She didn't see how that could be, but decided it gave her a convenient conversation stopper. "Then you know all about it."

Except it didn't stop the conversation. "Not entirely. Art, er, Mr. Worthington didn't entirely fill me in."

That figured. Worthington seemed to have his grasping fingers in everything.

"So," Maccarone continued, again pulling Pauli out of semi-hiding, "I'm just wondering what the plan is, and how I fit into it, and especially how *Don Carlo* fits into it."

Non sequitur, she was beginning to realize, was Maccarone's key strength. "Who's this Donald guy?"

"Our forthcoming opera. We'll be performing the Quasi-Postmodern Milan Streamlined version."

"The what?" She realized the mistake as soon as she'd asked, so as quickly as Maccarone opened his mouth to respond, she stopped him. "Never mind. I don't care. Opera isn't on my agenda, only security."

"Oh." Maccarone looked puzzled, as though not sure how opera couldn't be part of security arrangements. "So tell me—" He cast an irritated glance at Pauli, who had again started to edge back. Seeing the look, Pauli's head drooped and he shuffled forward again.

To say Omdahl's suspicions had been aroused would be lying. They'd been wide awake for some time now. This whole adventure had dripped suspiciousness from the start without Pauli skulking around and Maccarone asking strange questions. She dragged her foot off the desk, thumped it on the floor, and stood. Eyes fixed on Pauli, she slowly rounded the desk. He swallowed, hard, and closed his eyes. She stopped a mere hand's width from him. "What's with you?"

Pauli shuddered.

"He's just—" Maccarone started.

"Shut up." Omdahl took hold of Pauli's chin and lifted his face upward. "Open your eyes."

He did but apparently didn't enjoy the view, because he immediately shut them.

"Well?"

"Um. I. Um. That. I. Um."

"You don't say."

"Tranquilizers."

"Wow. Four whole syllables."

"Wearing off," Pauli said miserably.

That might explain a few things, she decided, but she didn't care. "Why does your pal keep shoving you toward me?"

"Um."

"You have something to say?"

Pauli shook his head a bit too vigorously.

"Just listening, huh?"

Impossibly, he looked even sicker now.

And that's when she figured it out. She grabbed Pauli by the shoulders and shook him. "You're wired!"

Maccarone stepped forward and put a hand on hers, possibly thinking he could pry it off of Pauli. "Now Ka, ah, General," he began.

Omdahl released Pauli and grabbed Maccarone's throat. His eyes widened about fourfold. "What are you up to?" But she didn't need him to explain. In a flash, she had it worked out. Froebisher had sent Pauli to do her dirty work, just as Worthington had sent Omdahl. Maccarone, mad as it sounded, must really be a StarBright board member and had hatched some lunatic scheme to take them both down. What did he want? Control of the company? Or freedom from it?

Maccarone watched the wheels turning, swallowed, and said, "So, er, could you let go of me please?"

She pushed him away. "What's your angle?"

"Angle?"

"What are you after?"

"After?"

"Real genius, aren't you?"

"I just want to produce an opera."

Omdahl felt like strangling him again, but remembering that she was a general and needed to project a professional bearing, she restrained herself and slapped his face instead.

"Honest!" he yelped.

"In the middle of a coup, you want to produce an opera."

"Yes!"

"With mercenaries all around."

"No! At Territory—"

He cut himself off so quick she wasn't sure he'd actually said what he'd said. "You've got to be joking. Nobody plays that theater!"

Maccarone seemed to be holding his breath. Pauli, too, except he looked like he might already be dead of asphyxiation. Omdahl leaned back on her desk, stunned. "What does this have to do with me?"

Maccarone cleared his throat and tried to regain his composure. "Nothing. I swear. Nothing at all. I just need to know what, what, what's, what, that is—"

"Spit it out!"

"What's going on?"

"Spit harder!"

"What." He turned away. "He's." He turned back and grimaced, although surely it had been meant as a smile. "Doing?"

"A trap," she said, wondering why she had to explain his own plan to him. "A trap for Worthington."

Maccarone nodded miserably and looked at his shoes. He probably thought she was going to arrest him now and order his head severely klonked by her mercenary goons. She considered doing just that for all of three seconds, but then a better idea occurred to her, and although she knew it was probably going to lead to further insanity, she really, really, *really* wanted to pursue it.

Naturally, both Maccarone and Pauli were thrown completely off kilter when she announced her decision: "Okay guys. Let's do this."

CHAPTER 18

"Hey Gordo," Murdock rumbled. "Long time no see."

He'd found his old friend in an interrogation room tucked away in the base police office surrounded by a score of his mercenary companions. Just beyond them, one terrified middle manager was cowering, back to the wall, shoulder pinned by one of Gordo's massive hands. At Murdock's greeting, Gordo released the man who crumpled to the floor and curled into a ball.

"Josh!" Gordo said. With a backward, downward glance at the manager, he warned, "No more of your backtalk." Then he turned his full attention on the newcomer, as did all of his companions. "What are you doing here?"

Murdock shrugged and waded through the clog of mercenaries, who parted with ease as he pushed them aside. The two big men clasped hands and eyed each other for a moment as though trying to determine which would have the upper hand in a duel to the death. "Was mining," Murdock finally said. "Until you showed up."

Gordo laughed uproariously. "Hey, I'm just paying the bills. Didn't know this was your place."

"Wouldn't have made a difference." Murdock smiled easily to signal no harm, no foul. Mercenaries gotta klonk heads.

"But I would've looked you up if I'd known you were here."

"Darya's here, too."

"No!"

"Yep."

"Who," BonBon asked, sidling up to Gordo and hooking her arm through his, "is Darya?"

Gordo grinned at her. "A former, um, colleague. In the end, she didn't like me very much."

"The feeling wasn't mutual," BonBon guessed, and Gordo shrugged.

"Hey, BonBon," Murdock said. "You folks staying long?" He noted with a casual glance that the manager had crept toward the door without uncurling himself. A pretty neat trick, the miner thought. He returned his eyes to Gordo so nobody would follow his gaze and notice the poor guy.

"Who knows?" Gordo said, sounding peeved. "Some woman named Omdahl is in charge. She won't tell us anything."

Murdock nodded. "Kaja never was too forthcoming."

"You know her?"

"Our foreman. Or was, before somebody promoted her."

Gordo and BonBon exchanged a puzzled glance.

"Truth," Murdock insisted. "One theory is, this whole mess is a Star-Birght power struggle." He glanced down long enough to see that the manager had made it to the door and was gradually uncurling.

"I don't like the sound of that," BonBon said.

Gordo squinted at Murdock. "Me neither. Are you sure?"

"Would I lie?"

The mercenary chorus chucked. They all would lie, certainly, so they couldn't imagine Murdock wouldn't. But Gordo had grown up in the same colony as Murdock and had been schooled with him, at least to the extent necessary to produce miners. He knew Murdock's fundamental goodness and honesty. Would Murdock lie? Not at all. He could be cagey, but he wouldn't outright lie. "We'd better be on our toes," he told his wife.

"Be ready to bug out," she corrected. "We've been paid half and done half the job. If things turn sour, I say we cut our losses."

Gordo smiled affectionately. "BonBon's our business analyst."

"Smart lady," Murdock agreed. "You take any hits on the way down?"

"A few, nothing much. The landing was rougher than I thought. There's debris scattered all over the place, like something exploded out there. Some of it's flying around in low orbit."

"Something did. A theater fountain. Big mess."

BonBon choked back a laugh. "A theater fountain?"

"With pink water. Took out the whole structure." He nodded at Gordo. "Need any help with repairs? My guys are top notch mechanics."

"So are mine, ol' buddy."

"But yours are occupied." He looked around, wondering just how they were occupied. At the moment, they were eavesdropping and not watching the manager, who had quietly opened the door and slipped out. As the fellow's hindmost foot vanished and the door gently closed, Murdock added, "Keeping order."

They all nodded agreement and looked hopefully at Gordo for confirmation.

"It wouldn't hurt," BonBon said.

Gordo considered her for a moment. "I guess. But just check for exterior damage. Nobody boards any of our ships without my say so. We run our own diagnostics."

"You got it," Murdock agreed. Negotiations concluded, the men shook on it. Murdock bid everyone farewell and lumbered back the way he had come.

Now for the hard part.

Comfortably ensconced in his faux forest office, Artemis Worthington kept tabs on the reports flooding in from TDY-41093-RRP. An endlessly entertaining stream of hysterics, pleas, gripes, and invectives paraded before his eyes as everyone from managers to custodial staff begged for help and, when no help came, lambasted the do-nothing imbeciles comprising the security staff, top management, and board of directors.

Serves them right, Worthington thought. Mining colonies had such a simple job: extract the goodies, keep costs down, and make company owners richer, richer, richer. And they couldn't even do that right. Lifters and theaters and who knew what else blowing up left and right, draining funds, slowing production, not in the least enriching anybody. It was about time a few heads got thunked down there. Besides, after this Worthington would control everything. He would be a hero. Best of all, nobody would ever again dare criticize as much as his wardrobe, knowing he could call in a mercenary strike to settle the matter.

An incoming message from General Omdahl put these happy thoughts on hold. Omdahl was the only person Worthington would speak with right now, and she wouldn't call unless a problem had reared its ugly head. Ensuring the connection was encrypted, he answered. "What is it, General?"

"I've received a small request."

That didn't sound too problematic. "So deny it."

"Your name came up in connection with it."

That did sound like a problem. "How?"

"Roberto Maccarone . . ."

"*What?*" Worthington didn't need details. "Lock him in his ship. Blow it up if he comes out or looks out or thinks about coming out. On second thought, blow it up regardless."

"He says he's a board member?" The way Omdahl's voice lifted in query suggested blowing up a board member might not be prudent.

Worthington drummed his fingers on the desk. "General. You are a general because..." He let it hang there, knowing she'd understand.

"I'm your stooge," she said miserably.

"You cease being a general when..."

"You say so."

"Maccarone's position is..."

"The same as mine," Omdahl replied. "I get it."

"Good girl." He offered that as a verbal pat on the head and piece of candy. He enjoyed taking that tone with inferiors, which included most everyone in the universe.

"He wants to know about their performance. It was scheduled—"

"Do you recall roughly what you're supposed to be doing?"

Omdahl didn't reply. Of course she recalled.

"Does that operation involve screeching sopranos?"

Nor did she reply to that.

"Exactly," Worthington said. "Keep Maccarone out of the way. I don't care how." A strange noise rippled in the background, as though several people were whispering. "Are you alone?"

"My guards are here," Omdahl told him.

"If they hear any of this, shoot them."

"They won't," she assured him. "Why is Maccarone such a problem?"

Worthington didn't like inquisitive minions. Omdahl ought to know better. "He's not a problem, just an irritant. Presumably we're done here."

"Yeah. Everything else is amazingly great."

Worthington cut the connection without further ado then spent the next fifteen minutes worrying over the background noise. Somebody had been with her, possibly Maccarone himself. If it had been him, he deserved to hear the putdowns. But if someone else had been there?

It was high time he had Omdahl watched.

Although, he had no idea what altitude had to do with the passage of time.

Mild pandemonium erupted among the mercenaries when they realized their captive had escaped. Irritated, Gordo dispatched the gang to retrieve him. He nearly blamed himself for it; Murdock's appearance had distracted him. Then again, a dozen other guys had been right there, any one of whom might have bothered to check on the prisoner from time to time. So really it wasn't his fault, was it?

BonBon assured him that it wasn't. "It's this whole operation. It's rotten to the core."

"What core?"

"The core of the operation."

"That's me," he protested.

BonBon's look wasn't far removed from that reserved for people who questioned her name. "Not this time."

"Well it sure isn't General Omdahl." Gordo made a face of his own.

"Of course not. She's taking orders from higher up."

"StarBright board, she said."

"She's lying."

"How do you know?"

They were sitting at the table now, seated next to each other, the only ones in the room. BonBon leaned into Gordo and smiled wearily. "Woman's intuition."

He grinned and put his arm around her shoulders. "If you say so, babe."

"I say so."

She hadn't liked this business from the start. It wasn't their style, blasting defenseless mining colonies, klonking corporate executives on the head. She didn't mind fighting, but there was neither honor nor sport in subduing the helpless. Other mercenaries didn't understand BonBon's sympathy for the weak, but Gordo respected her for it, even if he did have to put on a show for the gang sometimes.

"Who do you think it is, then?" Gordo asked.

She shrugged. "A particular board member, probably. It smells like a power struggle to me."

"With us in the middle, huh?"

"Yep."

Gordo stroked her hair. "You want out?"

She nodded.

"I got a better idea."

BonBon rolled her eyes toward him. "Uh oh."

"You know it, babe."

She closed her eyes and leaned further into him. "Well," she said. "You're the boss."

They listened to the recording three times, and with each repetition Pauli noted that Omdahl's expression darkened. She must really hate Worthington, he thought. Oddly, Maccarone seemed impassive, as though nothing Worthington had said upset him in the least. Both of them ought to be at his throat. Grateful for his invisibility, Pauli held very still and made no contribution to the discussion, which was easy since no conversation had yet broken out.

Neither of his companions asked for a fourth repetition, so he didn't provide one. He simply waited, pretending to be a tiny rock sitting far enough away to not be kicked should anyone assault the ground with their boots.

"He didn't tell us anything," Omdahl finally groused.

"He admitted to being in charge of us," Maccarone told her evenly. "That's something."

"It's not enough. What's he after? What does he get from this stunt? This little ice ball isn't worth that much."

Pauli suddenly remembered what Froebisher had said. He didn't repeat it, but apparently his expression said something, because Omdahl gave him a severe eyeballing and Maccarone studied his face thoughtfully. He sank down in his chair. Alas, that couldn't render him invisible.

"Let's have it," Omdahl suggested, anything but gently.

He shook his head.

"Don't shake your head at me."

He stopped shaking his head, but then the rest of him shook instead.

Omdahl rose and approached like she just might assist with the shaking. "What do you know? You work for Froebisher. You must know something."

Pauli wished she hadn't been so logical. Denials lost their power in the face of reason. "A hero," he said miserably.

"Not remotely."

"Not me."

"Worthington?" Omdahl asked.

"Yeah."

Maccarone rubbed his chin thoughtfully. "For putting down a rebellion that doesn't exist."

"Yeah," Pauli admitted. "A hero. With an army."

"That doesn't mean—" Omdahl began but then looked worried. "Or maybe it does."

"It does," Maccarone assured her. "The man has no scruples."

"So what good are recordings? Nobody would lift a finger even if he ordered the whole colony obliterated."

For a moment, Pauli thought he was going to pass out. Obliteration hadn't figured into his plans, nor would tranquilizers do much good should matters come to that. He could see fragments of ice and metal and people tumbling through space, disassociated from each other in a blinding flash triggered by a single word from that maniac. Some of the people fragments would be his, too, a state he couldn't comprehend except to be sure that arriving in said state would be unpleasant.

"I'm gonna hurl," he mumbled.

"Don't even think it," Omdahl warned.

"I agree," Maccarone said. "About the recordings, I mean. Well, about not hurling, too, but the recordings where what I meant."

Miraculously, that made the feeling go away. Pauli blinked at Maccarone, confused.

"So what's plan B?" Omdahl asked. "I sure don't have one. I didn't even have a plan A except do what I'd been told and try to limit the damage."

Maccarone pondered for a time, then turned a smile on Omdahl. It wasn't his usual everything-is-beautiful smile. It was somehow crooked, wicked, maybe even savage. Where had he learned to do that? Pauli could hardly wait to find out what it meant.

On second thought, yes, he could.

"Here's plan B," Maccarone told them.

Damn, Pauli thought.

"We take Worthington's toys away from him."

"Toys?" From Omdahl's tone, plan B ranked among the stupidest ideas she'd ever heard.

"Toys."

"What toys? He's a grown man."

"Every grown man has toys," Maccarone assured her. "I have an opera company, for example. Singers, musicians, stage props, instruments." A cloud passed over his face. "No marimbas, thank God."

"Get to the point, already!"

"Worthington has mercenaries."

Pauli tried not to gape, but Omdahl did, so he gave in and indulged.

"You're out of your mind!" Omdahl snapped. "You wouldn't stand a chance!"

"True." Maccarone's dark smile returned. "But you would."

"Me?"

"You. General."

Pauli suddenly understood. Hope returned. He wouldn't be blown to smithereens after all!

Omdahl turned to throttle Maccarone, but then she got it, too. "Ah," she breathed. "Maybe you're not a dunce after all. Yes. I like that idea."

Worthington, Pauli thought, was in for a rude shock.

Arne Slocum designed a neat, compact, even pretty little package that sparkled in the sun—or would have had there been sufficient sun to make anything sparkle. A miner could cradle the device in the palm of the hand. Murdock might cradle several. Although heavy for its size, it weighed no more than a mini watermelon—the little seedless kind that take the adventure out of eating watermelon. In this gravity, mini watermelons didn't weigh so much, so a sturdy miner like Pasternak—maybe not Tambe, but certainly Pasternak—could carry ten or twelve in a backpack, no problem.

They set to work building the devices and in no time had one for each mercenary ship plus several extras, just in case.

"Just in case what?" Tambe asked Slocum.

"You see," Slocum replied, carefully placing the cover on the last unit and locking it down, "the explosives are kind of touchy. If one goes off, it will take out the entire backpack. So you'll need more than one backpack."

Tambe's eyes grew a couple of sizes. "What about the back that's packing the pack?"

"That's what morgues are for."

"Er," Tambe remarked.

Pasternak put an arm around him and pulled him roughly to her side. "Don't worry kid. Explosives respect me. They won't dare go off when I'm around."

He could almost believe that.

Slocum packed up the last unit. "All set."

Murdock hefted one of the backpacks and slipped it on. "Ready?" he asked.

Pasternak followed suit and adjusted the straps. "Ready."

"Er," Tambe said, but he donned the last pack with only twenty three seconds of hesitation. Twenty-six at most.

Murdock led the way to the lifter, up to the surface, and into the staging area just inside the airlock. There they gingerly removed the backpacks and stuffed themselves into pressure suits. After checking oxygen supplies and refitting the backpacks, they each strapped on a toolkit belt and entered the airlock. Murdock locked the inner door and pushed the big red button that depressurized the room. When the exterior door slid open, they stepped out onto the surface.

Walking in TDY-41093-RRP's feeble gravity challenged the most skilled explorers. One careless stomp could catapult a person half a mile. Every step had to be placed just so—especially, Tambe thought, when carrying explosives on one's back. The trio didn't so much walk as shuffle the half kilometer across the tarmac to the cluster of black ships lurking in the dim daylight. Overhead, the universe blazed in the airless sky.

Murdock directed Pasternak to a cluster of ships on the right and Tambe to those on the left. He took the middle group himself. Dispersing to their appointed victims, the miners nestled each unit against the hull of a ship, activated the electromagnet, and carefully released it, ready to catch the device should the magnet fail. Everything worked perfectly.

As they placed devices of destruction, they checked for prior damage. Not much turned up. A couple ships needed small repairs. Murdock would dispatch a crew to handle those later, after the EMP worked its mayhem. Tambe found it an ironic plan: bust ships before fixing what they hadn't busted.

It took them no more than an hour to finish the job, then with a huge sigh of relief—at least on Tambe's part—they made their way back to the airlock. Safely in atmosphere again, they stowed their gear and returned below.

The rest lay in Slocum's expert hands.

After rounding up all of his troops and dispatching them to their ships, Gordo quickly and decisively led BonBon by the hand to the executive office General Omdahl had misappropriated. Magnetic boots clanking severely as they went, they kept up a quick pace until halting before her desk. Gordo set his face in an immovable display of determination. BonBon looked rather like she was pondering where to go for dinner.

"Oh, good," Omdahl said, looking up from her computer display. "We need to talk."

Gordo did his best to hide his surprise. But it no longer mattered what Omdahl wanted. He knew what he wanted and knew that nothing in the entire universe could deflect him from his purpose. "We're leaving," he said.

Carefully, Omdahl leaned back and placed her left leg up on the desk. Perfectly balanced, she smirked at him. "Yeah?"

Nothing in the entire universe, he reminded himself while trying not to look where he suspected she wanted him to look.

BonBon did look, then rolled her eyes and snorted. "If he wants that, honey, he's got me."

The guards shifted their weapons, once again suspicious that somebody had messed with their boss's image.

"Yeah," Gordo insisted, returning to the original subject. "We figure there's greener pastures."

Omdahl's smirk drooped. "Greener what?"

"Pastures."

"Pastures in space?"

"It's an expression," BonBon told her.

"Well it's a stupid one."

"Forget it," Gordo snapped. Wherever the conversation had wandered off to, he wanted it back on course pronto. "We're done with petty crime. Time for a big score."

Omdahl regarded him thoughtfully. "That's exactly what I was thinking."

"It was?"

"Yep."

"But..." This wasn't fair. Gordo wanted the big score for himself, not to share with Omdahl. He'd worked it out himself, too. Instead of attacking lucreless icebergs in space, they'd take their game straight to the treasure trove: Territory Headquarters. Everything StarBright held dear—its money, its money, and especially its money—lay exposed. Unprotected. No force existed capable of repelling the black ships of the mercenaries. Having formulated such a brilliant plan, he wondered why he'd never thought of attacking it before. The answer was simple. Mercenaries were Artemis Worthington's dogs, and Worthington had thrown sufficient bones to keep his dogs at bay. But even he valued himself more than his money. The time for biting the hand that fed them had come.

But why was Omdahl thinking the same thing? He hated to ask, but he had to. "Why are you thinking the same thing?"

"What are we getting here? Scraps and head thunking practice. It gets old fast, no?"

"So what's your plan?" Gordo figured it wasn't anywhere near as grand as his own. Saying no would be a cinch. Whatever a cinch was.

Before she could answer, a new voice intruded. "Excuse me, General."

Gordo and BonBon turned. Omdahl cast her weary eyes upon the newcomer. A petite young woman with jet black skin and lush curls of blue, orange, red, and silver hair stood in the doorway. Subtle red stripes circled her crisp yellow and green pant suit at random intervals. The outfit nearly made her glow. Several gold and silver devices were pinned to her lapels and cuffs, indicating that she was ready for any data-related task that might arise.

"Who the hell are you?" Omdahl asked.

"I'm your new minder." The woman briskly crossed the space to Omdahl's desk and stuck out her hand. "Miranda Miranda. Most people just call me Miranda."

"I'd call you something else."

"That would be unwise." Miranda dropped her hand, not at all bothered by Omdahl's lack of courtesy. "Mr. Worthington sent me. He expects your cooperation."

"Want me to blow her away?" Gordo asked in all seriousness.

"I have guards for that." Omdahl directed a cool smile at Miranda. The guards readied their weapons, just in case this wasn't a drill.

"Oh, calm down, you two" BonBon said. "Miranda's just doing her job."

"Thank you ma'am," Miranda said.

"BonBon," BonBon offered, if not exactly with enthusiasm.

"Of course, BonBon," Miranda replied.

BonBon nearly glowed. "Thank *you*."

Gordo mussed up his hair. "We're trying to have a business meeting here!"

"Certainly. Please proceed." Miranda pulled a chair from the side of the room and sat, legs crossed with one magnetic shoe firmly pressed to the floor, fingers of her right hand poised on the device on her left cuff. She watched the others with evident interest.

At first everyone stared at her, but that quickly proved unilluminating, and BonBon finally said, "So anyway."

"We can't talk about this with her there." Gordo tilted his head towards Miranda.

"Oh, go ahead. They'll find out soon enough anyway."

"You have a death wish, you know that?

Omdahl pulled her leg off of the desk. Her boot clanked on the floor. "Bottom line, we're taking our show on the road. Ready your team for take-off."

"And just where are we going?" Gordo asked. This was playing right into his hands. Once Omdahl ordered them into space, they could go wherever he wanted, specifically to Territory HQ.

"Territory HQ."

"What! Wait a minute!"

"It'll be a breeze," Omdahl assured him.

"I know it will! That's *my* plan!"

If that surprised Omdahl, she didn't show it. She rose. "Glad we're on the same page."

"No we're not! This is my plan, and I'm taking charge!"

"You and what army?"

He could do nothing but gape. *He* had the army, not her, and she knew it. Why would she say such an idiotic thing? Unless–

BonBon touched his sleeve. "Babe."

"What?"

"It's all good."

"What's all good?"

"Everything."

Grimacing at BonBon, Gordo puffed himself up to his full impressive size. "Nothing's been good since we started this venture!"

"We're going to Territory HQ. She's going to Territory HQ. Let's just go, okay?" She arched her eyebrows.

"Ooooooh," Gordo breathed. "You're one smart lady, you know that?"

"Uh huh."

"Do you people mind?" Omdahl snapped. "Let's just go."

"Right." Gordo figured it was best not to ask exactly what Omdahl had in mind. If he didn't know, he could do whatever he wanted when they got there. And if at some point she divulged her plans, well, he could ignore her.

After all, he was the one with the army.

Miranda Miranda tapped at her various devices and stood. "I'm all set."

Everyone but BonBon gave her a murderous gaze. BonBon flashed her sweetest smile, the one Gordo knew usually presaged mayhem.

"Everything checks out," Slocum told Murdock. "Ready?"

"When you are," Murdock acknowledged.

At Slocum's right, Pasternak watched with interest. At Slocum's left, Tambe waited for explosions with baited breath. On the array of monitors clustered haphazardly before him in the sink and on the counter, status graphs and images of black ships revealed, if not exactly all, then as much as necessary.

"Right," Slocum said, pressing a key. "T minus sixty seconds and counting."

On Gordo's orders, the mercenaries converged on the airlock, suited up, and trooped out to their ships. They marched in lines as highly organized as one might expect from a flock of headless chickens, joking and laughing over their comm links, meandering crazily in the feeble gravity, sometimes taking little leaps of fifteen or twenty feet to impress each other.

"Cut it out!" Gordo bellowed. "This is a military operation!"

That got a big laugh from the gang.

"Guys," BonBon added sweetly, and everyone suddenly calmed down. Gordo would have lobbed a few rocks at his gang, but that would just fire them off again.

"A well-oiled machine," Miranda Miranda commented.

"Shut up," Gordo affirmed.

Amazingly, the complement arrived more or less together. At the correct ships, even.

T minus twenty eight seconds.

"What are *they* doing there?" Slocum bellowed as he watched the mercenaries clamber on board, oblivious to the devices poised to wreak havoc upon them.

Murdock grinned. "Getting a surprise."

Pasternak nodded gleefully.

Tambe leaned closer. "Explode," he breathed. "Explode!"

Slocum shoved him back.

T minus thirteen seconds.

Outside, the ships were black. Inside they were black, too, aside from the lighting strategically placed to illuminate controls, steps, and other necessary components. On the deck of the control room in the lead ship, Gordo and BonBon oversaw the run-up to the departure of their fleet.

"Systems check," Gordo called.

Having verified information about their own ship, BonBon reported, "Ready."

The owners of the other ships called in, too: "Ready." "Ready." "Ready." Gordo noted General Omdahl shaking her head. It was a good thing, he reflected, that he knew everyone's voice, otherwise he'd have no clue who was ready and who wasn't. They didn't usually coordinate operations this closely, so they'd never worked out protocols or signals or even pleasantries.

"All right, let's be off."

On each of the mercenary ships, someone pushed the button to make them be just that. Power began to build.

T minus four seconds.

"Three," Slocum counted, "Two. One. Zero."

On the screen, nothing happened.

Then nothing else happened.

Finally, some modest blips of light flashed beneath the ships and were gone.

Tambe leaned closer to the monitors, squinting as though that might magnify the image. "Hey."

Slocum pushed him back. "What?"

"Hold on."

"Hold onto what?"

Tambe thumped the top of the monitor with his fist. "Just a second, now."

Slocum pushed his chair back from the sink. "What are you doing, Ajit?"

"That wasn't it, was it?"

"Yes."

"That was *it*?"

"Yes!"

Straightening, Tambe stomped a foot. "I want my money back!"

Pasternak slithered up behind him. She slipped her arms around him and pulled him away from the monitors. "Never mind, kid. I'll show you some *real* fireworks later."

Slocum leaned back, hands locked behind his head. "A job well done."

Pasternak's promise notwithstanding, Tambe didn't give the appearance of agreeing.

On board each of the ships, engines ignited and thrust built for all of three seconds, then for no apparent reason every system on every ship went dead at the same time. The vessels completely failed to take off. Even the lights went out, leaving the black interiors of the black ships very, very black indeed. Gordo tried to examine the walls, the floor, the ceiling, the instrument panels, but in fact he examined nothing because nothing was all he could see.

"Hey," he said.

"Hey," BonBon added, and he felt her hand on his shoulder.

"Hey!" Omdahl snapped.

"Hey what?" somebody boldly snickered, although since nobody could see who it was, it probably hadn't been all that bold.

"Did we lose power?" Gordo asked.

"How should I know?" a voice in the dark replied. "I can't see any-thing!"

"That's probably a good indication," Miranda Miranda opined, as though she knew anything at all about spaceships.

Beyond the viewport, the distant sun cast enough light to reveal that other ships hadn't moved, either. They all sat dead on the tarmac, as dead as Gordo's own.

"All right," he decided. "You guys get back to the base. Scrounge up some portable lighting units. We'll need at least four or five per ship."

"How do we find the airlock?" someone asked.

"You know where the airlock is!"

"Yeah, but—"

"Just go already!"

The control room filled with shuffling feet mixed liberally with mur-mured complaints, then all fell silent. That silence reigned for ten minutes until the feet shuffled back and the owner of at least two of them said, "The airlock won't open."

"Uh-oh," BonBon said with considerable concern.

Uh-oh's right, Gordo mused. With nothing working, the ship's atmo-sphere wasn't being scrubbed. "We'll have to cut our way out," he said.

"You can't cut a hole in my ship," BonBon complained.

"You'd rather suffocate?"

"There must be another way."

"Like what?"

BonBon didn't answer, but he could imagine frustration contorting her face.

"Nothing we can't repair," he assured her. "The miners will help us. Like they did—" An unsavory thought flitted through his brain. "—before."

After a moment, BonBon asked, "You think?" She wasn't inquiring about the likelihood of assistance from Murdock's crew.

"Yeah," Gordo said darkly in the dark. "I think."

And from somewhere in the gloom, Miranda remarked, "That would be a novelty."

Omdahl fumed silently in the dark. So the miners had helped, had they?

Murdock again!

CHAPTER 19

A respectable businessman like Roberto Maccarone couldn't be caught anywhere near the redirection of a coup against its owner, so he declined to accompany General Omdahl on her little adventure. Not that he'd been invited. Indeed, Omdahl seemed happy to abandon him. Since their plans matched so perfectly, he retired without complaint to the *Ponchielli*, there to await word of success. On board, he found Feng Shui Land contemplating the airlock with murder in his eyes. Why he should want to murder the airlock, Maccarone had no clue. Foot tapping erratically, Land's expression didn't change when Maccarone came into range, except maybe to harden.

"What now?" Maccarone asked.

"Including you, only ninety seven percent of the crew is back on board. But I suppose we can dispense with the rest of them. Let's be on our way."

Increasingly, Maccarone perceived a gap between Land's words and anything sensible about the universe. The poor fellow must be losing his grip. A reasonable response to events of late, Maccarone supposed. Gently, so as not to accelerate Land's downward spiral, he asked, "Where are we going?"

"The mercenaries fled the base. They're probably readying for take-off as we speak. Security forces must have rallied and—"

Maccarone cut him off with an unpretentious shake of the head.

"And—" Land faltered again.

"They haven't fled. They're preparing an assault on Territory HQ."

His grimace fixed unalterably to his face, Land pondered that. "Stupid," he decided, "but fine for our purposes. We can slip away unnoticed."

"Where to?"

"Home!"

"We have no home." Maccarone thought that sounded grand. With a grand sweep of his arms, he expounded. Grandly. "We are wayfarers of the cosmos, spreading good cheer wherever—"

"Oh, shut up! I mean Earth."

That didn't compute at all. Why would anyone aside from Chelsea Liwanu want to go there? There were no new frontiers to conquer on Earth, especially not new operatic frontiers. "The theater—"

"Forget the theater. With your luck, that'll be the first thing the fools demolish."

"Why would they blow up a theater?"

"Because they're morons!"

Maccarone sighed, took Land by the arm, and led him away from the airlock. "General Omdahl has matters well in hand."

Land yanked his arm out of Maccarone's grip. "Well in hand!"

"Sure."

"Matters are never well in hand out here! The Oort Territories are an insane asylum!"

Maccarone wondered why Land found that so disagreeable. The props manager's own flirtation with lunacy—or at least peculiarity—ought to put him right at home. But since it had not, some therapy was in order. "Let me show you something, Feng." He led Land to the entertainment area, a tiny rectangular room jammed full of consoles where crew members could plug into audio, video, virtual surround, or sensory deprivation as suited their tastes. "Earth, ripe for the taking." Maccarone lovingly tapped a console, then motioned Land to it. "Go ahead, give it a try."

"Get me a sledge hammer and I will."

Okay, so placating him might prove difficult. Maccarone leaned on the console. "Trust me, this will all blow over. Kaja gives Worthington the boot, Darya and the kid extract Irvine's remains from the wreckage, Chelsea takes Irvine back to Earth, we get our theater, and everyone lives happily ever after. Simple."

Land almost kicked one of the consoles. "As simple as making a fountain spray pink water without exploding?"

Maccarone searched for a snappy rejoinder, but before he found one, the disembodied voice of the ship's comm officer called him. "Go ahead," he told the ceiling.

"Mr. Worthington for you."

"Right on cue," Land muttered.

Maccarone rubbed his temples. "Have the mercenaries taken off yet?"

"Not yet," the comm officer replied. "It looks like they might have a problem."

"Several," Land agreed.

Maccarone ignored him. "What kind of problem?"

"Their ships all seem to be dead."

"Dead?"

"No power, no communications, no nothing."

Maccarone said no nothing in reply.

Land plopped himself into the seat at one of the consoles and picked at the edge of the screen as though trying to peel it back to reveal its innards. "Don't tell me you've forgotten your lines, Roberto?"

Actually, Maccarone felt like he'd misplaced the whole libretto.

Just then, Artemis Worthington would have talked to anyone on TDY-41093-RRP with one functional eye and a one quarter functional brain. How could the river of information flowing to him transform itself into a dry gulch in mere moments? No data streams, no reports, no video, not even a stupid kid making faces at a security camera. Oh, the cameras still functioned. But they showed only empty corridors and empty offices. Not a face, juvenile or otherwise, in evidence.

"Idiots!" He thumped on his desk. "What are they doing down there?"

A communications panel lit up as though awakened by the abuse. A cheery voice spewed forth: "Roberto Maccarone here."

One idiot located. "I take it from your tone," Worthington grumbled, "that you're oblivious to the whole universe."

"Not at all. I'm here with my properties manager in the *Ponchielli*'s entertainment area, where we were just—"

"Being oblivious."

Maccarone observed a moment of silence. "What can I do for you?"

"Open your eyes, look around, and tell me what you see."

"Entertainment consoles."

Worthington reminded himself that he'd wanted somebody stupid for this job, then questioned why he'd wanted somebody stupid, then scolded himself for being so stupid as to want somebody stupid. "Has martial law been declared?"

"Oh. Yes."

"Has management been arrested?"

"I think so."

"Have any executions taken place?"

Maccarone didn't reply to that one.

"Well?"

"I hope not."

Worthington gazed upward at his pleasant forest ceiling, which completely failed to comfort or relax him. "Where is General Omdahl?"

Maccarone didn't reply to that one, either.

Worthington drummed his fingers on his desk, loudly so Maccarone could hear. *"Well?"*

"I think she and Gordo went to his ship to, er, discuss strategy."

That better not be what it sounds like. "Get over there. Order her to contact me."

A silence nearly long enough to elicit another, "Well?" ensued. Before Worthington could throw him down the well, Maccarone spoke. "I can't. The mercenary ships are dead in the water."

"What water? It's an airless ice cube."

"It's an expression. It means—"

"Never mind! Get me Omdahl!"

"I don't think I can. Their ships have no power. Probably they can't even open the airlocks."

Why did so few truly semi-intelligent life-forms populate his world? Worthington frequently felt like pounding his head on his desk, but seldom had he come so close to doing it. "You didn't find that important enough to report?"

"Didn't think of it."

Stupid is as stupid does, Worthington told himself. *Or is it?* A nasty, fanged and clawed suspicion crept through the back of his mind. Nobody, it suggested, not even Roberto Maccarone, could be that stupid. "All of their ships?"

"Apparently."

"How did that happen?"

Worthington could hear Maccarone shrug in reply. Did the man truly not know? Or did he know all too well?

"Find out. Now. Get back to me ten minutes ago." He wished Maccarone could hear how savagely he cut the connection. But bluster couldn't mask his mounting dread. His future teetered precariously on the brink of a kilometer-high cliff. The slightest puff of wind might plunge him into the abyss. He needed to anchor himself, and he had two rock solid anchors.

Mina Ramsden.

Soumanwolo Jue.

Within moments of his summons, the duo arrived. Ramsden deposited her droopy self into a chair and squirmed to get comfortable. Jue perched on the edge of the chair next to her, ready for action.

Worthington always kept them briefed on operations, so he had only to update them. "Something's wrong. Miranda is incommunicado. Maccarone reports the mercenary ships have lost power. Omdahl and Gordo are trapped on board, allegedly discussing strategy."

Ramsden snorted. Jue flashed a thin smile. "I'll bet," they said simultaneously, then looked at each other, surprised. They sometimes thought the same thing but seldom said it in unison.

"Skip the wagers. Analysis."

Ramsden chewed on a fingernail for a moment. "Gordo is taking over."

Jue shook his head. "Omdahl."

Ramsden shot him a look of droopy disappointment. "He's seduced her. She'll let him call the shots from now on."

"No, Mina. She's seduced him. He's in her power now."

Ramsden snorted again but didn't argue the point. "Either way," she told Worthington, "they aren't following *you* anymore."

He'd reached the same conclusion, but hearing it from Ramsden and seeing Jue nod agreement bolstered his confidence in the assessment. It also made his stomach perform a triple somersault. "And the ships?"

"Gordo wouldn't sabotage his own ships," Jue said. "Omdahl might temporarily disable them until she has his loyalty."

Ramsden undrooped. "Don't be absurd. Omdahl is out of the picture. Someone else is monkeying with the mercenaries. Odds are it's Maccarone."

Worthington's stomach did another flip. "Why?"

"His board position may have gone to his head. He's had a taste of power. If he controlled the mercenaries instead of you—" She shrugged and redrooped.

Worthington wished his stomach would stop the gymnastics. "He doesn't strike me as anywhere near that intelligent." Or had Maccarone played him for a fool the whole time? That thought rankled as much as it unsettled.

"Or the rebels are striking back," Jue suggested.

"There are no rebels," Ramsden reminded him.

"Disgruntled miners, though." Jue nodded to Worthington. "We need more data."

Worthington slammed a fist on his desk. "We can't get any!"

"Sure we can," Ramsden told him. "Go there yourself."

Now Worthington drooped. Ramsden was right. He had spies everywhere, but none both trustworthy and effective. He had no choice. Alas, going there himself would morph the situation into a three-ring circus.

Whatever that was.

Trust among StarBright board members simultaneously soared to an all-time high and sank to an all-time low. That is to say—for the benefit of the mathematically disinclined—its numerical value sat precisely at its default of zero.

Let's put that in practical terms. Each board member kept close tabs on the others. Should one—say, Artemis Worthington—decide to take a little trip somewhere—say, to TDY-41093-RRP—where something interesting— say, a hostile takeover—was in progress, the rest of them quickly learned of it and reacted accordingly—say, by arranging their own trips to the selfsame somewhere.

Thus, Worthington's massively comfortable private shuttle embarked as the lead ship in a flotilla of massively comfortable private shuttles, and the whole comfortable armada voyaged to the uncomfortable little iceberg at a comfortable pace so as not to give the impression that any one of them was so uncomfortable as to want to arrive first. They descended more or less in unison, debarked more or less in unison, and convened a meeting of the board in the executive offices. The agenda? To consider how to achieve whatever goals had brought them here. Problem was, only Worthington knew the nature of those goals, and he wasn't talking.

"Why don't you tell us why we're here, Artemis?" Chairman Santamonica Amarillo suggested. A remarkably young woman surrounded by men and women of considerably greater age, she had her father's hard eyes and dark skin. On her they looked far less intimidating, far more alluring. Perhaps therein reposed the secret to her success. Whereas her father had driven his underlings like a severe if not insane stagecoach driver flogging a team of horses, she piloted them like a space racer guiding a precision ultratech craft. Demons danced in Phoenix Bakersfield Amarillo's eyes. You knew you couldn't escape them, no matter whose side you were on. The scales of justice reflected in Santamonica Amarillo's eyes. So long as you sat in the correct pan, you knew you'd be more or less safe. The only trick was figuring out which pan was which.

Worthington knew better than to vex Amarillo, but he wasn't about to let on that his plans for corporate domination existed, much less that they hung by a thread. *Although*, he reflected, *mentioning the thread business could be a good way to divert attention.* People would embroil themselves in a debate over the meaning of the phrase and quite forget for a time that they had no idea why they'd made this pilgrimage.

Before he could devise an answer, Lena Froebisher came to his aid. "Artemis put down the rebellion among the miners. On our behalf and at great risk to life and limb, he has now come to personally inspect the operation and take the necessary steps to guarantee its continued success." She turned a jaundiced eye on him. "Am I right, Artemis?"

"Precisely." He donned a self-sacrificial expression. It didn't come easy. He just hoped the look would convince.

From the gulps and widened eyes and wringing hands surrounding him, he gathered that the others hadn't dreamed this excursion might involve even the slightest danger to life and limb.

Amarillo, though, didn't flinch. She rated a trio of armed guards to protect her excessively important person. They stood behind her in brilliant gold body armor, heavy assault zap guns in their hands, eyeing everyone and every entrance as though itching for something to blast. "Excellent. Your itinerary?"

Worthington had no itinerary as he still didn't know what the hell was going on down here, but that was something he could fake. "Obviously the details must remain confidential."

Amarillo raised an eyebrow. "Come now, Artemis. This is the board of directors."

"My point exactly. But in brief, I shall verify that base management has been secured, inquire into the status of the miners suspected in the plot, and confer with General Omdahl and the leader of the mercenary forces regarding security arrangements."

Perfectly vague. The other board members nodded agreement and cast suspicious glances about the table. Worthington wished they'd drop the suspicion for once in their lives and play along. Only Froebisher seemed at ease. He ought to round the rest of them up and have them incarcerated along with the local managers.

"We may as well accompany you," Amarillo decided. "We all need to be in the loop."

Froebisher's eyes widened. "You must be joking, Santamonica. Fifteen of us trooping around the base? We'd look like a bunch of clowns. Not to mention there may still be rebels on the loose. What a tempting target we'd be! And you the only one with protection." She smiled as though imagining the entire board wiped out in a single stroke.

The others gaped and gasped and pushed back from the table, but Amarillo directed her steely gaze at Froebisher. The women locked eyes. Neither backed down. Everyone held their breaths, even Worthington. He had to admit, Froebisher seemed to be fully in his court now, although he had no idea why.

Amarillo didn't give in. She did an end run instead. "I suppose you're right. But somebody should go with Artemis, just the same."

"Oh, I don't think I need–" Worthington began in his most reasonable voice.

"Let's not play games. We all know you're up to something. If our places were exchanged, I certainly would be up to something. That goes for all of us." Amarillo's eyes dared anyone to deny it. Nobody could. When you're right, you're right. "I want you where I can see you."

"Well."

"Two of us should suffice for that," Froebisher suggested, and everyone raised their hands to volunteer. "But whoever it is should be willing to embrace the considerable danger."

All hands dropped suddenly.

"I'll go," Amarillo said. "As you pointed out, Lena, I have protection." She nodded back at her guards, who stood a bit taller.

"So will I." Froebisher searched the faces of the others as though disappointed. "Given the lack of volunteers."

"The rest of us should stay here," a man near the far end of the table bravely suggested in a quavering voice.

"Absolutely," Froebisher told him. "Where it's safe." She flashed Amarillo a knowing glance, then passed one surreptitiously to Worthington.

"Fine," Amarillo decided.

What, Worthington wondered, *is she suggesting?* She clearly wanted the board out of the way, but there had to be more. If only he could keep Amarillo out of the way. Maybe he could arrange her capture by the rebels. Better, maybe he could arrange the capture of...

...the whole board.

Who would be sitting right here.

Unguarded.

Lena, he thought with wicked glee, *you're a genius.*

"The *suits* don't work?" Darkness held Gordo in its disconcerting grasp. Not just physical darkness. Intellectual, emotional, and spiritual darkness, too. How could the suits not work?

"Nope," whoever it was replied in the dark.

"The cutting torch?"

"Nope."

"Why the hell not?"

BonBon touched his arm to calm him. "Computers."

Calm failed to wash over him. "Whaddaya mean, computers?"

"Computer chips. They're everywhere. They control suit pressurization, oxygen flow, and temperature. They regulate fuel in the torch for maximum efficiency. Even the galley toaster has a chip in it."

Gordo considered that. "So you're saying that whatever knocked out ship's systems knocked out everything electronic."

"Yes."

"You're fortunate," Miranda Miranda added from somewhere in the great dark. "All my equipment is dead in the water, too. Now I can't send Mr. Worthington my report on your so-called plans. Or my professional assessment of your competency."

"Dead in what water?" someone asked. "Water didn't kill the electronics. The water dispensers don't work, either."

Gordo cracked his knuckles for dramatic effect. "Good thing I can't see either one of you." But smart-mouthed minders and minions didn't much concern him right now. "Airlocks, pressure suits, water dispensers. Toasters. Everything. You're saying we're trapped in here until we suffocate."

BonBon put her arms around him in the dark and leaned on his shoulder. "Yes."

Deep below the surface, safe within spy headquarters, a.k.a. the abandoned restroom, Josh Murdock, Arne Slocum, Darya Pasternak, and Ajit Tambe concluded a similar discussion. They'd noted how the mercenaries didn't rampage off of their ships upon discovering they were dead in the wa—that is, dead in the vacuum of space, which amounted to the same thing except without much hope for breathing.

Actually, Tambe wasn't party to that discussion. Still miffed about the lack of explosions, he sat in a corner, sulking. But the other three were, and once they'd identified the unintended consequences of their actions, Murdock summed up the situation for them.

"Oops."

CHAPTER 20

Miners didn't often face serious moral dilemmas. Murdock found himself staring down several at one time, and unlike the humans who circulated through his sphere, abstracts such as moral dilemmas didn't much care that he resembled a ferocious carnivore. Stuffed into the cramped room with Pasternak, Tambe, Slocum, nonfunctional plumbing, and an electronic menagerie doggedly collecting intelligence on the goings-on far above their heads, Murdock chewed his thumb and considered each in turn.

First and foremost, they'd trapped a gang of mercenaries inside dead spaceships on landing pads in the vacuum of space. Asphyxiation loomed large in said gang's future. Not good.

Second, most of the managerial staff on TDY-41093-RRP had been locked up by the mercenaries. Only the mercenaries could release them. Said staff had air enough for the nonce, but food and water would soon become a problem. Not good, either.

Third, the entire StarBright board of directors had burst upon the scene to find the base largely devoid of personnel. What they were up to wasn't clear, but they presented a tempting target. Slocum's spy gear showed that three board members had wandered off with the only guards in their company, leaving the rest huddling defenseless in a conference room. Thoughts of kidnapping and ransom danced in Murdock's head. Kidnapping would be easy, but nobody remained to pay whatever ransom he demanded. Not helpful.

Last, Murdock considered Roberto Maccarone, who seemed to be playing all sides against each other while staying largely out of view. What was he up to? Rationally, he should be bound and gagged until Murdock could drain the swamp—not that any swamps existed here—but then what would become of the opera? It would be a shame to jeopardize future performances. Opera wasn't half bad.

Feeling a distinct need for consultation, not to mention a growing curiosity about how swamps were drained, he summarized these points for his crew, ticking them off on his massive fingers. "Trapped mercenaries. Trapped managers. Vulnerable board members. Maccarone."

"Blow them all up," Tambe said, still irritated over the lack of fireworks.

Pasternak flashed him an irritated grimace. "Oh, grow up, kid. Not everything in life is about explosions."

"None of it is so far." He shuffled over to the rest of the gang and stood there glowering.

"Can't save the managers ourselves," Murdock mused. "Mercenaries have the cell door codes."

"Can't kidnap the board with mercenaries and managers running around," Pasternak added.

"Can't watch opera without Maccarone."

"Can't do much else with him."

"Can't we," Tambe complained, "blow something up for real?"

Murdock covered Tambe's slender shoulder with his meaty hand and pushed, forcing the kid to slump into a nearby chair. Tambe had to snag the chair and shove it under himself on the way down. "Sorry, kid. Lives are at stake."

Tambe looked up, for once making the connection between bombs and death. "I don't want to kill anyone. I just want to blow something up."

Murdock's twisted grin belied his thoughts: *Ajit's not been right in the head lately. Must be Darya's fault.* "I know, kid. Gordo and BonBon, their folks, and everyone they locked up are in danger. Gotta do something about that first. Blowing things up can wait."

"Oh." Tambe did a fair imitation of a scolded puppy. "Well, can't we maybe blow a few holes in the hulls of their ships to let them out?"

"They don't have working suits," Slocum grumbled. He turned from his console and gave everyone in the vicinity a look of rebuke. Especially Pasternak. "I told you this wasn't smart." The rebuke slid off of her and onto Murdock. "I told her it wasn't smart."

Murdock stroked his beard thoughtfully. The hard part, he knew, would be getting the mercenaries off their ships. Once they were free, the staff could be released. "Let's start simple. They need spacesuits."

"Which we have," Pasternak agreed. "How do we deliver them?"

Murdock turned to Slocum. "Got any ship schematics? They're supposed to be on file, yeah?"

"Oh, yeah," Slocum replied. "And these guys always follow the rules, of course." He turned back to his equipment. He pounded commands into it and studied displays and pounded some more and studied some more and pounded a few more times and finally said, "This isn't exactly it, but it's a vessel similar to Gordo's. What are you looking for?"

"Emergency airlock. Manually operated."

"Even if they have one, they won't know how to find it. Nobody uses those anymore." But Slocum navigated through the schematics anyway until locating what he was looking for. "Here we are. Just behind the caudal transceiver package on the port side. It can be opened from both exterior and interior." He swiveled about on his chair, still dubious. "Assuming their ships actually have them."

Murdock wasn't about to let Slocum's negativity derail him. "We'll soon know."

Pasternak put up a hand. "Hold on, Josh. We should do things in order. Let's rescue Gordo and BonBon. Not the rest of them." Murdock was about to object, but Pasternak plowed on without giving him the space. "We take them and their guns to the board and make our demands. Once we get what we want, we release everyone else."

"And what, precisely," Slocum asked, "are our so-called demands?"

Now that, Murdock thought, *is a problem*. They'd spent so long being irked at just about everything that they'd never actually formulated a list of demands.

"Explosions," Tambe muttered under his breath. Everyone rolled their eyes. He jumped up and stomped a foot. "I mean it! Our lives are as dull as dish water!"

Murdock arched an eyebrow. "What's dish water?"

"I don't know! It doesn't matter! Our lives are dull, that's all. Look at our rooms, our work areas, our coveralls, our everything!" He pointed at one of Slocum's monitors, where the StarBright board minus three huddled around a conference table, talking in subdued tones. "Everyone gets to wear all the colors of the universe. Everyone gets to make the great dark as bright as a sunny day on Earth. Everyone but us. We're nothing. We're the ice we mine. No, that's got some sparkle. We're the soot in the ice." He flopped back into the chair. "They all get explosions. Why can't *we* have explosions, too?"

Wide-eyed, Slocum stared at Tambe as though he'd discovered a fascinating new life form hiding under his left boot. Murdock's face revealed nothing, as usual, but he nodded and stroked his beard thoughtfully.

Pasternak sidled up to Tambe and put a hand on his shoulder. "You're right."

Tambe looked up in surprise. "I am?"

"Yeah, kid. You are. That's exactly it. What do you say, Josh?"

Murdock wasn't sure how it would play, but he couldn't argue with the sentiment. He got his fireworks from sparring with Kaja Omdahl. Slocum got his from gizmos and gadgets. Everyone had their way of coping with the grayness of life in the mines and the frigid black of the Oort Territories. Even the managers and maybe the board of directors itself. They might understand, after all.

"Sure," he decided. "Explosions it is."

Having spent so many years in the terrifying trenches of artistic warfare, Roberto Maccarone held his own strategic acumen in high regard. Still, the goings on presently going on flummoxed him, and he had no qualms about saying so.

"I'm flummoxed," he told Feng Shui Land.

"I'm flabbergast." Land sounded hardly flabbergast at all.

It didn't matter. Maccarone had received word that the entire Star-Bright board of directors had descended upon TDY-41093-RRP and that three of them, Artemis Worthington among them, were now wandering aimlessly through the facility. The rest, he'd been told, were huddled in a conference room in the administration center. So Maccarone knew what he had to do. "Come on." He motioned Land out of the entertainment area. Far from budging, Land just stared at him. "No time to lose," Maccarone added. Still Land didn't budge. "What?"

"Given your general state of cluelessness, where could you possibly be going?"

"Not me. We. We're going to see the StarBright board."

"Why? Are they performing the ballet of dead nuns from *Robert le Diable*?"

Poor fellow, Macarrone thought. *He's really off the deep end now*. Then he wondered what a deep end was before deciding it wasn't worth wondering about. "Just come on." Without looking back, he set course for the airlock. Once he got there, he glanced back and found to his amazement that Land actually had followed him, albeit looking thoroughly miserable. Maccarone led onward, using the navigation lines to find his way to the administrative center, and poked around until stumbling upon his target: a room full of annoyed executives arguing among themselves about the goings on, although they actually didn't know what was going on.

Pleased to find that he wasn't the only flummoxed one, Maccarone cleared his throat and interrupted with a powerful pronouncement: "Excuse me?"

Silence fell. Land grumbled some inaudible something.

An ancient scarecrow of a man stood and poured disdain over Maccarone and Land. "Who are you?"

"Roberto Maccarone. I have some news for you."

"Worthington's yes-man," someone in the back snorted, and the others chattered loud enough to be heard but not loud enough to be understood.

"What's he up to?" The time-worn one approached Maccarone slowly, seemingly growing taller with each step. He tugged his gold and purple lapels and thrust his chin upward so he could look down his pointy nose at Maccarone.

"Subterfuge."

The others snickered. "Obviously. What exactly?

Maccarone trotted out his most amiable smile, "Who do I have the pleasure of addressing?"

"If you came to board meetings, you'd know. Vanderbilt Morgan Snodgrass, CFO." Snodgrass tugged at his lapels again and grew even taller. "Answer the question."

Maccarone wondered just how tall Snodgrass could get. "Something so diabolic that it's probably illegal. You should have him arrested."

"Specify."

"He's manufactured a rebellion among the miners and brought in mercenaries to crush it. He hopes you'll think he's a hero."

Suspicion filled every eye in the room. Well, not every eye. Not Maccarone's, of course. And not Land's. Irritation filled his eyes. As usual.

Snodgrass turned, took a step toward the table, and addressed the gathering. "Clearly there *is* a rebellion. Things have blown up. Theaters, even. It's a wonder nobody was killed."

"No," Maccarone began, but got no further.

Spinning on his heel so rapidly it was a wonder he didn't fall on his face, Snodgrass jabbed a bony finger at Maccarone. "We all reviewed the evidence. We voted for this police action. You voted for it, too."

"That was before I understood Ar, er, Mr. Worthington's plan. I've done some independent research. There is no rebellion. Just things being pushed off cliffs."

Land tugged on Maccarone's sleeve. "That doesn't make sense," he whispered.

"Sure it does," Maccarone whispered back.

Amazingly, Snodgrass's chin pointed even higher and he looked even more sharply down his sharp nose at Maccarone. "Young man, theaters can't be pushed off cliffs."

"Even if they could be," someone in the back said, "they wouldn't explode."

"That's right," another chimed in. "They'd sort of smash."

"It's an—" Maccarone began.

"In fact," Snodgrass told him, "in the absence of a landslide, a theater wouldn't budge at all."

"A sinkhole, maybe?" yet another board member opined. "I don't know if they have sinkholes here, but I seem to recall an incident about a decade ago on Titan where a sinkhole swallowed the pizza concession at a methane processing facility."

Maccarone tried again and got the whole thing out before being interrupted: "It's an expression."

Land tugged on his sleeve. "It's a stupid expression," he whispered

"Is not," Maccarone whispered back.

Snodgrass turned to the guy who had suggested sinkholes. "Sinkholes don't spit fire and spew debris all over the place."

"But they make theaters move, sort of like falling off a cliff does."

"The presented evidence dealt with explosions, not sinkholes!"

"Enough!" Maccarone's bellow shocked everyone to silence, including himself. It took him a moment to find his original thought. "Worthington wants control of the company. That's all that matters."

None of them could argue with that, at least. Except that Snodgrass did. "Where is your evidence?"

"With General Omdahl."

"And where is she?"

Land tugged on his sleeve. "It won't work," he muttered.

"Shut up," Maccarone snapped.

Snodgrass looked offended. "I beg your pardon?

"Not you." Maccarone jabbed his thumb at Land. "Him."

"And who is he?"

Maccarone nearly introduced Land as Mr. Fang, but stopped himself just in time. "Nobody."

"Thanks," Land grumbled.

"Shut up," Maccarone repeated. "General Omdahl is trapped on a mercenary spaceship."

"What do you mean trapped?"

"I mean trapped. The mercenary ships have lost power. Nobody can get out."

"How convenient." An ironic smile stretched across Snodgrass's face. "Why should we believe you?"

Now that was an unfair question. Why *shouldn't* they believe him? "Because I'm an artist. I live for truth."

Land smacked his hand against his forehead and muttered something unintelligible.

At this point, Maccarone might have had the upper hand—which wasn't the same as the hand slapping Land's forehead, of course—but if so it did him no good. Before the slap concluded, a small hoard of armed miscreants burst into the room and totally fouled up his clever plan.

Heavy wrench in hand, Murdock rapped the standard rescue code on the hull of Gordo's ship: *rap rap rap* [*pause*] *rap rap* [*pause*] *rap rap rap rap* [*pause*] *rap*. The shock of each blow reverberated soundlessly through his pressure suit. He waited half a minute, repeated the sequence, waited, repeated. The crew couldn't signal back, but they would know help was just outside the emergency airlock. Motioning Pasternak forward, he stood aside while she manually cycled the hatch open, then followed her in. Tabme and Slocum brought up the rear, each lugging a bulky equipment bag that weighed hardly anything in the feeble gravity.

Their helmet lights illuminated the tiny compartment, a sterile gray space barely large enough for the four of them. Pasternak closed the outer hatch and manually opened the vents. Air from within the ship flooded the compartment. She watched the blinking red light on the oxygen sensor strapped to her wrist. In a moment it turned green, and she opened the interior hatch.

Although the rescuers couldn't hear it inside their suits, the conglomeration of mercenaries gathered before them, suddenly blinded by the headlamps, clearly cursed the light. The miners fumbled their way out of their helmets and aimed the beams in a less painful direction.

"Murdock!" Gordo pushed forward and pounded Murdock on the back. "About time you showed up!"

Murdock grinned. "Your fault. Everything's gone to hell since you got here."

"That's what I do best."

Omdahl pushed forward. "Murdock? Just our luck."

Murdock grinned at her. "Hey boss. I hear you got a promotion."

"You'd better not forget it."

BonBon insinuated herself into the reunion. "You got anything useful in there?" She nodded to the bags Tambe and Solcum had dropped on the floor.

Murdock shoved one of the bags toward her with his foot. "Lights, emergency power packs to get your air scrubbers going, food and water. Also two pressure suits."

The mercenaries grumbled.

"We got more waiting. We couldn't bring more than two this trip out."

"That's fine," Gordo narrowed his eyes at his crew and the rumbling melted into muttering, then evaporated. "I'll send a couple guys to help with the next load."

Murdock motioned Gordo aside with a wave of his hand. "Just you and BonBon," he whispered.

Gordo glanced back at the others. "What're you up to, Murdock? Me and BonBon figure this was your doing."

Murdock shrugged, but didn't deny it. "Need your help with a problem."

Gordo glanced back again. The gang of thugs looked edgy. Omdahl looked ready to kill. "Not sure that's a good idea."

"Won't take long. Besides, I took care of your ships, yeah?" Murdock figured it wasn't a lie. He certainly had taken care of them.

The mercenary leader mulled that over. "Okay. But it better not take long."

"Scout's honor."

"Who's honor?

"Scout's."

"Who's Scout?"

"Who cares? Old expression. Let's go."

Gordo shook his head and turned to his men. "BonBon and I will help bring in the next load. We'll try to get enough suits for everyone. Just sit tight."

"I'm going with you," Omdahl commanded. "BonBon can stay here."

Murdock smiled easily. "General has to stay with her ship, right?"

Ignoring them, Gordo and BonBon began to suit up.

"That's the captain, which I'm not. *He* is." She jabbed a finger in Gordo's direction. "Anyway, somebody needs to keep an eye on you."

"I'll do it," BonBon assured her. "Josh knows better than to mess with me."

"Pardon the interruption," a completely different woman interrupted. She slipped from concealment behind the mercenaries. Though far below the level of Murdock's eyes, she met his impassive gaze with unyielding determination. "Your fascinating dispute notwithstanding, I require one of those pressure suits."

Murdock smiled easily at her. "That so?"

"Completely so. I'm Miranda Miranda. Mr. Worthington sent me here to monitor the progress of the operation. My equipment was affected by whatever caused the ship to lose power. As I've been unable to report back to Mr. Worthington, I require the base's transmission facilities to—"

Murdock held up his massive hand. "Sorry, no can do."

"You'd better do."

"Or what?" Murdock asked pleasantly. "I'm already on everyone's naughty list. General Ohmdal's for sure, Gordo's probably, BonBon's maybe. I'll be offending Mr. Worthington next. Don't need your help for that."

Miranda probably had never encountered anyone so totally oblivious to the might of the StarBright board. She stared at Murdock, comebackless.

"Let's go," Murdock said, motioning to Gordo and BonBon, and after that nobody from General Omdahl down had room to object.

Step one proved easy: Worthington verified that base management had been secured. He found every last one of the bumbling fools, from the head honcho to the lowest administrative assistant, locked in overcrowded holding cells in the detention facility, clamoring and pleading for release. Lena Froebisher patted one of the massive steel doors and silently approved of the arrangement. Best this gang wasn't underfoot while she sorted out Worthington's mess.

Chairman Amarillo appeared less convinced. "Shouldn't we let them out?" she asked nobody in particular.

Behind the grate covering the door's tiny window, a frantic chorus of agreement sounded.

Worthington shrugged, feigning powerlessness. "How can we? We don't have the security codes."

"I do!" one of the prisoners yelled. "Eight five seven seven three two nine eight nine one five zero six zero two four!"

Worthington glowered as Amarillo tapped the numbers into the keypad by the door. "You shouldn't have said that. Now we'll have to change it."

The lock refused to disengage. "Repeat that," Amarillo said. "Slowly." The prisoner complied, but no to avail.

Froebisher winked at Worthington, an action that required swallowing far more pride than she expected. "The mercenaries probably changed it for us."

"So blast it open!" the prisoner with the code wailed.

Amarillo's body armored-guards snapped to attention, weapons at the ready. All they needed was the command to fire.

Worthington put his face to the grate. "You enjoy dancing in rains of superheated steel shards?"

"Don't blast it open!"

"Good boy. We don't want to hurt anyone."

The guards looked less than sanguine about that. Froebisher figured it had been a long time since they'd been allowed to blast much of anything.

Amarillo arched her eyebrows. "Especially not when we have them right where you want them."

"Really, Santamonica."

"I'm not criticizing. If only they could do their work in there. What's next?"

"General Omdahl."

"And where is she?"

Worthington rubbed his chin. "God only knows. I thought she'd be in the executive suite with her feet up on the desk."

"How could she put her feet on the desk without floating away?"

Froebisher had stopped listening after the security code didn't work. Now she pondered how to get to Omdahl ahead of her companions. Omdahl controlled the zap guns, so she alone could remove the obstacles from Froebisher's path. Given time for a heart-to-heart with the general, she had no doubt she could win her over. Arranging for privacy would be the tricky part. That, and making incarceration of the StarBright board, Amarillo and Worthington not excepted, look like Omdahl's idea. But first things first. She had to slip away.

"I'm sure the general is more than capable of maintaining balance." Worthington motioned the group down the corridor toward the detention facility exit. "Now where would a group of armed thugs go after seizing control?"

Amarillo followed his lead, and Froebisher fell into line behind them. "Wherever the alcohol is stashed," she suggested.

"Excellent point." Worthington slapped the wall. "Bar," he commanded, and a blue line flared to life on the floor. The party followed it, but when they turned the next corner, Froebisher held back. She listened to the clanking footfalls fade away, then struck out in her own direction. They had seen nobody moving in the facility. With the staff under lock and key and the miners likely cowering in the depths, where would Omdahl and her mercenaries go? The safest place would be their ships. Tapping the wall, Froebisher said, "Landing pads," and followed the yellow line.

Within ten minutes she was staring out a viewport at the collection of lifeless ships on the tarmac. They were no more than indistinct shadows in the feeble sunlight. Odd. She'd never seen a ship without some measure of exterior illumination, even when docked.

The ships were not alone. Also in the gloom, a small band of pressure-suited figures picked its way toward the base. Who were they? Mercenaries? Maintenance crew? Why did the ships look dead?

While pondering these puzzles, she heard the clank of feet on the metal floor. Turning quickly, she caught sight of someone slipping around a corner. "Who's there?" she demanded. "Come out where I can see you!"

"Oh!" a familiar voice squeaked. "Ms. Froebisher! What are you doing here?"

"Perry?"

Perry Pauli scrambled to her, eyes flitting between the floor and her face, his whole body shaking.

"Where are your tranquilizers?" She hadn't meant to say it; upon seeing Pauli's pathetic condition, it had sprung of its own accord from the recesses of her brain.

Fortunately, he didn't mind. "Lost." He grabbed for her arms. "This place is a looney bin!"

"Get off me!" She pushed him away. "Did you record anything useful?"

Pauli nodded. Hard. He couldn't seem to stop.

"You still have the equipment?"

He nodded onward.

"What's going on out there?" She pointed through the viewport to the ships.

Still he nodded.

"Stop that before your head falls off."

Somehow he got his head under control. "Sorry. I'm scared."

Froebisher knew that already. "Just give me your report."

Pauli started nodding again, then stopped and shuffled his feet, eyes on the floor. "Mercenaries took control and locked everyone up. Some miner named Omdahl was hired by Worthington to lead them. I have a recording about that. I think. Maccarone convinced her to use the mercenaries against Worthington. I have a recording about that, too. I think. The mercenaries are trapped on their ships with no power. I don't think I have a recording of that part. And I lost my tranquilizers. I definitely don't have a recording of that. Too bad, or I'd know where they are."

Froebisher gaped out the window. "What, all of them?"

"They were in a bottle together."

"Not the pills, the ships!"

"Oh. Yeah. I guess."

How could an entire fleet of ships loose power all at once? Undoubtedly sabotage. But by who? "Where are the miners?"

"Down below, I guess. They're scary. Maccarone's working with them, too. "

That was too much. Roberto Maccarone, idiot extraordinaire, simultaneously playing three sides against each other? Froebisher began to wonder if his bumbling was just an act. Could be. He ran an opera company. He knew about acting. "Very well. Since we can't get to the mercenaries, let's visit Maccarone. Where is he?"

Pauli shrugged. "I slipped away when he wasn't looking. He could be anywhere by now."

Not with the mercenaries, she was sure. He hadn't been with the board members. That left only the miners. But before she could command Pauli to lead her to them, a horrid clash of dozens of magnetized boots erupted. Pauli grabbed Froebisher's arm and pulled her behind a pillar. The boots thundered by.

Though quivering, Pauli dared to sneak a look.

"Who was that?" Froebisher demanded once the din subsided.

"Miners. With BonBon. And guns."

Froebisher couldn't deny Pauli had reason to go bananas, although she had no idea what fruit had to do with one's mental state. An awful lot of old expressions made no sense to her. Or to anyone. Be that as it may, she needed information, not lunacy. "What do you mean, bonbons?"

Wide-eyed, Pauli looked like he expected the miners to come thundering back and stomp him into oblivion. "A mercenary."

"Why not call them mercenaries, then? Why call them bonbons?"

"BonBon is one of them. A nice lady. I think. Anyway, she told Gordo to stop scaring me."

"Except he didn't," Froebisher guessed. "Where's Omdahl? She's supposed to be in charge of the guns."

"Maybe on the mercenary ship?"

If so, Froebisher wouldn't get to her anytime soon, but maybe this BonBon character could arrange a meeting. "Come on, let's follow."

Pauli tugged her arm to prevent her.

"Now, Perry!"

"Without my tranquilizers?"

She shook off his grip, grabbed him behind the neck, and pushed him after the miners.

Maccarone could tell from the narrowed eyes, gaping mouths, quaking limbs, and tight-lipped grimaces—not all of which adorned any single body at the same time, fortunately—that nobody relished this situation. Nobody with the possible exception of Murdock, who smiled easily at the billionaire lords of the outer fringes of the solar system and told them, "We got demands."

Gordo, one of those wearing narrowed eyes, leaned over and muttered, "What's this about, Murdock?"

The miner continued to smile at the board members. "You'll see."

Whatever it is, Maccarone told himself, *it better not take long.* Miners and mercenaries had horned in on his show at the worst possible moment. He'd very nearly had this gang eating out of his hand. Which, when he thought about it, proved a nauseating metaphor.

Vanderbilt Morgan Snodgrass, nose still high in the air, scowled down from the empyrean at Murdock, although it wasn't so much down as across. The two men were nearly the same lofty height. But he faked it well. "You are in no position to make demands."

Maccarone wondered how anyone could miss the fact that Murdock sure was.

"Sure I am." Murdock motioned the mercenaries forward. "These guys are in charge of your new base police force. Gordo and BonBon, say hi to the folks."

Gordo squinted at Murdock. BonBon smiled politely and nodded.

Snodgrass's nose lowered a few inches. "BonBon? You must be joking."

BonBon's smile slipped into a warning signal.

The CFO didn't get it. "What kind of name is BonBon?"

"Stop right there," BonBon cautioned.

"What are you, a stripper?"

A moment later, a pair of shivering board members pulled Snodgrass off the floor while he gingerly probed his nose for breakage.

"Girl's got a good arm," Murdock observed.

BonBon turned on him. "That goes for you, too."

He smiled and put up his hands in surrender. "I'm on your side."

"What side is that?"

"These two," Murdock told the board, "hold all the cards. And—" He winked at BonBon. "—they don't like backtalk."

A chorus of murmurs followed as the board tried to decide what degree of compliance was in their best interests, not to mention what cards were being discussed, since none of them could see anyone holding any cards whatsoever. In spite of his injury, they apparently regarded Snodgrass as the best spokesperson, because they all looked to him. He was now sitting in a chair, still prodding his nose and checking for blood. But all was well. BonBon had pulled her punch. Toppling an old geezer on a low-gravity world didn't call for enormous force.

"What do you want?" Snodgrass grumbled.

Tambe raised his hand. "Can I tell them, Josh?"

Pasternak shook her head and smiled.

Murdock motioned him forward. "Sure, kid."

Tambe cleared his throat and enunciated carefully: "Explosions."

As one, the board looked ill. Maccarone wondered whether Tambe meant it literally, and if so whether he literally meant it literally.

Murdock let them fret for a moment before assuring them. "Figure of speech. Life's dull out here."

Another round of murmuring ensued, then eyes turned to Maccarone, which set him on edge. What did they expect *him* to do about it?

Snodgrass explained in his inimitable way. "The culture ministry brought you an opera. Hell, the opera even blew up for you."

"Good start," Murdock conceded. "But not enough."

"I'm sure Mr. Maccarone can arrange for something else to explode." Snodgrass eyed Maccarone with distaste.

"Now wait a minute," Maccarone objected.

Murdock gave the board a disconcerting smile, as though pondering how far he could throw them. "You guys are supposed to be smart. Put your brains together and figure out a plan to make us happy. And remember, if we're not happy, the cops aren't happy. And if the cops aren't happy?"

Snodgrass probed his nose again. "You realize, of course, that we can't do anything without the rest of the board."

That, Maccarone figured, put him back in the picture, so he seized the moment. "Sure you can. Worthington is the cause of all this. Turn him over to the, er, police."

Gordo gaped at him. "What? Murdock!"

Murdock, naturally, had the answer. "Don't worry, friend. These folks won't give us trouble. BonBon gives 'em one of her looks, they'll do whatever we ask. Right, folks?"

BonBon gave the board one of her looks. "We should stash them in the slammer with the rest of their stooges. And let them rot there."

Snodgrass gazed thoughtfully at Maccarone. "You're Worthington's puppet."

"Hey, now."

"In his absence, could you vote his shares?"

"Is that legal?"

"Who cares? Legality fled at its first sight of these baboons." Snoodgrass pointed his nose at Gordo who looked about ready to cut that nose off. "But we must have a vote, and any proposal must win by simple majority of shares."

A new voice intruded: "Which you won't get without me."

Everyone turned or craned their necks to see the interloper.

Dismayed, Snodgrass rose. "Lena! Where are Artemis and Santamonica?"

Froebisher brushed between Murdock and Gordo, trailing a cringing, crouching Pauli who tried without success to simultaneously keep an eye on everyone and everything.

"Perry?" BonBon asked as he pushed by.

"Perry?" Maccarone echoed, wondering if the scriptwriter was still wired for sound.

"Perry?" asked several board members not entirely in unison.

"Urp!" Pauli squeaked.

Froebisher stopped in front of Snodgrass and sneered at him, but Pauli's quivering distracted her. "For God's sake, Perry," she said. "Hide under the table or something."

Relieved, Pauli scampered under the table.

Snodgrass watched him go. "I'm sure we can count on your support in ending this madness."

"Not me!" Pauli squeaked from his hidey hole.

Froebisher looked past Snodgrass to the rest of the board members. "For a price."

"How about we just do what's best for everyone."

"Be serious, Vanderbilt. You'd establish a dangerous precedent."

Snodgrass put on a good show of bristling.

"Worthington deserves to be locked up," Maccarone said in his most reasonable voice. Surely they couldn't object to that?

"Be quiet." Froebisher shot him a glance that, he figured, was just cause for being quiet. "We aren't locking up a fellow board member. Not even Artemis. Not yet, anyway. However." She turned to Murdock and eyed him, then gave Gordo and BonBon the same treatment. "If it's order you want, we should regularize our security forces."

"Look, lady," Gordo started, but BonBon put a hand on his shoulder and he shut his mouth.

"How much does it pay?" BonBon asked.

"Lots, including cash and company stock."

Maccarone wouldn't have thought it possible, but the naturally pale Snodgrass seemed to pale even paler. "Lena! You can't give these thugs ownership! Not a smidgeon!"

"I wasn't going to give them a smidgeon. I was going to give them enough to help me outvote Worthington. Or anyone else who doesn't think I deserve to be made permanent CIO."

Maccarone watched the shifting eyes and pursed lips and figured that an awful lot of them didn't want her in that position.

"And just where," Snodgrass asked, footing marginally regained, "are you going to find the shares? You can't dig them out of the ground, you know."

Froebisher replied with a thin-lipped smile. Maccarone had a pretty good idea what she was thinking. What a brilliant woman. He could almost fall in love with her.

Fortunately, he knew better.

CHAPTER 21

Worthington had long since lost track of their location, and the multicolored lines wending along the facility's floors had long since lost utility since he didn't know where he wanted to go. Mercenaries and miners were nowhere to be found in this relentless expanse of gray steel. "It's a good thing *we* don't have to live here," he commented. "It's enough to drive one mad. The board needs to maintain at least two sane members."

"Me and who else?" Santamonica Amarillo looked bored, while her trio of guards looked edgy. They were standing at the intersection of five corridors, none of which met the others at quite the same angle nor ran quite level into the distance. "Your brilliant plan lost most of its wattage somewhere along the line. Didn't it?"

Rather, it had been completely disconnected from its power source, but he couldn't admit that. "Not at all. The rebellion has been quelled." He swept all five directions with a flourish of his hand. "Look at how quiet the place is."

"Now all this mining operation needs is a mining operation."

"We'll get there."

"Get where? We're lost."

Worthingon took a moment to remind himself that Amarillo outranked and outearned him, and that she had armed guards. Armed guards who looked like they just might shoot something on general principles. "The mercenaries might have returned to their ships."

"Or plundered and gone home."

He slapped the wall and said, "Landing pads." A friendly yellow line pointed the way. "Come on." He indulged in the idea that he was giving her a command for once.

She followed, but not in silence. "If they're there," she told him, "I'll promote you to facility tour guide."

"What about the pressure suits, Murdock?" Gordo was about ready to shove his old friend out an airlock without one. They clanked along the corridor in exactly the wrong direction to get back to his ships. Murdock and Gordo lead, Pasternak and Tambe brought up the rear, and BonBon walked in the middle as though she were a VIP warranting protection.

"Priorities," Murdock told him. "Your guys are fine."

"General Omdahl will be furious." Not that Gordo thought Murdock cared, but it was worth a shot.

"Kaja has me pegged for a troublemaker. Don't want to disappoint her."

"Josh, dear," BonBon said reasonably. "We could spend hours looking for Worthington. He's probably lost."

"Arne will find him."

"Who?" she asked.

"You'll see."

While Gordo appreciated that BonBon's more diplomatic approach sometimes worked miracles, nothing swayed Murdock once his mind was made up. *If only we'd brought some weapons*, he scolded himself. But no. Murdock would have confiscated them. Whatever his plan was, it didn't involve permitting mercenaries an upper hand. Nor could he figure how Lena Froebisher fit in. Murdock must be using her somehow, but it sure looked the other way around. She had told Murdock to find the missing board members and return them. Murdock went along with it so readily that it must have been his own idea.

Murdock herded the gang into a lifter, which dropped into the interior at a rate that made Gordo's stomach rebel. He then marched them through a system of tunnels through the ice and soot to an empty room with a door that led into another smallish room stuffed with castoff equipment and a few functioning terminals attended by a wiry older man. Arne, Gordo presumed. But what was up with all the plumbing?

"What's up with all the plumbing?" he asked Murdock.

Ignoring the question, Murdock confirmed the man's identity. "This is Arne Slocum. Need your help, Arne."

Slocum grunted an acknowledgement. "They're almost to the landing pads."

"Who?"

"The people you're looking for."

Tambe edged forward. "How do you know they're—"

"Because they're the only ones moving, aside from yourselves. Everyone else is either in hiding or in jail. Here's the video, if you're not sure." He enlarged one of the security vid images.

Gordo nodded. "That's Worthington."

"Shut them in," Murdock ordered. With a few taps of the keys Slocum elicited a yelp from Worthington, followed by pounding on the now closed doors.

Slocum leaned back and locked his hands behind his head. "They'll keep 'til you get there."

Gordo chewed on his lip while Worthington railed at the universe. "And I thought *we* were scary."

Murdock smiled easily. "You are. Like I said before, this is all your fault. We're just riding your wake."

"My what?"

"Wake. It means—" Murdock looked puzzled. "Don't know what it means. We're just riding it."

Whatever it was, Gordo really, really wanted to push Murdock off of it. Or into it. Whichever was apropos.

You could think of it as a happy family reunion, aside from the snapping, snarling, and yelling, the threatening gestures, and, especially, the zap guns the miners eventually trained on the loudest of the group to get them to shut up. Even that didn't completely work until Darya Pasternak roared, "Shut the hell up already!"

That did the trick.

Everyone that mattered—the reunited StarBright board of directors, the four miners with their guns, the two mercenaries without their guns, and Maccarone with Land, whose grimace suggested he would rather have been without Maccarone—fell silent. For all of three seconds, the crowded conference room felt like an empty cavern.

Then Santamonica Amarillo cleared her throat dramatically. Maccarone thought she just might launch into an aria. "Being the chair, I'll run this friendly little meeting, shall I?"

"Sure thing." Murdock waved his zap gun around. "But I set the agenda."

"What do you know about agendas? You're just a miner."

Land gave Amarillo a frosty look. "He's advanced his agenda farther than the rest of us."

Amarillo countered with a bland smile. "And you are?"

"Nobody," Maccarone said, waving Land to silence.

Land slumped against the wall. "We really must figure out who I am. Being nobody is incredibly tedious."

Returning her attention to Murdock, Amarillo relented. As if she had any choice. "So what's the agenda, then?"

"Better lives for miners. Attention to safety regs. A few explosions."

"I beg your pardon?"

"They want excitement." Vanderbilt Morgan Snodgrass looked like he might spit on everyone within spitting distance. "I suggested Mr. Maccarone blow up another theater for them, but apparently that wasn't quite what they had in mind."

"I would hope not." Amarillo tried to skewer Murdock with her steely eyes, but he simply smiled his hungry bear smile and waited. "We already pay you and give you life's essentials. Why should we give you anything more?"

"We've got the guns," Pasternak explained. She held hers up, just in case anyone wasn't sure. The pale faces and frightened eyes suggested most of them absolutely *were* entirely sure.

Lena Froebisher came to Amarillo's side. "You won't for long. We're turning General Omdahl's mercenary gang into a regular security force."

Artemis Worthington had been uncharacteristically silent so far, but he could hold his tongue no longer. "Stop right there. Those are *my* mercenaries. General Omdahl is *my* general. You can't have her."

"We've got the guns," Pasternak repeated. "And the mercenaries. And General Omdahl. None of you have anything."

Froebisher eyed Worthington. "We have the money."

Worthington could get on board with that. "Of course. General Omdahl already makes obscene amounts of money. These two could join her in obscenity." He pointed to Gordo and BonBon, who looked interested if not entirely pleased with the phrasing. It couldn't have been easy, Maccarone thought, to simultaneously grin and snarl.

"And ten percent of your shares," Froebisher added, "divided equitably between the three of them."

"*What?*"

"You want a security force or not?"

"I will *not* sell as much as one share to these goons!"

"Who said anything about selling? You're donating them out of the goodness of your heart."

Worthington's face took on an unappealing shade of red. "What goodness? What heart? How dare you!"

Froebisher pointed to Pasternak, who waggled her gun and grinned.

The redness quickly faded to something a tad greenish.

Maccarone watched the negotiations, such as they were, with increasing puzzlement. "I don't understand something."

"That goes without saying." No one person had said it. It had been simultaneously uttered by (at least) Amarillo, Froebisher, Snodgrass, BonBon, and, under his breath, Land. But Maccarone had experience in ignoring his critics. "Why would miners—"

Land grabbed Maccarone's arm. "For once in your life, quit before you get further behind."

Shaking him off, Maccarone started over. "Why would miners with guns help mercenaries without guns get all the compensation *and* the guns, leaving the miners without even a vague promise of something?"

"Gordo 'n me are pals," Murdock rumbled pleasantly. "We do this, he'll owe me big time. Right, pal?"

Gordo chewed on that for a moment. He cast a questioning glance at BonBon, who shrugged her shoulders. "Yeah, okay. But what about Omdahl?"

"Kaja'll be okay with it."

Another pronouncement sounded in unison, this time by Slocum, Pasternak, and Tambe: "Are you *nuts*?"

"Trust me," Murdock assured them.

They looked like they trusted him about as far as they could throw him, which with all three of them working as a team was probably about three centimeters.

Worthington, having had time to think through the situation, came to a decision. "No shares. Not one, neither freely given nor sold at a hundred times their value. Shoot me. I dare you." He puffed up his considerable girth as a target. "Go ahead. Murder me in front of everyone. See what it gets you."

Murdock gazed evenly at the defiant marketing director, trigger finger not twitching in the least. "We aren't about killing."

"You're damn right you aren't," Worthington agreed, triumph writ large upon his face.

"We'll just lock you up."

"On what charges?"

"Arranging this fiasco."

Worthington puffed up even more, his confidence growing by the second. "You have no proof that I've done anything other than put down your rebellion." A number of board members, hiding behind him in case Murdock changed his mind about the killing thing, murmured assent.

The ensuing silence was broken by a small, tremulous voice. "I have recordings."

Worthington's head snapped around. "Who said that?"

"Uh. Nobody."

"Where are you?"

"Under the table."

"I'm afraid, Artemis," Froebisher said none too confidentially, "the game is up."

Worthington scowled at the ceiling. "Up where?" Then deciding it wasn't worth pursuing, he settled into his old routine. "I'm not assigning any shares to anybody."

Froebisher shrugged. "Suit yourself."

Murdock smiled a nice, friendly, famished bear smile.

To everyone's surprise, Worthington stuck to his guns for a long time in spite of being incarcerated. Two and a half days, in fact. He spent that time complaining about the food and the service and the lack of computer facilities and his general inability to do anything useful like talk to his attorney. But even he had to admit, in the end, that capitulation was the only alternative. Oort Territories courts were, by and large, stored in the hip pockets of StarBright board members, and for him that presently meant any judge taken out of storage to hear his case would be at best unfriendly, at worst malevolent.

Thus, he grudgingly relinquished control of sufficient stock to put two mercenaries and a mining supervisor turned general onto the board, weakening his position while giving Lena Froebisher enough clout to secure her permanent appointment as CIO. Still, he reflected, the situation wasn't a total loss. Having forfeited so much, he now had opportunities in spades—

whatever they were—to machete his way back to the top. Only this time, he'd play the metaphorical game of laser tag with non-metaphorical live weapons.

Roberto Maccarone, meanwhile, discovered that the King's Ransom was only one of three insanely expensive restaurants at Territory HQ, the other two being Everest and The Deeps. Everest proved a scary place, an environment of unrelenting white and gray, the only color a dark blue sky-ceiling almost close enough to touch. Periodically wind howled through the dining room and the temperature plummeted just long enough to make diners feel they might die of exposure, then all would return to normal. All, that is, except the oxygen level, which for reasons Maccarone couldn't fathom hovered on the low side. Diners spent a lot of their meals gasping for breath. Oddly, the locals ate up the ambiance with their food. "It's so *real*," he heard one diner comment. "Just like being there!" Maccarone didn't think he'd ever want to be wherever there was.

But The Deeps offered something wonderful. In a vast space of shimmering blues and greens, holographic fish swam among the diners, ducking in and out of beds of holographic plants, darting around holographic coral reefs, and playing in the golden sunlight that seemed to trickle down from above. He couldn't have asked for a more perfect setting for his final pitch for the theater.

Seated at a coral table adorned with coral place settings, they ordered lobster, calamari—Maccarone suspected Liwanu might be addicted to calamari—and assorted sides, then settled in for a cozy chat.

"I assume," Froebisher said, "you want something from us."

Maccarone flashed his smile. "Must everyone have an ulterior motive, Lena? May I call you Lena?"

"To your second question, don't even think it. To your first, yes."

Back to that again, Maccarone thought, although he laughed lightly. "All I want, really, is to break an impasse." He glanced at Liwanu, who frowned at her napkin but for once didn't come out swinging.

Frobisher took a sip of her water. "Yeah, I heard about that. It's none of my concern."

"In a way it is. Worthington thought he'd control the theater, but after the accident—"

"It's no longer safe. I know. Poor Artemis." She smiled with her mouth, but not with her eyes.

Maccarone shook his head. "It's perfectly safe. Isn't it, Chelsea?"

Liwanu glared at him.

"But before it can be used as a theater, one small detail needs attention. Some of the miners I've talked to think they can do it."

"Nobody can do it." Liwanu's voice was as empty as space.

Froebisher leaned forward. "What's this about?"

"Irving Ignatius Irvine," Maccarone told her. "The theater's architect. His body was never recovered from the wreckage. I want to help Chelsea take him home to Earth for the honors he deserves."

Liwanu discreetly dabbed at her eyes with her napkin.

The waiter glided up to Maccarone's side. "Are we ready to order?"

"Not yet," Froebisher said before Maccarone could reply, and with a polite nod the man withdrew. "Are you saying—" But she didn't need to ask. She had it worked out in another second. "My God, Chelsea, you think it was Artemis' *fault*?"

"It was his money. He was in charge." She folded her arms, leaned on the table, and stared at her plate. "Of course it was his fault."

Maccarone gingerly touched her shoulder in support. "Out here in the dark, corners get cut all the time. Don't they Len, ah, Ms. Froebisher?"

"I wouldn't put anything past Artemis. Regardless, this has nothing to do with me. Get your architect out if you can, but keep the theater shuttered. So long as Artemis can't get his hands on it, we all can be happy."

"Not me," Maccarone objected.

"How sad for you. There are other theaters. What's so special about this one?"

Maccarone smiled a sly smile. He hadn't practiced that smile as much as the other one, but he didn't doubt its effectiveness. "Let's order and eat. Then we'll take you there. You can see for yourself."

Froebisher blinked at him. Liwanu frowned at the table, but slowly her expression morphed into something more thoughtful.

"Imagine it," Maccarone said. "You'll see something Artemis Worthington never has."

If that didn't convince her, he didn't know what would.

The instant the lights came up, Maccarone knew he had Froebisher right where he wanted her. Awe-struck, she stood unmoving five full minutes, taking in the sweep of the stage, the rows of seats awaiting an audience, the balconies, the lights playing on the massive curtain, and especially the incongruously beautiful shaft of light marking Irvine's resting place.

"I had no idea," she breathed.

"Nobody did." Liwanu's voice sounded small in the emptiness. "Until Mr. Maccarone." She twisted her hands together. "Roberto."

The concession surprised Maccarone, but he held his silence.

"Why let him of all people in on the secret?"

Froebisher might have forgotten Maccarone was standing right beside her. Or maybe not. StarBright board members didn't have to care about anybody. Maccarone made a mental note to avoid slipping down that road himself.

"I don't know." Liwanu gave Maccarone a sideways glance that looked a bit more like her usual frozen self. "But the cat's out of the bag now, and he says he wants to help. Oddly, I believe him."

Maccarone would have been touched had he not been thrown off by the cat. "What cat?"

Still lost in the theater's beauty, Froebisher said, "There isn't one."

"If it was in a bag, there must have been."

"There was no bag."

"But Chelsea just said—" Fortunately, he stopped himself. *Don't do the marimba thing again.*

Liwanu looked like she regretted having mentioned the nonexistent cat in the nonexistent bag. "The point is, Roberto is going to help Irving and I go home, in exchange for which I'll let him play the theater. But there is one caveat."

Froebisher nodded. "There always is."

"Worthington doesn't get the theater. His name doesn't go on it, he doesn't manage any aspect of its operation, he doesn't get to scalp tickets or even sweep the floors."

"He put his money into this place."

"He put his money into the wreckage. He refused to pay for cleanup. He refused to pay for reconstruction. He refused to pay to recover Irving's body. I put my money into this." Liwanu took in the theater with a sweep of her arms. "It belongs to me now, and I'm giving it to Irving."

"But legally—" Froebisher began, but Maccarone interrupted.

"Le, ah, Ms. Froebisher. Worthington put his money into the stock you took away from him, too. Surely he has more right to that than to this theater."

Liwanu blinked at them. "You took stock away from him?

The corners of Froebisher's mouth curled upward just a bit. "He gifted it. At my suggestion."

Although she tried to hide it by turning away, Maccarone noted that Liwanu's eyes fairly sparkled. "Once the work is completed," she said, "we'll christen this the Irving Ignatius Irvine Theater. I'll turn over the keys to you, Lena. Only to you. And you, Roberto, can stage the opera of your dreams. Hell, I'll even attend opening night."

Maccarone felt like crowing. He felt like leaping into the air, running up and down the aisles, mounting the stage and singing "Le vin de Syracuse" from *Béatrice et Bénédict* even though it was better suited to Josh Murdock's voice. But that wouldn't have been professional, so he contented himself with a mischievous smile. "Fa, ah, Feng will be so disappointed. I told him we could call it the Land-Maccarone Center for the Performing Arts."

Liwanu pinched her lips and shook her head.

"Who's Feng?" Froebisher asked.

"Oh," Maccarone explained, "nobody."

CHAPTER 22

Aida, act two.

The victorious Egyptian army, led by the resplendent Radames in his blazing golden armor and magnificent flaming red, orange, and gold cape, paraded onto the stage in time with the music of the triumphal march. Radames sat astride an oversized robotic horse that pranced exuberantly before the Pharaoh's retinue, which stood at rigid attention on the palace steps. Pyramids rose in the background. Soldiers followed, mounted on horses and elephants, a seemingly endless column of military might bristling with spears and swords and war clubs and bows and arrows.

The spoils of war followed. Caged lions and tigers and antelope, monkeys and gorillas, aardvarks and kangaroos and penguins and a dozen other exotic species. Chests overflowing with gems and gold doubloons. Strong Ethiopian men in chains. Beautiful Ethiopian women in flimsy nightgowns. Whiny Ethiopian children complaining of tired feet.

The procession flowed onto, around, and off of the stage, taking so long the orchestra repeated the march. The audience ate it up. They'd never seen or heard anything like it.

"It's like," Vanderbilt Morgan Snodgrass gasped.

"It's like," Chelsea Liwanu marveled.

"It's like," Santamonica Amarillo purred, "gaining control of *two* StarBrights."

Roberto Maccarone smiled and winked at Liwanu, who for once smiled back at him. Still in black—Maccarone wondered if she would ever upgrade her color scheme—she no longer looked as cold as space itself. Darya Pasternak and crew had accomplished the allegedly impossible, carefully untangling and separating the mass of fused debris beneath the theater, gently extracting the remains of Irving Ignatius Irvine, and honorably placing them in a coffin of special design that commemorated his greatest architectural achievements. None of this had come cheap, but Maccarone had paid for it all, refusing a last-minute pitch by Artemis Worthington to help cover the costs. Following that, Maccarone had, with the help of Lena Froebisher, mercenary shareholders Gordo and BonBon, and even General Omdahl, defeated Worthington's angry attempt to kick him off the board.

So life was, for the nonce, amazingly good.

The music and the parade went on and on, and Maccarone lost himself in its glory.

Until, that is, a commotion erupted somewhere in the recesses of the procession. An out of key yelp sounded from somewhere on stage, followed by a chorus of similar yelps from the audience, and then Lena Froebisher leaped from her seat and barked, "What the hell?"

Maccarone felt his chest tighten.

He didn't want to look.

He looked anyway and instantly regretted it.

On stage, actors and singers scattered in every direction as a robotic elephant stomped around in a circle, reared up, and pitched its hapless rider into Pharaoh's retinue. The gaudily costumed dignitaries leaped aside, fell down steps, and otherwise tumbled ungracefully all around ancient Egypt.

"Turn it off, turn it off!" someone screamed.

A moment later, the elephant halted, one rear leg lifted, its tusk defiantly thrust upward toward Maccarone's box and his assembled VIP guests.

All eyes in the box turned toward Maccarone for explanation.

He shrugged wearily. "Divine retribution," he told them.

What else could it be?

THE END

Thank you for reading! Please leave a short, honest review wherever you purchased this book. I greatly appreciate it, and it will help others discover my books.

ABOUT THE AUTHOR

Dale E. Lehman is an award-winning writer, veteran software developer, amateur astronomer, and bonsai artist in training. He principally writes mysteries, science fiction, and humor. In addition to his novels, his writing has appeared in *Sky & Telescope* and on Medium.com. He owns and operates the imprint Red Tales. He and his late wife Kathleen have five children, six grandchildren, and two feisty cats. At any given time, Dale is at work on several novels and short stories.

Visit https://www.DaleELehman.com to find out more about Dale's books.

www.ingramcontent.com/pod-product-compliance
Lightning Source LLC
Chambersburg PA
CBHW071145180726
48291CB00007B/2348